Those who give have all things. Those who withhold have nothing.

—An Amish Proverb

SUGARCREEK AMISH MYSTERIES

Blessings in Disguise
Where Hope Dwells
The Buggy before the Horse
A Season of Secrets
O Little Town of Sugarcreek
Off the Beaten Path
Peace Like a River
Simply Vanished
A Stitch in Time
Mason Jar Mayhem

MASON JAR
Mayhem

TRICIA GOYER
&
CARA PUTMAN

Guideposts

New York

To Grandma Dolores:
You are an example of love and service to others.
Ever since I was young you've modeled how to give
from a cheerful heart. I'm so thankful for
your generous example in my life.
–TG

To Grandma Audrey:
You are the foundation of our family and a woman
who lives her faith with love. Thank you for loving me
and the rest of the clan. You've shown me what a life of
service looks like, and I'm grateful for your example!
I love you,
–CP

CHAPTER ONE

I'll be back in a bit for you, Beau." Cheryl Cooper's Siamese cat turned his back on her and flounced toward the long wooden counter at the back of the Swiss Miss as she watched. Then with one smooth motion, the cat jumped onto the counter, landing next to a large jar candle that infused the room with a mix of floral scents, mimicking the spring air she'd breathed yesterday. She'd strolled with Levi through the wild lupine, foxglove, indigo, and purple coneflowers on the Millers' farm, pleased with both the beauty of the farm and the company. It had only been a short walk, since Cheryl's mounting to-do list hadn't allowed more. She tugged the list from her purse and scanned it, hoping she hadn't forgotten anything. She also hoped that the slight throbbing at her temples would ease by the time she got to the job site.

Behind the counter, Cheryl's faithful employee, Esther Miller, priced the small boxes of fudge her mother, Naomi, had made. Her other usual employee, Lydia Troyer, was away visiting a close friend who'd moved to Shipshewana. Cheryl had encouraged Lydia to go and enjoy her trip, but now Cheryl was wishing Lydia was back to help at the store. The Swiss Miss had been so busy lately, Cheryl had asked Naomi to double her typical order. And now with this new community project, it was as if Cheryl added a second job to her first. *Why did I volunteer for this too?*

Cheryl hung the purse strap on her shoulder and turned the sign to Open on the front door. She must have forgotten to turn it earlier as she'd rushed in—not that Closed had stopped the flow of Saturday customers. As the plastic sign rested against the glass door, she wished she could hang a sign around her neck and turn it to Closed—even for a day. What she wouldn't give for a nap and then a few hours within the pages of a good novel. But with the work on the Cedar Creek Cottages in addition to running the Swiss Miss, that wasn't to be at least for a while yet.

"Are you sure you'll be fine, Esther? The morning has been so full with tour buses."

"*Ja.* I can call if I need help." Esther brushed a strand of dark hair back under her *kapp* and then made a shooing motion. "Go on yet. I know your mind isn't here anyway. It's running ahead in other directions."

Cheryl laughed as she reached for the door handle. "I know the Swiss Miss is in good hands with you."

The bell above the gift shop's door jingled, and Cheryl walked into the bright, early afternoon sunshine. She'd meant to arrive at the Cedar Creek Cottages much earlier in the day, but the hours had slipped by as tourists and locals wandered her shop. If she didn't know better, she'd believe every non-Amish couple in town was planning a May or June wedding. Aunt Mitzi hadn't warned her about wedding season. She'd have to make sure she asked Naomi and her other suppliers for more gift ideas perfect for bridal showers. Customers were searching for everything from beautifully detailed quilts to sweet preserves to bless celebrating couples.

Cheryl walked past the plate-glass windows, noticing smudged fingerprints dotting them. She smiled, imagining a passel of children leaning over the window box and pressing against the window to examine the display of Amish crafted toys. Cleaning the windows was another task to add to Monday's to-do list.

She sighed as she continued. It wasn't very many months ago that her days had revolved around her job at a bank in Columbus. Cheryl had enjoyed it, but she'd never found the fulfillment there that she'd discovered managing the Swiss Miss. If only she didn't feel pulled in so many directions, within the store and beyond.

With each passing week, Sugarcreek had become more like home. As she turned to walk up Main Street, she couldn't imagine returning to her life in the big city of Columbus. Instead, she pictured spending the next years here—working in Aunt Mitzi's gift shop and becoming woven into the fabric of this unique community. Having lunches at the Honey Bee Café, and taking drives out to the Miller farm to visit her closest friends.

Even though it was a short walk to the Cedar Creek Cottages, Cheryl decided to drive. She was eager to see the first stages of renovation, and she was already running later than she planned.

When Cheryl had met Johnson Williamson in November, she'd become captivated by his passion for working with abused women and their families. Now that he'd bought the deserted Cedar Creek Cottages to turn into emergency shelters, she wanted to help. Remembering the cautious gazes of the children she'd met, and the weighed-down, burdened frames of the mothers who'd fled to protect themselves and their children, caused the hairs to prick at the back of her neck. The idea of leaving all you had and knew to find safety made her long to give those families a chance for a better life.

As soon as she'd heard about his project, Cheryl had signed up to help. With encouragement from her friend Naomi Miller, the Amish community had adopted the renovation of the cottages as their own—similar to how they'd join forces for a barn raising. Empty for the past fifteen years, the small cottages were in desperate need of updates. But if she guessed correctly, the dedicated Amish workers would move quickly and efficiently.

Just last week, John-John had shown her his plans for the cottages. The dark, paneled walls would be stripped and freshly painted. New wood floors would replace the stained, tired carpet. But most exciting, the non-weight-bearing walls between the kitchens and dining rooms would disappear, giving the small cottages an airy feel. She smiled as she parked her car and got out, imagining how they'd look when ready to welcome women and their children. Comfy oases to weather the storms in their lives.

Cheryl had spent the last few weeks sharing the vision with volunteers, even while she still considered how she could help in this new phase of construction. She might not be good at hitting nails into drywall, but maybe Naomi needed help setting out lunch for the volunteers. Just the thought of her friend's delicious homemade bread and her Amish sandwich spread made with onions, cucumbers, peppers, carrots, and green tomatoes caused Cheryl's stomach to rumble.

As Cheryl neared the cluster of cottages, a bustle of activity filled the roadway. Trucks parked beside buggies. Construction workers with yellow hard hats worked alongside Amish men with their homemade trousers and shirts and straw hats. Machinery buzzed, voices called out, and the aroma of freshly cut wood welcomed her.

The six small cottages clustered around a small cul-de-sac at the end of a residential neighborhood. The location was perfect. Kids could run without disturbing neighbors. Mothers wouldn't worry about traffic, and any vehicle entering could be monitored.

Yet as Cheryl neared the cottages, the peeling paint and frayed screens became clearer. There was a lot of work to do to make them welcoming.

Maybe I should buy some zinnias and marigolds to plant near the front steps.

Cheryl mentally added the idea to next week's to-do list. The warm colors and cheery blooms would be a nice touch. And maybe they could use those same colors on the inside to make the cottages more homelike too. She imagined cream-colored walls with red curtains fluttering in open windows. A small couch with gold and orange throw pillows. A patterned quilt hung over the back of a rocking chair. Her lips curled into a smile, and she paused outside the nearest cottage.

"I see something has you smiling." Levi's rich voice startled her as he approached, stopping next to her.

Heat warmed her cheeks, and her heartbeat quickened. The quiet Amish man unsettled her. Perhaps because Cheryl never knew if he was a friend or if something more grew between them.

Cheryl crossed her arms over her chest. "I suppose I let my imagination run away with me. These cottages will be such a lovely respite when we're finished."

Levi cocked his head and squinted as if trying to see what she did. Then he shook his head. "Your vision is better than mine. The work inside is immense. *Cozy* is not the first word I think."

A man dressed in traditional Amish garb hurried by with a sheet of drywall resting on his shoulder. In the middle of the cul-de-sac, more drywall rested across wooden sawhorses and two more Amish men measured and cut. In one corner of the street, a temporary dumpster was already filled with a small mountain of debris, ready for the trash service to cart off. Standing by the dumpster, talking to another man, the visionary of this project—John-John—wore a grin as big as Ohio. Finishing his conversation, he hurried to the nearest cottage and offered a helping hand as another man lugged out a kitchen sink. Mimicking busy ants, workers surrounded Cheryl, and she could barely take it all in.

"I can't believe so many are helping."

"Wait until you see inside." Levi chuckled. "You and my *maam* can be quite persuasive. I am almost certain a member or two from every family in our district has helped."

His approving words warmed her.

"Where is Naomi?"

He pointed toward the cottage that appeared to be least active. "You will find her in the backyard of the third cottage. She is setting up the lunch picnic along with some other ladies."

"Thanks."

Levi moved toward the men cutting the drywall, and Cheryl hurried to the cottage he'd indicated. Surely Naomi needed help. Cheryl wasn't much of a cook—only some of the recipes she tried turned out edible—but she could help her friend.

When she rounded the corner, she found three long tables set up underneath two walnut trees. The leafy branches provided an avenue of shade in the recently trimmed backyard. Each table had a white tablecloth. An array of casserole dishes and Tupperware bowls covered the space. The aroma of delicious food met her, and Cheryl deemed there was enough to feed a small army.

Sitting next to plastic plates and utensils were mounds of sandwich bread and platters of meats and cheese. There were a dozen different salads and fried chicken. Baskets of apples, oranges, and bananas rested next to platters of homemade cookies. Ten pies, each cut into generous slices, sat near pitchers of water and lemonade. Naomi and her Amish friends had certainly outdone themselves. The women stood in a cluster near the tables, sharing the latest news. Naomi stepped away from the group as Cheryl approached.

"I thought I'd help." Cheryl hugged her petite friend. "I should have known you'd have everything well in hand."

"Ja. Like my mother always said, many hands make light work. With so many willing helpers, it is not so difficult."

Cheryl cocked an eyebrow as she considered the feast. "Doesn't look simple to me."

"That is why we are all gifted in different ways."

Cheryl's stomach rumbled a happy assent. "It looks great."

Naomi picked up a plate and handed it to her. "You must eat."

"Not before the others."

"You are here now…"

Cheryl's stomach growled again.

"And hungry." Naomi's eyes widened, and the two broke into laughter.

"Guess I am." Cheryl accepted the plate and quickly built a ham and swiss sandwich, adding a large scoop to her plate of what Naomi declared was Mary Raber's famous baked beans. She slid a piece of apple pie next to the sandwich. "Thank you for your help."

"Of course. Johnson is doing a good thing here."

Cheryl nodded as she chewed a bite of sandwich. He really was doing something valuable. Something she could wholeheartedly support.

Naomi walked to the cottages. "While you eat, I will gather the others."

A mechanical song filled the air, and Cheryl put down the plate on a table then dug her phone from her purse. Her mother. "Happy birthday, Momma."

"Thanks, sweetie." Her momma's soft Southern accent filtered from the phone. "I love the charm bracelet and box of chocolates you sent."

"Glad they arrived." Cheryl had known the moment she saw the charm bracelet in the gift shop at Heini's Cheese Chalet that it was the perfect gift. Each charm listed an attribute of God—the perfect reminder to have jingling on one's wrist. And of course, she'd included a box of chocolates one of Naomi's friends made for the Swiss Miss.

"So how are you relaxing this Saturday?" her mother asked.

Cheryl sighed. "I don't know that I'd call it relaxing. I spent the morning at the Swiss Miss helping a couple tour buses of customers find the perfect mementos. Now I'm at a cottage raising."

"Cottage raising?"

Cheryl could picture her mother's quizzical expression.

"The Amish usually hold barn raisings, but this weekend Naomi and I helped organize a work party for some cottages that need some serious work and updating."

"Why would you do that, sweetheart? That sounds like so much work."

"But it's a good cause, Momma. A friend is starting an emergency shelter to minister to women and children. Some people need safe places to escape." Cheryl struggled with how to convey her commitment in a way her mom could understand. "I saw the need at the main shelter in Millersburg. These families need safe places. Sugarcreek and these cottages are the perfect answer." With her view through an open kitchen window, Cheryl watched a man knocking a hole in a wall. "Well, they will be perfect when we're done."

"I'm glad you're involved in your new community and giving to others, Cheryl. But what are you doing for you? How are you taking care of yourself?"

"I'm doing just fine." Cheryl bit her lip as she said those words, noting the headache at her temples hadn't let up.

Her mom's silence conveyed the woman's doubts.

"Really, Momma. I'm fine. I'm just still finding my place in Sugarcreek and figuring out the ins and outs of the Swiss Miss. The store has been busy too. I had no idea how many people would be buying bridal shower and wedding gifts this time of year." She started telling Momma some funny stories about different customers who'd shopped in the store that week, but her mother wouldn't be deterred.

"Cheryl, you have to take care of yourself. You can serve yourself right into a health crisis if you're not careful."

"I won't do that. I promise."

"You won't mean to, but it will happen all the same. Start blocking out time on your calendar for white space, sweetheart. You are so much like your father. If I don't put a hold on his calendar, his schedule fills and the poor man can't breathe. If he's not healthy, he can't serve our congregation. You can't either."

"I don't have a congregation."

"Sure you do. And it's not just the church you attend. There are people who come in the store. To be ready to serve them when there's a need, you have to be rested and able to hear God's still, small voice. Pray about it, okay?"

"Yes, ma'am." She'd think about it, but this was one time Momma was wrong. She was doing exactly what she needed.

"Good. So did Matt tell you about the gift he got me?"

"No." Cheryl settled down with her pie while she listened to her mom describe the photo calendar Matt had made along with a gift card to her favorite restaurant. "Sounds creative."

"Oh, it is. Truly one of a kind."

A screen door slammed, and Cheryl looked up. An Amish man she didn't recognize ran toward her. His eyes were wide in his astonished face. "Have you seen Mr. Williamson?"

"Not recently, although he was up front a bit ago. Why?"

"We need him to come see something we found."

"Momma, I've got to run. Happy birthday. I love you!"

Cheryl waited until her mother hung up, and then she returned her phone to her purse. She set her plate to the side, and then she led the man to the front yard, quickly approaching her friend. "John-John, this man wants you to come look at something in one of the cottages."

John-John turned toward the man, curiosity in his eyes. "Yes?"

"You won't believe it, sir." He started walking toward the second cottage from the left, his steps hurried. "We were opening a wall in the kitchen and found something you have to see." He motioned John-John to follow.

John-John did with quickened steps. "Is it damage we'll have to repair?"

"Nothing like that, sir. Well, you have to see it."

As they entered the cottage, the front room seemed in fairly good repair. A coat of fresh paint was drying, and new flooring leaned against the wall waiting to be installed. Soon this cottage could welcome a family.

As they walked into the kitchen, the demolition crews remained hard at work. Countertops had been ripped out, and the cabinets were missing doors. Behind the spot where a refrigerator would go, the drywall had been ripped out, exposing bare studs.

What rested between the studs stole Cheryl's breath.

John-John looked to her and shook his head. "If I wasn't seeing this for myself, I'd never believe it."

Chapter Two

Dust stirred the air as Cheryl eyed row after row of filthy, quart-size mason canning jars. They sat stacked on top of each other from the floor to waist height.

Cheryl knelt next to the man who'd found them. He introduced himself as Dan Dekker and said he worked at the tack and saddle store.

"How many jars are there?"

He yanked off his hat, wiped a handkerchief across his forehead, and then settled the hat back on his dark hair. "Haven't moved 'em yet, but there's at least two layers and five deep. Probably forty jars in all."

John-John whistled. "That's a lot of jars to store inside a wall."

Cheryl moved closer and stopped short when she realized what filled the jars. "Are those coins? In all of them?"

"Looks that way." Dan rocked back on his heels. "See why we called you in here, Johnson? This is way above my pay grade."

"Mine too." Cheryl turned to John-John. He'd leaned against the back wall of the kitchen, as if trying to put as much space between him and the jars as he could. "What do you want to do with the jars? I'm assuming we won't leave them here."

Dan nodded. "We'll need to remove them before we can return to work in this room. Besides, if all those jars are filled with coins, they could contain quite a sum. Not safe to leave them lying around."

"But someone hid those in the wall long before I bought the cottages." John-John rubbed between his eyes. "The money isn't mine."

His words hung in the air as Cheryl evaluated John-John and then the jars. Based on the thick layer of dust that discolored and clouded the mason jars, he was probably right. Those jars had rested in the walls a long time. They'd come with the sale. Wouldn't that mean they belonged to the cottage's owner?

"Daniel, the food is going to disappear if you all do not come outside soon." Naomi stopped in the kitchen doorway and blinked. "What are you looking at? Why…what is that?" She took another step forward, disbelief clear in her gaze. "Are those jars inside that wall?"

Cheryl leaned forward and ran a finger along the rim of a jar. Then she wiped the dust on her jeans. "Yes, can you believe it, Naomi? Somebody left these jars. I wonder who? There has to be a story behind something that unusual."

"*Ach, ain't so?*"

John-John pushed off the wall. "Well, I don't know who left them or who those belong to, but I can't do anything about it on an empty stomach. Ready to grab a quick bite, Dan?"

Cheryl's mouth fell open as she watched the men head for the door. "Are you really leaving? Now? This…this is a big discovery."

John-John shrugged. "They're not going anywhere, and I'm just getting food. Maybe I'll think better with a full stomach. Anyway, you're better at solving puzzles like this, Cheryl."

Dan looked over his shoulder. "I'll grab a quick bite too and be right back. Holler if you need anything."

Naomi must have found something amusing in the situation because laughter burst from her lips. She shook her head and covered her mouth. "I am sorry, Cheryl, but the look on your face tickled me. You seem so upset, and all they are doing is filling their stomachs."

"But they left all this money. Here. Exposed. Anyone could walk in and grab it."

"Nobody will. Who knows it's even here? Only a few of us, ja?"

"I suppose." But Cheryl wouldn't leave until the men were back and they'd decided where to put the jars. They certainly shouldn't be sealed up inside the walls. She picked up a jar and rubbed the thick dust, but it only smeared. So many years of grime had accumulated, it was almost impossible to see inside the mason jars.

Cheryl did a quick count and confirmed Dan's earlier number. Forty quart jars had been stacked between the walls. Even if a couple hundred dollars of coins filled each, it would equal a sizable sum.

As she finished restacking the front row of jars, the men returned. "Where do you want to put these, John-John?"

He shrugged, his hands shoved deep inside his pockets as if to keep from reaching out and touching a jar. "The bank's already closed. It's too much to leave these locked inside the cottage. I don't know where to take them."

Cheryl rubbed her chin. "How about the Swiss Miss? We might be able to get the coins in the safe if we remove them from the jars. And even if they don't all fit, I've got the alarm system. Everything should be secure."

Naomi nodded. "That is a good idea—a way to keep them safe, Johnson, while you evaluate what to do. This may be *Gott's* provision for your project."

John-John looked at her hand and then at the jars. "I've asked God for funds. The renovations are looking to take more money than I've raised. I can only stretch a dollar so far before it squeals." He turned to Cheryl. "But I can't accept it if someone out there has a stronger claim to the funds. It wouldn't be right."

Dan faced him squarely as he pointed at the jars. "These cottages were abandoned for quite a time." He rubbed his brow. "Maybe this is God's way of providing."

"Maybe." John-John worried his bottom lip. "But I can't take it until I'm sure. Otherwise it feels like stealing from someone I don't know. What if their need for the funds is deeper than mine? Will you help me, Cheryl?"

Cheryl looked at the jars. She wished there were a good place to start. From her quick perusal of the jars, there was no name, no information on them. Still, she could tell John-John wanted to do the right thing. And he was right—she loved a good puzzle. This had all the markings: someone who needed help, a question no one could answer, and a reason that compelled her to help.

"I'll be glad to do that. I can take the jars to my shop for the weekend. Then on Monday you can take the coins to the bank for safekeeping."

"If you're sure, that would be a relief to me." He stared at the jars as if they might somehow hurt him. "I don't know where else to put them."

Naomi looked at the mason jars. "You will need help. I'll have Levi escort you to the store. You should not be about with all that money on your own."

John-John crossed his arms over his chest. "We don't know that it's a lot."

"At the same time, we don't know that it isn't."

"If we washed the jars, we might find they're filled with pennies." Dan hefted one in each hand. "These are better than weights."

"More fragile too." Cheryl reclaimed her jar from his hand then turned to Naomi. "I'd appreciate Levi's help." Her gaze moved to the door, and she paused.

A pretty young woman stood in the doorway. Her legs looked long in designer shorts. Her hair was pulled back in a bouncy ponytail topped by a bow that would make any college cheerleader proud. How long had she stood there? More importantly, who was she? Cheryl frowned as she shuffled to stand in front of the tower of jars. John-John's gaze followed hers, and he smiled.

"Cheryl, I'd like to introduce you to Sadie Rivers. She's a college student who will be interning with me this summer."

Sadie stepped forward and held out a delicate hand. "It's nice to meet you."

Cheryl shook her hand, and more questions than answers about this young woman flashed through her mind. "It's wonderful to meet you. What will you be doing this summer?"

"Whatever Mr. Williamson needs." Her voice rose an octave. "I'm excited to work with an organization doing such important work."

Cheryl added "perky" to her observations. Sadie matched the perfect cheerleader image. Would the girl get her hands dirty when the work required it? As she examined the young woman's spotless clothes in the middle of a renovation zone, Cheryl had to wonder. "It's nice of you to volunteer. I'm sure John-John is thankful for your help."

"Cheryl and her friend Naomi Miller have been a big help to me as we get these cottages renovated." John-John sneezed and then wiped his nose with the back of his hand. "I'm not sure what I'd do without them."

Sadie's gaze met Cheryl's. "Mr. Williamson has said a lot about you. It's great to meet you and put your faces with your names." The girl smiled, but the edges seemed forced rather than natural.

Cheryl swallowed down the additional questions she wanted to ask, like just why was Sadie Rivers so excited about this dirty mess?

Naomi clamped her lips together, as if remembering what they'd been talking about. Then she picked up a jar. "Let me get Levi to help you, Cheryl. Then you can get the jars transported."

"Do you need any help?" Sadie stepped forward, an eager note in her voice.

Cheryl couldn't quite figure out why, but she didn't want the girl's help. "I'll be fine with a little help from Levi."

The girl's expression fell, and a pang of guilt cut through Cheryl's gut.

"All right." Sadie turned to leave the room. "I'll be in the first cottage if you need me, Mr. Williamson."

"She's certainly eager," Cheryl chirped.

"And an answer to prayer." John-John spread his hands. "This job is much bigger than I anticipated. There's just so much. And making these cottages livable is just a start. I don't really know how to make them welcoming once we've got the renovations done."

"I'll help, John-John." Even as Cheryl said the words, echoes of her momma's comments about adding white space to her calendar flitted across her mind. "I've learned a little about decorating and color schemes since running the Swiss Miss."

"I know you would like to help, Cheryl, but you've got a business to run. You can't be here every day too."

He was right. Still she wondered at the intense expression on Sadie's face. She'd been staring at the jars before anyone even knew she was there. Cheryl would be glad when the jars were safely tucked away at the Swiss Miss. *I just need my big, strong helper.*

As if he'd read her thoughts, Levi appeared in the doorway, followed by Naomi and her husband, Seth Miller. With their help, it didn't take long to trundle the jars to Cheryl's blue Ford Focus. When the last jar was in the car, the trunk seemed to sag from the weight.

Cheryl brushed her dusty hands against each other. "All right. I'll get these to the shop."

"Not without help." Naomi turned to Levi. "You will go, will you not?"

Levi's dark blue eyes met Cheryl's gaze, and her protests stilled before she could voice them. "Yes. She should not do this alone."

"Good. Thank you, Levi." Naomi turned to John-John. "We will return on Monday to continue to help."

"I deeply appreciate it, Mrs. Miller, Mr. Miller." John-John's eyes misted as he faced them. "You all know how much this is a personal cause. These women and their families need these cottages. With your help, we'll finish much sooner."

Seth Miller nodded toward the cottage he'd been working in. "It is my pleasure. Nice to use some skills Gott gave me to help others. And Naomi would not leave me alone otherwise, right, Wife?" He winked at her.

"Of course, Husband."

Cheryl smiled at her friends. God had truly planted her in a great community when she came to Sugarcreek. "Let's get the jars to the Swiss Miss then."

"I'll stop by as soon as the work is wrapped up." John-John glanced at his watch. "Probably within a half hour or so."

"No problem." As she climbed into the car and then turned it out of the cul-de-sac, questions circled through her mind. Where did the money come from? Who was the rightful owner? How could she find him or her?

But even as those questions came, she heard her mother's voice prompting her. *"You're taking on too much, Cheryl."*

Not if it meant helping her friend. And John-John needed her help to find the owners of the jars and their contents. He needed to know for certain if their discovery was just something interesting or if it was a treasure, coming at the perfect time for the perfect need.

CHAPTER THREE

The Swiss Miss was quiet as Cheryl entered. Esther dusted a front display table while Levi and Cheryl carried the first jars inside.

"What have you found?" Esther wrinkled her nose and stepped back. "Please keep the dust outside. I was about finished here."

Cheryl laughed. "With these jars I think we'd have better luck if we simply hosed them off. A utility sink would be perfect. Unfortunately, the Swiss Miss doesn't have one, so we'll make do with a wet rag."

As Levi made repeat trips to her little car to carry in the remaining jars, Cheryl wiped each one. While she didn't get all the grime, she at least knocked off the loose dirt. After he brought in the last three jars, Levi crossed his arms and watched her.

"Cheryl, those jars will not fit in the safe." He made a measuring motion with his arms. "They are simply too big. Too bulky."

The same thought had floated through her mind. In fact, she wasn't convinced she'd have room for all of the coins even if she took them out of the jars. She had some gallon baggies on one of the office shelves. Maybe if she separated them in a balanced way, she could use those bags to contain the coins. It only had to work until Monday. Then she could get the coins to the bank, and the money would be someone else's worry.

"Let's see how many will fit." She turned to the wall safe and carefully turned the knob until it clicked and opened. Then she took a jar and placed it inside. She could only slide in fifteens jars before the door wouldn't close properly.

"Sugar and grits! I'd hoped more would fit." She stepped back. "I guess we'll have to try baggies. Levi, can you get me that box of them from the shelf beside you?"

"Sure." He handed her the box.

She took and opened a baggie and then twisted the lid on the closest jar. The bag quickly sagged as she upended the contents of the can into the baggie. "This is heavy, but the bag should hold the coins at least until Monday." It would be easier if she could get the coins rolled, but she didn't have a machine to do that, and from the few she'd seen, the jars contained a wide variety. "We might need to have the coins appraised."

Levi handed a jar to her as she placed the first bag in the safe. "Why would you appraise them?"

"To see how much they're worth. These coins look old." She lifted one in the air, but it was hard to read the date on it. "I'm not a coin expert, so an appraisal could help."

"I suppose." Levi grabbed the next jar. As he twisted the lid off, something rustled. He frowned and slowed down his movement. "What else is in this jar?" He eased the lid off, and a smallish piece of mimeographed paper was folded on top of the coins. "Wonder what this is?"

"Let me see it." After Levi handed the folded envelope to her, Cheryl carefully examined it. Across the top of the envelope in blue ink was a V-mail symbol and in the middle a window for an address that was too faded to read. She flipped the envelope over and opened it. The creases were yellowed with age, and the paper frail, like it wore its age cautiously. She squinted at the page and shifted it to try to see the words in a better light.

Dear Maam and *Daed*,

Es dutt mir leed. I know you are disappointed that I accepted the medic position with the [blacked out words]. I felt it was my duty to do as my country asks. But I know you do not agree. I wish I could honor you and your wishes, but this time it was not possible. Tomorrow we head out to [blacked out words]. I have never been to a [blacked out word] location. It will be an experience.

Know that I will do my best to honor you and my country. I like my job. If I can help the injured, then I will. It is valuable, brave work.

Beau crawled in her lap and batted at the page. Cheryl gasped and lifted it out of his reach. "Beau, get down. This is a piece of valuable history!"

He meowed his displeasure and flicked his tail in her face. She brushed it down and laughed. "You may sit in my lap, but please let me read."

Levi shook his head as he watched them. "That cat thinks he owns you. He should be in a barn."

"Not my kitty." Cheryl rubbed his black ears and then put the letter up so she could finish reading.

I have listed you as my wage recipients. The checks will be sent to you. Use the money to care for the farm. I will return as soon as I can. *Kumme* the end of the war. Pray it kumme soon.

Your Humble Son

The censored parts made the content hard to decipher. Still, Cheryl teared up as she read the letter. "This letter must be from World War II."

"You know this from the words?"

Cheryl shook her head. "No, but it fits. I can hop online and see if the envelope looks like V-mail from that time. I thought the envelopes were bigger and all one piece though." She shrugged. "I can find out. If I'm right, I wonder if that means the jars were put in the wall during World War II?" The thought both intrigued and bothered her. "If that's the case, then it would be so sad. The soldier who wrote this was so clear that he wanted the money spent. So maybe there is another connection to the money."

"Maybe." Levi shrugged with a smile. "It is a mystery for you to solve. I am just here for the heavy lifting." He winked.

"And you're good at that." She smiled and then scanned the letter again. "I wish I could read the signature." Then she flipped it over. "Or the address. It's impossible to read that scribbled signature. I wonder where the man served. How could I find out?"

"You're assuming the letter is tied to the money," Levi said. "It is possible they are unrelated."

Levi had a point.

Cheryl sighed. "We shouldn't leap to conclusions. Not that I've ever done that before."

He rolled his eyes, and she laughed in response.

"Do you think the author could be Amish?"

Levi leaned closer and his hand brushed hers as he reached for the letter. "Why?"

"Some of the phrases are German or Dutch, right? And what about the way it's written?"

After a minute of quiet as Levi read, he nodded. "I see what you are thinking. The writing is formal. Maybe it is because of the time it was written."

"True. But what about the phrases?"

"Es dutt mir leed means 'I am sorry'. I am not sure it means the person is Amish. An Amish man would be a conscientious objector since we are pacifists. I cannot see how one would serve even as a medic. It would go against the *Ordnung*."

"All the time?"

"Yes."

Levi's answer was so direct and clear it left little room for interpretation. Cheryl's shoulders slumped, and she considered all the mason jars and coins. "Well, we'd better get these in the safe so we can leave."

Maybe when she read the letter again, she'd find a clue. It was too simple to suppose the answer to who owned the money would be contained in the letter. And if it was, it would be too much to hope its contents would be clear and easy to interpret.

The time passed quickly as they worked together to move the coins into the bags. Esther came back to tell them that she was leaving for the day. She told Cheryl she'd lock up.

More time passed, and soon Levi handed a sagging bag to her. "Here is the last one."

Cheryl puffed out a breath as she eyed the safe. "One last hurtle, trying to figure out how to fit these all in." She attempted to shove it in, but it slipped right out. "Sugar and grits," she mumbled again.

She plastered on a smile as the weariness of the day overwhelmed her. "I'm ready to get out of here. I'm ready for peace. I'm ready for quiet." The smallest yawn escaped, and she told herself she'd get to bed early and make her mother proud.

Levi examined the safe too. "I am sure we will figure something out. Then I will leave you be."

"Oh! I didn't mean that. I don't need quiet from you. You're no trouble at all. In fact I appreciate you being here—helping. Can I give you a ride back to the cottages or to your house when we're done?"

Since the Millers didn't have a cell phone to call, she had no idea if they were on their way as they said, or if she should meet them back at the cottages. Or maybe they should just stay put. She wouldn't mind the time with Levi. "Or, since your parents said they'd be by, we can just wait." Their friendship had definitely developed and was comfortable most of the time. She'd enjoy a few more minutes with him.

"I can walk back when we are done. Exercise is good for the soul."

Cheryl refused to let disappointment rush over her. Instead she eyed him. "You've been swinging a hammer all day on the cottages. The least I can do is get you home."

Levi set the plastic bag of coins down, and then he reached down and pulled an envelope from under the office chair. "Did you see this?"

Cheryl reached for it. "No. Look—it's another V-mail envelope. And there are two letters inside."

"Shall we read them?" He quirked an eyebrow at her as if daring her to say no.

"We shall. I can think of nothing better to do." Maybe it would have a better clue than the first letter. "I wonder how we missed this."

"I do not know, but they look much like the first."

He was right. The envelopes were the same, as was the chicken-scratch handwriting. She pulled out one of the letters. "This man should have been a doctor. His writing is even worse on this letter."

Cheryl turned the letter over, and then a loud banging caused her to jump.

CHAPTER FOUR

The banging continued, incessant and demanding. Someone pounded on the door of the Swiss Miss, and whoever it was didn't seem happy.

Levi looked at Cheryl. "Would you like me to see who it is?"

She was tempted to ignore the pounding. The shop was closed, and whoever it was could wait until they were in a better mood and the store open. Instead, as Levi pushed to his feet, she waved him back. "I'll see who it is. No need for you to do that. It's my store, so I should be the one to check."

Cheryl tucked the letters into her purse and turned to the office door. She considered letting Levi handle this, but her curiosity got the best of her. She had to see just who was so determined to get in the store.

As Cheryl left the small office, her gaze landed on Aunt Mitzi's bulletin board display of family photos. How would Aunt Mitzi handle someone pounding on the store door after hours? Likely with grace and goodwill.

Realizing that the coins were not yet locked up, she shut the door firmly behind her. Cheryl took a deep breath and prayed for both as she strode across the store's wooden floors. She skirted a display table and not a single jar of homemade preserves rested out of place. Esther had done a great job setting the store to rights at the end of a busy Saturday. The pounding continued on the door, hard enough for the glass to shiver in the frame. Whoever was out there was certainly determined.

Heavy footsteps approached behind her. "Let me open it." Levi strode up to her. "I do not like that someone is this forceful."

The same thought settled in Cheryl's mind. What could be so important that breaking the door of the Swiss Miss was a real possibility? It was her aunt's store and her responsibility until Aunt Mitzi returned from her mission work in Papua New Guinea. Cheryl flipped the lock then stepped back as Levi's broad form filled the doorway.

"Oh, good, someone is here." A woman with long frizzy blonde hair pushed around Levi and into the shop. She looked vaguely familiar, but Cheryl couldn't immediately place her. "I was beginning to wonder if I'd knock until Monday."

Cheryl and Levi exchanged glances, and Levi stepped back to make room for the forceful spitfire.

Cheryl cleared her throat. "Can I help you?"

"I certainly hope so." The petite woman patted a strand of hair away from her cheek. "I wouldn't have come unless I was convinced we can help each other."

"Oh." Cheryl considered the woman. "And how is that since I don't even know who you are?"

The woman giggled, the sound like something a twelve-year-old would make. Levi winced. "I'm Suzanne Marshall. I thought for sure we've met somewhere before."

Cheryl stared at her blankly. The woman shrugged and continued.

"Anyway, I'm here because I was helping at the cottages this morning. Just as I was ready to leave, there was quite the ruckus. Naturally, I hung around. That's when I heard about the coins." Her smile widened like Cheryl should be thrilled.

Instead, Cheryl felt like she was caught in a bizarre episode of *Candid Camera*, a show she'd watched years ago when visiting Aunt Mitzi. She glanced outside, but didn't see anybody lingering on the sidewalk as if trying to capture her reaction.

She turned to Suzanne. "I'm sorry, but I don't understand what you think you can help me with."

"I'm a coin collector and appraiser. My hobby has grown into a vocation." Her gaze darted between Levi and Cheryl. "Everyone in the Dover area knows that."

"Okay. Is there something we can do for you?"

"Do for me? I'm here to help *you*. I've come to examine the coins. I should be able to give you a quick assessment of whether any of the coins have real value." Suzanne smiled so wide a dentist would be proud. "Then you'll know if you have anything worth protecting."

Something didn't feel right. How exactly had Suzanne learned of the coins? Only a few people saw them in the cottage. Cheryl stopped herself. But a few others had paid attention when they were lugging the jars to her car. Word of such an unusual find was bound to spread. It wasn't every day that a potential treasure like old jars filled with coins was discovered during renovations. While

Cheryl couldn't place a finger on what bothered her, she couldn't shake the feeling that she needed to learn more about Suzanne before she showed her anything.

Suzanne's fingers played with the strap of her large leather bag as she watched Cheryl. Her smile slipped as the silence stretched.

"Don't you want to know if any of the coins have value?"

"Yes." That would be an important part in the process. However, the coins weren't hers. "But that's really a decision John-John should make." Cheryl pulled out her cell phone and found his contact information. "I'll try him now."

After his phone rang a few times, the call cut out. Cheryl frowned then slid her phone back in her pocket. "I'm sorry, Suzanne, but I can't reach him. Do you have a card you could leave with me? Then when I talk to him, I can see what he wants to do with the coins."

Suzanne straightened and jerked her chin up. "I only want to help. Coins are a commodity that are tricky to appraise. You want to make sure you work with someone who knows coins and how to assess value." She took another step into the store, her red high heels clicking on the floor. "Where are the jars? We can get to work right away." She pulled a camera from her monstrous purse. "All I'll need to start are high-quality photos I can snap with this."

Cheryl's mouth dropped as the woman strode past her and moved farther into the store. Would she push her way into the office? If so, she'd see the coins sitting there all bagged up.

"I'm not so sure we want to do that!" Cheryl called after her.

"Oh, but you do. Every day that dawns brings something to do that can never be done as well again," the woman spouted and then looked to Levi. "Isn't that an Amish proverb? You should know that." Then without waiting for a response, she turned to Cheryl. "Aren't you coming? I have a coin show tomorrow over in Canton, so let's start. Then I'll have what I need to do some basic research."

"I..." Cheryl turned to Levi and mouthed *what do I do*?

He shrugged but then stepped forward and raised his hands in a placating motion. "Ja, we appreciate your offer. However, as Cheryl mentioned, she cannot make decisions like that since the coins are not hers. *Danki* for coming." He swept his hand toward the door.

Color flooded Suzanne's cheeks. Her eyes narrowed.

Levi took another step forward. "It has been a long day for all of us." He brushed drywall fragments from his shirt. "A long day with much accomplished. Why not give Cheryl your card? Then she can contact you after she knows John-John's decision."

Suzanne stood her ground as she looked deeper into the store. "You must have them somewhere around here. Why waste time? Just a few photos and I can get started."

"But I can't let you do that." Cheryl firmed her jaw and stepped in the aisle that led to the office. "I really must talk to John-John first."

"Well, if that's what you want. Don't presume I'll be available at your timing."

Cheryl bit back a grin at the words. That was exactly what Suzanne had presumed they'd do for her. Drop everything so she could examine the coins.

"You need not worry about that." Levi opened the front door. "Can I help you to your car?"

Cheryl could almost see steam pour from Suzanne's ears.

"What an absurd thing to say. I can get there without assistance. What a rude man!"

Cheryl held out a hand. "Do you have a card or Web site? In case John-John does want to contact you."

The woman cocked an eyebrow. "Of course he will. Who else around here knows a thing about old coins?" The woman huffed as she dug through her voluminous bag and yanked a business card from a side pocket. She jutted it toward Cheryl. "Here. Have a good weekend."

Cheryl took the card and nodded.

Without another word, Suzanne pivoted and headed out the door.

Levi stepped just outside the door, keeping his eyes on Suzanne. Cheryl followed and watched Suzanne's progress down the sidewalk to a white Mini Cooper. "That was, uh, interesting."

Levi chuckled. "I do believe that woman is almost as stubborn as you can be." One corner of his lips lifted in a half grin.

"Hey!" Cheryl swatted his arm then turned back to watch Suzanne pull out of her parking space. "I wonder what she really wanted."

Standing this close to Levi, Cheryl noticed the slightest blond stubble on his chin—his five o'clock shadow. She tried to picture Levi with a full beard—that of a married man—and an unexpected heat filled her stomach as she did. She quickly pushed those thoughts away.

"She heard about the coins and wanted the job of evaluating them?"

"Maybe." Still, as she watched the small car disappear down Main Street, she had to wonder. "Why hurry over now? The shop is closed—most of downtown is. There's no hurry to look at them before Monday."

She tapped the business card. "I'll see what I can learn about her when I'm home." Cheryl turned back toward the office. "I'm beat, but I have to get those coins put up, and then you need to find your family."

"Only after I know you are fine." Levi's rich voice calmed her turmoil but only for a moment.

As she returned inside, the hair on her arms rose as she replayed the encounter in her mind and paused. Levi paused beside her.

That Suzanne whatever-her-name-was had pushed her way into the store. She'd disrespected Levi, and she'd left in a huff. Cheryl was glad they hadn't given in to her demands. She placed a hand on her hip. "Something isn't right."

"I agree."

They moved back toward the office, and she placed her hand on the doorknob, pausing. There was something bothering her, something she couldn't put her finger on.

Wait a minute. A soft gasp escaped her lips. Suzanne had been wearing red high heels. Those weren't the kind of shoes anyone would be allowed to wear if they were working at or around the construction site. Even Cheryl's beat-up tennis shoes hadn't felt quite protective enough once she'd understood just how much demolition and construction was being done inside the cottages. Surely no one would have allowed the coin collector to hang around the cottages all day wearing those.

Cheryl slid the card from her pocket and examined it. *Suzanne Marshall. Coin collector and appraiser.* After that came the usual e-mail address and phone number.

Which role had she come to the Swiss Miss in? Coin collector? Or appraiser?

Her intent in seeing the coins would vary greatly based on that answer.

CHAPTER FIVE

The bell over the front door of the Swiss Miss jangled, and Cheryl startled. "Did we forget to lock up?"

Surely after watching that intense woman stride from the store she would have locked it. But as she thought about it, Cheryl couldn't remember twisting the deadbolt.

Levi was already headed into the main store. "I will check."

As she watched him walk back to the front, Cheryl saw him puff into protective mode. She smiled, appreciating having someone here watching over her. She'd gotten so used to taking care of herself and the store that she hadn't noticed how heavy the burden was. She opened the door and turned on the lights. She eyed the coins for a moment, wishing she hadn't volunteered to keep them safe. This was turning out to be a much bigger deal than she'd imagined.

The murmur of voices filtered to her from the store. Flipping off the light, she left her office. As soon as she entered the store she saw Naomi and Seth standing next to Levi. Her friend's normally perfect kapp looked askew as if Naomi had rushed from the cottages to the store. Still, when Naomi glanced up and met Cheryl's gaze, Naomi's eyes danced with curiosity.

"So you already are having excitement without me? Levi just mentioned you had an unexpected visitor." Naomi stepped toward Cheryl, her skirt swishing against a display of tablecloths and napkins. "I thought we agreed you would not have all the fun yourself."

"Oh, I shared with Levi."

Levi's dark blue eyes glinted as he nodded. "Cheryl allowed me to escort our bold and excitable guest to the door."

Seth Miller shifted and scooted closer to Naomi. "I am glad you were here to help."

"Me too. I'm not sure what I would have done without Levi's help. The whole encounter was odd. It felt like I was supposed to know her, but I can't imagine why."

Naomi leaned into her husband's side. "Why do you think you should know her?"

Cheryl recounted how Suzanne Marshall had swept into the store as if expecting Cheryl to be delighted to see her. She recounted how the woman had been pushy to the point of obnoxious, yet Cheryl simply couldn't agree to show her the coins. "As I thought about it, I realized she couldn't have been at the cottages. Well, she couldn't have been working there."

Naomi leaned forward slightly as if to catch each word. "Why not?"

"She was wearing red heels. Those aren't working shoes, and definitely not for a construction zone."

"Maybe she went home first. Cleaned up."

"It's possible." Cheryl's brow furrowed, but the answer still didn't seem plausible. "We hadn't been here that long when she arrived. I'm not sure she would have had time to go home and change."

Levi nodded his confirmation. "We were here just long enough to get the coins in bags. And read the letter."

"Letter?" Naomi grinned. "I knew there must be more to your coins."

Cheryl straightened an Amish doll that sat next to its twin. She might not have mentioned the letter yet if Levi hadn't said something. There was so much she didn't know after that one quick read. She wanted more time to analyze it, but she was being silly. Naomi was always a good source of ideas when it came to a good puzzle. And using the letters to learn the identity of the author would be exactly that.

"Would you like to see it?"

Naomi nodded, a cautious light in her eyes. "If you are sure . . ."

While she hadn't meant to be rude, it looked like she'd done just that. Now her closest friend in Sugarcreek was uncertain Cheryl valued her. "Of course. I'm sorry. It's in the office."

She motioned for her guests to follow her to the office. Naomi and Seth followed her inside, and Levi waited in the doorway.

Cheryl took it from her purse and carefully opened it. The safe was still open, and the extra bag of coins still rested on the desk, but everyone's attention was fixed on the piece of paper in her hands. Cheryl cleared a spot, carefully laid the fragile sheet of paper on her desk, and then stepped back. Naomi and Seth leaned toward the letter, their heads nearly touching as they examined it.

"You could read this?" Naomi looked up with a slight frown marring the skin between her eyebrows. "It is quite faded."

"Levi and I were deciphering it when Ms. Marshall's pounding startled us." Cheryl shrugged as she noted the tight penmanship. "It seems to be from a soldier to his family back home."

"Cheryl believes he may be Amish." Levi's voice soothed the anxious feeling rising inside her.

"I can't be sure, but it seems like he used a couple phrases that would make more sense if he was Amish."

Naomi nodded. "I can see why." Her finger traced above the paper. "Here…and here. Still, anyone from this area with Amish friends would know the phrases. They are common."

Cheryl skimmed the page again. Could Naomi be right? If so, Cheryl really had no idea how to begin her search for the author. "Es dutt mir leed." She glanced at Levi. "What did you say that meant again?"

"I'm sure you'll know it as soon as I say it," Naomi jumped in. She smiled as she repeated the phrase.

Cheryl shook her head.

"It means 'I am sorry'. It is a simple phrase that we say all the time. You may not have noticed it yet, but someone who grew up around Sugarcreek would not think twice to use it. It would be like saying *bitte* or danki if you knew someone German."

"So a very common phrase?"

Seth and Levi nodded their agreement. "Ja."

"*Hmm.*" Cheryl frowned as she repeated the phrase. "I guess you're right, Levi. It doesn't mean the person is Amish."

"It does not mean they are not." Seth's eyes twinkled. "Things are often exactly what they seem."

"And sometimes they are not, Husband." Naomi shrugged, but then pointed at the next phrase. "The only other Pennsylvania Dutch word is kumme. That is common."

"I translated that on my own." Cheryl grinned at her friends. "I'm learning a few things while I'm here."

"Ja, you are." Naomi patted her hand then glanced back at the letter while Seth stepped away from the counter. "I do not know that these words are enough to convince me that your author is Amish, but it is possible."

Seth ran a hand down his beard. "Ja. But the fact that this man is a soldier moves it to uncharacteristic."

"I told Cheryl we would not serve if drafted. I've never heard of an Amish man doing so." Levi leaned casually against the counter, and Cheryl inhaled the faint odor of a man who had spent the day working, yet somehow with Levi it was appealing.

The bell over the front door jingled, and Cheryl stiffened. She'd forgotten to lock the door for a second time. Could it be Suzanne returning? "Who could it be this time?"

Cheryl moved past the others to the hallway leading to the store area. A smile lifted on her lips when she spotted John-John walking through the store in her direction.

"I hope it's all right that I walked on in. I saw Seth and Naomi's buggy parked out front. The front door was still unlocked, but I dead bolted it after I entered. Sugarcreek is safe for the most part, but you don't want to welcome trouble."

"No, of course not." Cheryl noted a tenseness around his eyes. Was it just the busyness of the day? Or something more? She hoped for the latter, motioning him back to her office. "Come on back. I bet you're tired at the end of a long day." Levi stepped aside so John-John could enter the office. "Can I get you anything? I don't have much, but there are a few cans of soda and a few bottles of water in my fridge."

Naomi caught Cheryl's gaze and gave her a slight nod. Warmth welled inside at the confirmation she'd done well.

"I'm fine. Just ready to head home. Before I do, I thought I'd come see the coins. Make sure you had what you need."

"I'm glad you stopped by. And I have something to show you that Levi and I discovered as we moved the coins to the safe." She motioned to the desk, and they all shifted to allow John-John closer to the desk. Cheryl and John-John stood inside the office next to the desk, while Naomi, Seth, and Levi clustered in the doorway.

"I couldn't get many jars to fit into the safe, so we took the coins out and bagged them. We're still trying to figure out how to get them all in." She pointed first to the bags of coins and then to the jars lining the floor by her desk. "And all of the jars are here."

"I can see that." John-John grinned.

"That is quite the leaning mountain of coins in there." He picked up the extra bag of coins that didn't quite fit. Then he carefully held the bag to the light and manipulated it as he looked at the coins. "My daddy was a coin collector. I never took it up as a hobby, but some of these look pretty old." He squinted as he looked closer at one coin through the clear bag. "This one looks like it's dated 1939."

"That matches the timeframe for the letter we found."

He turned and looked at Cheryl. "Letters? I thought we were dealing with coins."

"We are, but a few V-mail letters were shoved alongside the coins. I'll show them to you, but first do you know much about coins? Because I don't." She turned and met Levi's gaze. Something in his knowing gaze made her think he was remembering the pushy coin collector who'd pushed her way into the store. Should she mention Suzanne to John-John now? She decided not to. They had many other things to do before they broached getting the coins appraised, and she'd need to research the woman before she decided whether to suggest Suzanne to John-John as an appraiser.

"I know a little. Just what my daddy told me." He sighed. "I wish I would have paid better attention. I was just a kid. All I wanted was to get to my favorite fishing hole. At the time staring at old pieces of metal trying to learn their stories wasn't interesting. Now . . . " He turned the bag over again. "Now I could be persuaded to learn more—especially why these were hidden inside a wall."

Naomi cocked her head as she studied the coins in his hand. "I bet John-John would find that letter interesting, Cheryl," Naomi said, turning their conversation back to the other items that were in the jars.

Levi nodded as he squeezed a broad shoulder through the doorway. "The author served in World War II. Cheryl believes he may have been Amish. I am not convinced."

"Do you want to read it?" Cheryl asked.

John-John rubbed his brow. "Maybe another day. I wouldn't know much 'bout that—about World War II." He shrugged, an uncomfortable grimace on his face. "I'll leave it to you to determine who the letter writer is."

He turned to Naomi, who had knelt beside the jars and was wiping more grime from the side of one. "Ma'am, would you like to take those jars? Do you have any use for them?"

She smiled up at him, her smile stretching her cheeks. "I can certainly use them if you don't have a use for them. I won't can with them, but they would look nice on top of one of my cabinets. At least a few of them... maybe not all forty."

"I wouldn't know what to do with them other than break them with these big paws of mine." He held up his large hands for examination. "I think anything you do with them will be better."

"Thank you." Naomi picked up a jar and turned it from side to side. "I cannot tell for sure until I get home and clean them, but these look unique. I might take one to the sewing frolic Monday and see if anyone there recognizes these—where they came from or how old they are. Surely someone will."

Naomi handed six of the jars to Seth, who with a long-suffering sigh but a twinkle in his eye began carrying them to the family's buggy.

Cheryl placed the remaining jars in one of her low cupboards and turned her attention back to John. "Would you like to take a few coins home? Maybe you can examine them and see something I don't. After all, your father collected coins. That's more than anyone in my family has done." She just couldn't imagine her preacher father or prim mother spending time bending over tiny coins.

John-John shook his head. "No thank you." He pointed to the safe. "They'll be safer here, and you have a much better chance of actually making heads or tails of them. Thanks for making room for them."

"At least take a few photos of the coins, in case you get interested."

A slow grin spread across his face as he tugged a simple cell phone from his pocket. "If it'll make you happy." He opened the bag and took out some of the coins. He snapped several shots and then put them back into the bag.

"Now to get them in the safe."

Levi handed the last sagging bag to her. "Here is the last one."

Cheryl puffed out a breath as she shoved the last bag back on top of the pile of other bagged coins inside the safe. The bag slid back down the mountain of coins, and she grabbed it before it fell out of the vault.

Heat rose up her neck as she sensed all eyes on her. She had to get the coins all in the safe. She didn't want to leave them out, and she didn't want to leave the Swiss Miss with them.

Levi shook his head. "You are not going to get that in there."

She moved the bag of coins back and forth in her hands and eyed the safe. "I think I can. I have a plan. I'll stick it in, move my hand quickly, and then you slam the safe."

Levi stroked his chin. "And slam your hand in the process?"

"No...I'll move it out quickly. I promise."

Behind them Seth cleared his throat, but no one said a word.

"If you want to try, but I don't know the numbers if your fingers get stuck. And you will be crying too hard to tell me."

"The numbers?"

Levi pointed to the dial.

"Don't worry about the safe code. This will work. I promise."

Cheryl moved to the side of the safe and placed the last bag inside. She held it there with one hand. "On the count of three."

Levi nodded and placed his hand on the safe door. "One, two..."

She wasn't expecting him to count, and she quickly pulled her hand away. The bag slipped, and she jerked her fingers out of the way.

"Three!" Levi slammed the door.

The safe clanged shut, but it didn't sound right. Her heart pounded when she realized that her fingers almost did get slammed inside.

"Did it lock?" Levi asked.

She barely touched the door and pushed. It gave the slightest wiggle. "I think so. I'm afraid to try to push any harder, let alone spin the lock. I don't want to jam it."

Levi's eyebrows shot up. "Should we try again?"

"No!" The word shot from Cheryl's mouth. She glanced down at her hand and flexed her fingers, fully appreciating that she still had all of her digits. "That's good enough. It feels secure. Besides, the store has an alarm system too."

His dark blue eyes fixed on hers with both amusement and concern. "If you say so."

She turned to the others around them. Seth and Naomi both glanced from one to another, as if amused by the playful banter between them. John-John smiled. "It looks secure enough to me."

That done, he slapped his ball cap back on his head. "Well, I'd better head home and plot out the next tasks at the cottages. We made a lot of progress today thanks to everyone's help, but there's much to do." He nodded at Cheryl and Naomi. "See you early on Monday. I'll get the coins out of here and in the bank then."

Cheryl nodded. It was a sound plan, and as she looked at the bulging safe, she had to admit she'd be glad when the coins were no longer her responsibility.

CHAPTER SIX

It felt like hours later when Cheryl finally reached her home even though it had only been thirty minutes since the Millers had left the Swiss Miss. She set down Beau inside the front door. He glanced back at her with displeasure. His unhappy meows echoed inside her pounding head. Sometime in the last few hours, a drummer had taken up residence on her skull.

"Sorry, boy. I didn't plan to be gone so long. I'll get your dinner right away."

He high stepped it toward the kitchen and his food bowl. When she reached the kitchen, she saw that his bowl was empty. If Beau could have one wish, she guessed he'd appreciate a bowl that magically never emptied of his favorite kibble. She retrieved the bag from the pantry, and Beau curled around her legs, purring as he pranced. When she poured the kibble into his bowl, he was lost to her, eating as if he hadn't seen food in weeks rather than hours.

Her stomach rumbled in response to seeing Beau so happily eating.

Maybe if she made time to eat and took a few ibuprofen, her head would stop pounding and she could begin thinking.

What had she had for lunch? She didn't want to duplicate that for dinner.

She stood in front of the refrigerator and nothing came to her. Maybe she hadn't eaten anything. That's right, she'd only had one bite of her sandwich when she'd been summoned to the cottage. It hadn't felt right to eat before the workers, but now as Cheryl thought back over the day, she realized she'd careened from the Swiss Miss to the cottages and then back to the Swiss Miss with the mason jars of coins.

How many days flowed just like today? Without the time to grab a needed bit of food?

Was Momma on to something with her challenge that Cheryl was too busy?

Cheryl shook the thought away as she opened the refrigerator and grabbed a strawberry yogurt. She'd start with that quick treat after she added a little granola to the top for crunch. Then she'd take the ibuprofen and figure out what else to eat. Maybe her thoughts would be clearer when her stomach wasn't so rumbly.

After she scraped the last bit of yogurt from the container, Beau rubbed against her legs. His purr seemed to thank her for his meal. Cheryl glanced out the window at the back patio. A cushioned chair provided the perfect vantage point to watch birds flying to and from the white birdhouse atop a tall pole. Cheryl made a mental note to wipe off the chair before she used that spot for devotions again. Now that the weather was warming up and spring seemed here to stay, she could imagine many mornings of devotions outside Aunt Mitzi's backyard.

The chair looked like the perfect place to relax, and Cheryl considered doing so now, but she knew if she settled into it she might not be able to get up again.

Her momma's words flitted through her mind again. *"Cheryl, you have to take care of yourself. You can serve yourself right into a health crisis if you're not careful."*

Surely Momma was being dramatic. Overstating to catch Cheryl's attention. She'd done that more than a time or two when Cheryl was a teen. Momma had all the lectures about boys and keeping her nose clean and out of trouble down pat—so much so Cheryl imagined she practiced them in front of a mirror. But now Cheryl was thirty-one years old. She didn't need Momma to watch over her like she did when Cheryl was a child.

No, she was a grown woman and could stand on her own.

The weariness though... the weariness could press down hard. She covered a yawn that threatened to stretch her face in half and then shook herself.

"I still need food." Not much sounded good, so she settled on a simple BLT. Quick, easy, and tasty. Add an apple and it was a full meal when she considered the yogurt and granola she'd already had.

After she grabbed a glass of water and took the pills, Cheryl wondered if she should lie down. Yet her mind whirled with all that had happened. The day that should have been much like any other in Sugarcreek had erupted with the discovery of the coins.

Could she possibly locate the owner or the person who had hidden them?

She tried to imagine why someone would tuck that many jars filled with old coins between the walls of a cottage. True, the Depression had just ended as the letters were written. If the money was somehow tied to the letters, that might explain why someone had chosen to create their own safe rather than use a bank. So many banks had failed during the Depression, it could easily make a person who'd experienced that leery of the long-term safety of an account.

At the same time, she couldn't quite imagine someone stashing so much between the walls and forgetting about them. That was equally as hard as believing someone had intentionally left them buried between the studs. What could possibly motivate someone to do that? Cheryl might not have a great grasp of how much money the jars held, but it had to be several thousand dollars. That was a sizable amount today, let alone when the jars were hidden.

She grabbed a notebook and pen from the junk drawer in Aunt Mitzi's sunny kitchen then settled on the couch. After shifting to make sure she was comfortable but not in danger of immediately relaxing to sleep, she wrote the date at the top of the page.

She would use this notebook to track everything she'd learned and make sure nothing slipped from her mind. If she would help John-John figure out who might claim the coins, then she'd need to start laying out what she knew now and add to it as she learned more.

As she stared at the blank page, it seemed pretty clear she didn't know much of anything. What she really had was a list of questions.

Where were the mason jars from?

Who filled the jars with coins?

Why would they do that?

Was the letter writer somehow tied to the coins or were the letters shoved in the jars for another reason? Safekeeping maybe?

Could the coins tell her something?

She supposed if she looked at the dates on them, she'd at least be able to limit when the coins were placed inside. It would provide an end point for the deposit inside the walls.

If she could identify something unique about the jars, she might be able to further limit where the coins came from. She noted that Naomi was going to check with her sewing circle friends on Monday, so she could follow up with her friend after that. If anyone could sweetly ferret out the information, Naomi could. She was an expert at making her friends comfortable and willing to share what they knew. The question was whether they'd know anything about the jars. As far as Cheryl knew, canning jars pretty much looked the same.

Next she wrote *appraiser* with a question mark.

Should she get an appraiser involved? Why? Who? What would she hope to learn from them?

The questions seemed to multiply as she captured them on paper.

She flipped the page on the notebook and titled the clean one *Things to Investigate*.

First, she needed to see if she could trace the title to the cottage. All of that should be in writing in some office in the county courthouse. Then she just had to trace back to who owned the house in the years before and after the letters were written. That would give her an avenue to explore. If she were lucky, it might even lead her to the person who put the jars in the wall—or someone who was around at that time.

Then she should try to figure out who wrote the letters. If that soldier was still alive, she could find out whom he'd written. Or at least try to track down his family.

The pounding in her head picked up pace again. She rubbed the back of her neck then her temples, praying for relief.

Maybe if she went to bed a little early, she could kill the headache and start Sunday fresh. When she looked at the silver clock hanging in Aunt Mitzi's white kitchen, she startled. Could it really be ten already? She hadn't realized she'd spent that much time on her notes. The calendar on the refrigerator caught her attention as she filled a glass with water. The next week was packed. If she thought about all she had to do between the Swiss Miss and helping John-John with the cottages, she might have to sit down and cry. Or clone herself. Had scientists made enough progress for that? She shook her head to clear the loopy thought.

She shouldn't feel this overwhelmed at the thought of the next week. Yet how could she be available to help the people God placed in her life if she was always telling them no?

Had her momma figured out that balance? As she thought about how Momma ran from church meeting to committee meeting to school activity, Cheryl couldn't believe that her mom had determined the correct mix of home, church, and work. At least not while Cheryl and her brother, Matt, were still home. No, she remembered lots of times when her mom seemed more than a little submerged by all of the events she had to manage. Of course, it made sense. Her father was the lead pastor at a church for all of those years, a church that continued to grow and add to his responsibilities.

So how should she do it?

How could she care for her shop and care for those around her without becoming overwhelmed?

Cheryl carried her glass of water to her room and sank onto the edge of her comfy bed. This wasn't a question she could answer quickly. Certainly not while she was helping John-John at the cottages and Aunt Mitzi with the shop and discovering what happened to the coins.

Maybe if she dreamed about white space on her calendar and free time in her days, she'd get to discover what that really meant.

Until then, she had a mystery to untangle so she could tell John-John whom the coins belonged to. If she were really lucky, she'd tell him they were his to use for his ministry to battered women and their children. That would make all of this worth it.

CHAPTER SEVEN

The next morning, Cheryl barely made it to church and spent the service attempting to focus on the sermon. Instead, the questions she'd written about the coins invaded her mind. By the time she got home, she was ready to dive into her investigation. Today, she'd start with the V-mail. Maybe if she transcribed the letters, she'd pick up on a nuance she'd missed in the quick reads at the Swiss Miss.

She opened and read the second letter.

Dear Maam and Daed,

I have received a letter from Larry, and they started planting. I am out of the hospital but still taking treatments for rheumatism. Guess the weather is too wet and cold here. This is the first time that I had to bother with it since I came overseas. I know you have not written much, but if it is possible I would appreciate you sending some of that Soretone Liniment. I will send a gift and a postcard. I hope you are receiving the deposits. Please write and let me know.

I like my mates well enough. Some of them are actual mates. From Australia. It has been incredible to meet guys from way beyond the good ole US of A. I guess I never stopped to think about that bit. Still, I like it. For a boy who never thought he would see much beyond Ohio, I have experienced much I could not imagine.

I long for home though. More than the farming, I miss your noodles, Maam. And Daed, I even miss helping you with your woodworking. Never thought I would write that. Yet here I am doing so.

[Blacked out paragraph.]

Cheryl stopped. He'd gotten through several paragraphs before the government censors stepped in. She wondered what he'd started to say, but no matter how she held the letter up to the light, she couldn't make out anything past the black block.

As she read back over it, nothing in particular stood out to make this one seem like the author could be Amish. Well, other than the use of *maam* and *daed* to address the writer's parents. That might just mean he had Amish friends and had picked up their terms of endearment. No, that was unlikely. But no other Pennsylvania Dutch phrases had slipped into this letter.

She still had one more letter after this one. Maybe it would give her more clues. Puffing air past her lips, Cheryl turned back to the letter.

I do not have much more to say. I miss you. I even miss the *kinder*. I never thought I would write that either. It helps to know that I am providing help for everyone even from far away. I know money is only a tool, not a goal, but I hope it is keeping food on the table since I cannot be there to help. Anyway, greet everyone for me. And tell Josiah to take good care of Dutch. I miss that dog, but he would not have enjoyed the cold here.

Your Loving Son

She read the letter one more time and then carefully folded it and put it next to the other thin letter. He'd used *kinder*, but she wasn't sure that would count. And Josiah certainly was a name the Amish used. But those were slim details to presume the author was Amish.

The simple fact was she had little to go on.

Cheryl thought about reading the other letter, but she was almost afraid to. It would likely just lead to another dead end. Besides, she had to get some housework done. Today was her one chance before the busy week ahead.

Cheryl spent the next hour putting the cottage back together. It wasn't a terrible mess, but during the week she put in such long hours at the Swiss Miss that it needed a bit of attention to feel like it was cared for the way Aunt Mitzi would do it. It didn't take long to run a broom and then a mop over the small kitchen floor. Another fifteen minutes and she'd run a cursory vacuum over the space. A bit of dusting to knock Beau's fur down now that he was shedding, and the house was ready to welcome Aunt Mitzi if she chose to walk through the door. Next weekend Cheryl would need to find a few minutes to plop some spring flowers in the ground around the front gate. The pop of color would be a welcome addition.

She looked at her watch and put the last of her cleaning supplies back under the kitchen sink. It was time to Skype with Aunt Mitzi and see how her aunt's mission work was going.

Part of Cheryl still struggled to believe that her aunt was halfway around the world on a remote island. The other part was so proud of her willingness to go where she felt led and serve the people God had placed on her heart. Cheryl only wished she could help speed up the process. Aunt Mitzi was still finding it a challenge to connect with the people she longed to serve. This was Cheryl's opportunity to encourage her aunt in her work.

She did a little Meg Ryan boxing move a la *You've Got Mail* and then fired up her computer. She opened Skype and then selected Aunt Mitzi from her list of contacts. A quick message to see if she was available, and Cheryl settled in with her calendar and to-do list while she waited for the call to connect.

Soon Aunt Mitzi's smiling face popped on to her computer screen.

"How's my favorite niece?" Aunt Mitzi's short hair looked spiky—almost as spiky as Cheryl's usual style. She was wearing a blue cotton blouse over a tank and looked happy, if warm.

"Doing fine."

Aunt Mitzi leaned closer to her camera and frowned. "Doesn't look that way from here. What's got that frown line between your eyebrows?"

"Nothing much." Cheryl straightened and forced what she hoped was a perky smile. "Besides, I didn't call to talk about me but to hear how you're doing. How are things in Papua New Guinea?"

"Everything I'd hoped, sweet girl."

"Really?" Things certainly seemed to have changed since the last time they'd chatted. While Aunt Mitzi was usually upbeat, she still had moments of melancholy and days of homesickness. She hadn't exactly eased into her mission work. "Has something changed?"

"I have." Her aunt chuckled, the sound crackling a bit over the connection. "I asked God to use me. In the process He's changing me. I'm calling this my pruning season."

"Ouch." Cheryl winced at the thought of someone taking shears to her aunt.

"Oh, I'm not saying I've been the most willing participant at every step of this journey. But I asked God to use me, and He is. He's definitely showed me that." Her aunt launched into a story of how she'd helped a village that had been flooded in a monsoon. As the villagers began to put their hovels back together, she was there with hugs, food, and elbow grease. "You should have seen how much I glistened at the end of some of those days. There's no deodorant strong enough to help a gal out in the jungle."

Cheryl smiled as she noted the dots of perspiration on her aunt's forehead just sitting there talking to her.

"It's unreal how much a person needs to drink. My friend tried to warn me, but I think I had to live it to truly understand."

"Was this friend with the mission board?"

"Oh no. Though I'm sure a few of them did try to tell me as well. They really do try to train and equip you. Maybe I'm just one of those stubborn types who has to experience something personally to get it."

"I know I'm that way sometimes."

"We all are." Mitzi paused and looked past the camera for a minute. "There are so many times if I'd just taken God's prompting the first time, I could have saved myself some stress and heartache.

Instead, I had to learn the lesson over and over again. Journey around that particular mountain a few times before I truly understood it." She looked back at the camera and at Cheryl. "Catch me up on the Swiss Miss. How's it going? Any questions I can help with?"

Cheryl launched into a story about how she and Esther had helped a little girl who'd gotten separated from her mom earlier in the week. Somehow she'd missed her mom in the flood of people moving off a tour bus.

"All's well that ends well since we found the girl's mom in under an hour. No easy feat when you consider all the people who enjoyed tours and shopping in Sugarcreek."

Then they also talked about how to freshen the stock for summer. Cheryl ran a few ideas for new products past her aunt but was surprised to hear Mitzi going along more and more with Cheryl's ideas, offering counsel on only a couple of her thoughts.

"If you execute all those ideas, it could be a very successful summer for the shop."

"I hope so!"

The picture cut out for a moment, and Aunt Mitzi's face was frozen with her mouth open. Cheryl paused, waiting for the connection to smooth out, hoping it would. Finally, thirty seconds later the picture started moving again.

"You're doing so well with the shop, Cheryl," Mitzi continued without missing a beat. "Everything I'd hoped and more. I'm proud of you." Mitzi's words felt like a balm to Cheryl's heart.

Why couldn't her momma see things that way? It would be so nice to have her mom support and encourage her rather than challenge her lifestyle and decisions.

"Are you working on any mysteries?"

"Maybe." Cheryl grinned. She quickly filled in her aunt on the jars they found within the walls of the cottages. Aunt Mitzi's eyes widened to hear that the jars were filled with coins.

Cheryl leaned closer to the computer screen. "It seems so odd that the coins were stored like they were and that the V-mail letters were inserted in a few of the jars."

"People do things for lots of reasons. They don't have to make sense to us."

"I know. But I wish I understood why the coins were there."

"Maybe someone was sending their pay home. Lots of soldiers did that during the war. What did they need with the money when they're marching across Europe or fighting their way across Pacific Islands?"

Cheryl pointed a finger into the air. "True, but if that's the case, why store coins and not just deposit the pay in the bank?"

"Can't answer that one." Mitzi cut in and out on the computer. "Do you have the letters?"

"We've found three so far, but I've only read two." Cheryl grabbed them and quickly read them to her aunt. There wasn't much too them. Except for the use of Pennsylvania Dutch or German phrases, there weren't many clues. Cheryl folded up the letters after she finished reading them. "What do you make of that?"

"Not much, but you'll figure it out. You've got a knack for it." Then Mitzi paused, looked off in the distance and tapped her lower lip with her pointer finger. "Although, there is something about the letters that reminds me of a friend who fought in the Pacific. He was ill when he was overseas too. Maybe it was rheumatism. I just don't remember now." She frowned, and the picture cut out again.

Mitzi came back on midsentence. "...about how wet it always was. And surprisingly cold at night, but horribly hot during the day. Now that I've been here almost a year, I finally understand what he meant. The dampness really has a way of seeping into these old bones. In fact, if it wasn't for my friend..." The picture and sound cut out again.

"What's that, Aunt Mitzi?"

The connection died.

Cheryl glanced at the clock on her computer and was shocked to find she'd Skyped an hour with her aunt. Frustration built that the call had cut off—just when they were getting to the good part. Just when her aunt was sharing about someone she'd known from the war.

It would be a long shot to think that the soldier her aunt Mitzi knew was the person who'd written the letters. Then again, Sugarcreek wasn't a very big town, and Aunt Mitzi had lived here for years and probably knew almost everyone in Sugarcreek...so maybe it was a new possibility.

Excitement bubbled up in Cheryl's chest. She tried to reconnect the call, but it was no use. Mitzi didn't pick up. Cheryl knew that the Internet was spotty where her aunt was, and she wasn't surprised. She *was* disappointed. She quickly e-mailed her aunt a short note:

> I can't wait to hear more about the World War II soldier that you knew. I'd love to hear more details. Looking forward to Skyping again.

Cheryl closed her notebook computer and pushed it to the side. Being away from all those friends had been hard on Mitzi for a time, but she sure seemed in a good place now. Cheryl reached out and stroked Beau's back, then her gaze landed on the calendar and she frowned.

Just before saying good-bye at the store, Naomi had invited Cheryl over for dinner Monday night to share whatever she learned at the sewing frolic. As Cheryl looked at the rest of the packed week, the thought of adding on a visit to the Millers' farm overwhelmed her. She loved the family but didn't think she had the energy for one more thing this week.

Before she could change her mind, Cheryl grabbed her phone.

When the answering machine in the phone shed picked up, she cleared her throat. "Naomi, thank you so much for the invitation to join you tomorrow night. Something's come up, and I need the time to work on this mystery for John-John. Also, to tell you the complete truth, my mom's challenged me to watch how much I'm doing—she thinks I'm doing too much, and I've decided I'll try to follow her advice. I have been burning the candle on both ends lately."

As soon as she hung up, Cheryl's neck muscles loosened a bit. Maybe Momma was on to something. Maybe she could find a bit of freedom as she learned to open up her calendar a bit.

This was a start. Every change had to start somewhere.

Chapter Eight

Monday morning, the sunlight filtered through the sheer curtains in Cheryl's bedroom. Ready or not, here came a new day, a new week. She took a moment to sink deeper into her pillows.

"Father, help me be a light for You today."

She inhaled deeply and then slowly exhaled. A feeling of peace settled over her. Now she could start her day. Based on her conversation with Aunt Mitzi, she wanted to examine the inventory at the Swiss Miss and make sure she had a few extra items not just for bridal showers but also for high school and college graduation gifts. She hadn't thought about those milestone events that would come at the end of May, but she wanted to make sure the store was prepared. It might take a little imagination to come up with the perfect gift for graduates. Maybe someone had books of Amish wisdom that could be paired with homemade lotions for the young women and a leather Bible cover and bookmark for young men. Also, with so many gift books available, she was willing to bet somebody had created one that was Amish-themed and would fit perfectly with the current merchandise at the Swiss Miss.

She prepared a bowl of granola and yogurt and paired it with the perfect mug of coffee, then Cheryl settled on the patio with her Bible and devotional book. The morning was perfect, and the birdsong added the perfect back note while she read her devotion for the day. It spoke about rest and peace, confirming all her mother had been trying to tell her.

Seeing she had a few minutes left before she needed to leave, Cheryl retrieved the third letter.

Pacific Asian Area
April 24, 1945

Dear Maam and Daed,

Just a few lines. Hope that this letter finds you well and happy. It's hard when so many letters are sent and none are returned. I am in a new place. It is sort of a hard grind to get along here now. Maybe someday we'll have our new Air Base built and live in the jungle. We've got a pretty good start already.

The engineers are building the runways and also helping us build the camp. We have to do most of that ourselves though. Sure is swell to be doing something else other than caring for injured men for a change.

Suppose you folks are all busy in the fields now. I can almost see you getting up out of bed to get ready for a good day of work. I imagine that I get up before you do though? Not counting the change of time between here and Ohio.

Even as I work, I'm thinking about what I will do after the war. Everything's changed, hasn't it? Your silence has proved that it has. But I have peace. Deep down I know I've done the right thing. I pray that someday you both will believe that too.

Cheryl put down the letter. There weren't many more clues, but it did confirm a few things. Whoever wrote the letters was in a conflict with the people he wrote the letters to. She couldn't imagine what type of conflict could keep a father and mother from writing their son away at war, unless both she and Levi were right—the writer was Amish, and he'd joined the war against his parents' wishes. Her heart ached at the thought of being so far away and feeling so alone. It was just the opposite problem than she had—too many people, too much to do.

After praying for the people God had placed in her life, she was ready to head to the store. Beau strolled willingly into his cat carrier, and soon they were covering the few blocks to the store. The sky had the perfect blue color that promised a beautiful spring day. She smiled as she tipped her face toward the rays. A light breeze played in her spiky hair, as if God had sent it to kiss her and remind her how wonderful her life was.

To think a year ago she'd lived in Columbus and worked in a bank. Now she lived in charming Sugarcreek and got to walk to work each day. What a blessing.

She waved at Mr. Gruber, who worked in his yard pulling weeds from a flower bed. Another block, and she stopped to say good morning to Marion Berryhill as she pushed her young daughter, Eden, in a stroller toward By His Grace Christian bookstore.

"Sounds like you've been busy." Marion's ebony face smiled as she glanced at Cheryl. "Working on those cottages is a good thing."

"I'm glad I can help John-John. His vision is one worth embracing."

"So what do you think of the coins?"

"Coins?" How did Marion already know about those?

"The grapevine is alive and well in this town." She chuckled. "I heard about the jars from several people at church yesterday."

"Of course." Cheryl felt a little silly for getting defensive. "I'm not sure what to think about them. I can tell you I'll be glad to give them back to John-John today so he can put them in a safety deposit box at the bank. It's a huge responsibility to have them."

"I can imagine." The women chatted for another a few minutes then separated, each heading to their stores.

The Swiss Miss looked cheery in the sunlight as she approached. The window boxes needed to be filled with red geraniums to complement the red shutters. Cheryl made a mental note to get that done this week. It was definitely time to welcome the flowers. She smiled as she walked past the turret and then turned in front of the store. She quickly unlocked the door, entered, set Beau's carrier down, and then hurried to the security system.

It was as she reached the security panel that she realized it wasn't beeping. She frowned as she punched in the code. The crazy system beeped its warning, stating that it was now fully armed. Hadn't she set it Saturday?

The security system had seemed a necessary addition to the store a few months ago. Now it just seemed to give her more fits as she tried to remember to turn it on and off. But surely she would have remembered to set it Saturday, especially with all the coins in the store.

She closed her eyes and tried to think back, but the thing that stood out the most was Naomi's invitation to dinner and the hopeful look in Levi's eyes at the question. No wonder she'd said yes so quickly and easily.

Beau meowed, and Cheryl hurried over to unzip his carrier. He stretched his front legs and then goose-stepped out of the carrier. His tail went straight up, and he sauntered around the tables and displays as if inspecting to make sure nothing had changed since the last time he'd been in his domain away from the cottage.

She turned back to the security panel. She thought over the sequence as she'd left the store Saturday night. After Levi and his parents had left, she'd reentered the store and loaded Beau in his carrier. Making sure the coins were secure, she'd walked through the main floor of the shop and she was certain she'd stopped to arm the security system.

Over the last few months she'd worked hard to install that in her closing-the-store routine.

Cheryl closed her eyes and went through the sequence again. Yes, she was positive she'd secured the system.

So why wasn't it armed when she entered the store?

A growing feeling of dread crept over her as she thought about how Marion Berryhill had known about the coins. If she did, then there was a strong likelihood the word had spread throughout the small community. If that were so, somebody might have decided that they wanted the coins.

No, she was being ridiculous.

Crime like that didn't happen often in Sugarcreek. This was a safe community where people cared for each other. It wasn't unusual for business owners to help each other out as needs arose. In fact, she'd seen it happen many times in the nine months she'd been a part of the town's life.

If the security system had failed, there was another reason. Maybe the power had surged and knocked it off. Though wasn't the security company supposed to call her if that happened?

Or maybe a storm had blown through town and flashed the electricity. Had she needed to reset a clock? She didn't think so, but some days that seemed a common occurrence since Beau could knock her clock's plug out with a simple brush past the wall socket.

Wait. Maybe Esther had arrived before her. While Cheryl had come in early to find the volunteer list for the cottage project, Esther could have arrived even earlier. She knew Cheryl liked to have the shop in perfect order before they opened the doors for the locals at nine. Even though the shop had looked great Saturday, Esther might have one more thing she wanted to do.

"Esther?" Cheryl flipped on the lights and took a step deeper into the shop. "Are you here already?"

Nothing but Beau's purr reached her. Esther would respond if she were in the shop, so that couldn't be the case.

Why would the security system be turned off?

A sinking feeling settled in Cheryl.

This could only mean one thing.

She tried to shake off her concerns as she picked up Beau's carrier and marched toward the counter. She skirted display tables as she went then set Beau's carrier on the counter.

A minute passed as Cheryl braced herself. She was probably being ridiculous. The fact that the security alarm wasn't set didn't mean there was a problem. Yet she couldn't shake the feeling something was wrong. Fear caused goose bumps to rise up her arms, and all the peaceful thoughts from this morning's quiet time vanished. Cheryl felt alone and almost too frightened to check on her office. She squared her shoulders and told herself to be brave, but even as Beau marched forward, Cheryl's feet stayed planted.

Chapter Nine

Time to quit being ridiculous and just go in the office. Cheryl turned the corner and stopped.

The office door stood open, even though she *knew* she'd firmly closed it like she did every night when she finished her work in there. The office wasn't a place for tourists to wander, the usual chaos not matching the beautiful displays in the front of the shop.

The fact the door was open made her pause. Someone had entered her office since she left Saturday night.

Maybe her assistant had gone into the office for something and forgotten to pull the door shut behind her. "Esther? Where are you?"

She waited, but still nothing. Beau sauntered by, not worried at all. Big help he was. She grabbed her cell phone from her pocket and made sure it was on. Just in case.

Then Cheryl took a deep breath and dared to step inside. Her breath stuttered to a stop on the exhale.

The normally tidy office looked like a tornado had blown through the small space. Her desk chair had been knocked against the wall, leaving a dent. The cupboard doors all stood open, with the contents pulled on the desk and floor. But the part that stopped her heart was the open safe door. The safe was horribly empty, as if she'd never put anything on top of her stack of papers. As if the coin-filled baggies were merely figments of her imagination.

Cheryl scrambled into the small space. Her knees trembled. Her heartbeat quickened. Her hand reached in and she felt around the safe, pulse throbbing as she felt for anything but paper. All that was left was a paper that looked like one of the V-mail letters and another folded piece of paper on top of her few files that had remained.

Nothing else.

She looked under the desk, righted the chair and scanned the office.

Nothing. Anywhere.

The coins were gone.

The bell over the door jingled, but Cheryl's feet stayed planted firmly in place. John-John had entrusted the coins to her care for the weekend...less than two days...and they were gone.

"Cheryl?" Esther's cheerful voice reached Cheryl from the store area. "Is everything okay?"

"No." The word wavered as if she didn't possess enough air to push it out. What was she going to tell John-John? Should she call him first or the police?

She searched each cupboard then slammed their doors shut. No coins inside. Where had they gone? Who would want to break into her store to steal them? It didn't make any sense. "Please, God."

Dread at having to tell John-John what had happened pushed down on her heart.

The sound of Esther's footsteps neared.

She shook her head. She had to focus, had to figure out where the coins were. Her gaze shifted back to the safe.

Nope. It was still empty. Except for the papers. The V-mail and another piece of paper that she didn't remember seeing before.

It must have been left intentionally. She needed to read it, see if it contained clues about who had taken the coins. Even though that didn't make much sense to her, it was the only way it could have gotten in the safe over the weekend. It hadn't been there when she shoved all the coins in the safe.

She was absolutely certain.

Well, as certain as she'd been that she'd set the security alarm. As certain as she was that she'd firmly closed the safe. As certain as she could be that the coins should have been safe in her office over the weekend.

Esther entered the office and knelt beside her. "You are scaring me, Cheryl. What has happened?"

"Someone stole the coins."

The girl's eyes widened. "All of them? You're sure?"

"I can't find them anywhere."

"But how would someone have gotten into the store? We were closed yesterday."

"I know, but they must have broken in somehow." Yet nothing had been smashed at the front of the store. Had they broken in the back door? Why hadn't she thought of that earlier? It felt like her thoughts were mired in the thick molasses that she sold out front.

Cheryl pushed to her feet and hurried down the small hallway to the back door. It was fully intact. No broken glass from the small window next to the door. No broken lock that had been jimmied. Nothing to indicate someone had forced his or her way inside.

"Well, we will keep looking. I will help." Esther smiled, one of her cheery efforts, but it didn't reach her dark brown eyes.

"Thank you. I guess we should start in the office. Maybe I missed something." Cheryl returned to the office and made a halfhearted effort to search the cupboards and drawers again, even though she knew someone—a thief—had taken the coins. No one would open the safe simply to move the coins from one location to another. This wasn't a game of hide-and-seek, no matter how much she wished she could believe it was. After Cheryl had searched every inch, she stepped out to let Esther repeat the process.

"So the safe was open when you got here?"

"Yes." Cheryl nodded.

Esther turned to the safe and then back to Cheryl. Her nose wrinkled in a cute manner, reminding Cheryl of Naomi. "Did you tell anyone the code? I have not told anyone, I promise. But if you told someone..."

Was that a hint of betrayal in her voice? "I promise, you and I are the only ones who know the combination."

"All right. The coins are not in the safe, but these notes are." Esther handed over the V-mail and another folded sheet of paper. "I can check the cupboards and floor. Maybe someone is playing a prank."

It might be a prank, but it wasn't a harmless one. If those coins were truly gone, it would harm John-John and the work he was trying to do. She fingered the V-mail and paper, but then set them on the desk.

She had a call to make before she read them. Even the thought burdened her.

While John-John had insisted the coins weren't his, she'd seen the glint of hope in his eyes. He'd known as well as she did that the coins could solve many of his financial concerns about finishing the cottages. The project was so expensive. And the coins surely valuable.

She worried her lower lip between her teeth then squared her shoulders. This call wouldn't get easier, even if she waited.

She punched in his number and listened to the phone ring. When it kicked over to voice mail, she left a short message asking John-John to call her as soon as he could.

Then she returned to the office. "Did you find anything, Esther?"

The girl laid a hand to her collarbone as she turned from a cabinet. "No, but I have organized these files a bit." She nodded toward the cabinet. "How do you find anything?"

Cheryl shifted to lean against the wall. "I guess I have a system. I usually manage to find what I need." She sighed. "There's nothing left to do but call Chief Twitchell." She could only imagine his response. The man must be getting so tired of her. "Well, here goes nothing." She punched in his number, shaking her head at the thought that she actually had the police chief's phone number memorized. That had certainly never happened in Columbus, and that wasn't a point she'd bring up to her mother.

After a minute, she heard his gruff voice. "Twitchell."

"Hi, Chief. Would you mind sending someone to the Swiss Miss?"

"What's happened, Cheryl?"

She glanced around the small office as she cleared her throat. Something glinted on the floor, and she stooped down to pick it up. "Somebody must have broken into my shop yesterday. Johnson Williamson asked me to keep some coins in my safe after they were discovered in the walls of one of the cottages."

"I heard something about that at church."

"Word seems to have gotten around." The wonders of the small-town grapevine. "When I got here this morning, the safe was open and empty." She turned the coin over in her hand. It wasn't anything special, just an ordinary coin that must have fallen out of her wallet. Disappointment flooded her chest.

There was a hint of humor in the chief's voice. "Did you forget to set the alarm again?"

Cheryl tried not to bristle at his question. "No, I didn't forget. I'm certain."

Yet as she looked at the coin, her body stiffened. She held it between her fingers, understanding that if there had been any fingerprints she'd ruined them. Her curiosity had gotten the better of her. Emotions rose in her throat, and she swallowed hard. Her office was now a crime scene.

The coins were valuable—they had to be. No one would have gone to the effort to break into the Swiss Miss and steal them if they weren't.

"You still there, Cheryl?" Chief Twitchell's raised voice grabbed her attention and pulled her back to the conversation.

"Yes, sir. I guess my thoughts ran away with me."

"I'd say so. Look, I'll be there in a few minutes."

"Thank you."

"And Cheryl?"

"Yes?"

"Don't touch anything."

CHAPTER TEN

The bell jangled, and Cheryl glanced at her watch as she hurried around the corner to the counter. She tucked the coin that she'd found into her pocket. "How did it get to be nine already?"

Ben Vogel nodded at her as he settled at the checkerboard in front of the heart-shaped window.

"Morning, Cheryl." Rueben Vogel joined his brother.

Cheryl shifted her weight from side to side and hoped the brothers couldn't tell that anything was wrong. The last thing she needed was word spreading about the theft too. "Can I get you anything?"

Ben grinned up at her. "I'd love a few of those peppermints you've got in the candy case. I've heard Rueben likes those."

"Don't let him waste his money on me, Cheryl." Rueben shook his gray head. "I get enough sweets at home."

"Tell him he can never get enough sweets from you."

Cheryl grinned. "All right, Ben. I'll be right back."

She filled a small white bag with a scoop of the sweets and then carried it back to him. Maybe the brothers would share the treats while they played their quiet game.

The bell over the door rang again, and Chief Twitchell entered the store. Tall and thin, he reminded Cheryl of the man who played the Scarecrow in *The Wizard of Oz*, except the chief had salt-and-pepper hair.

"I'd ask how you're doing this mornin', but I think I have a sense of that." His eyes were kind as he took off his hat. "Care to explain the trouble?"

Cheryl eyed the brothers, offering a smile, and then she walked the chief toward the office. "Like I mentioned, when I got here this morning the coins Johnson Williamson asked me to store for him in my safe were gone. The safe was open, but it doesn't look like anything else was taken—at least nothing obvious."

They paused at the sales counter.

"And no sign of a break-in?"

"No, sir."

"I'll take a look around. First, have you contacted the security company?"

Cheryl brushed an invisible crumb from the counter. "No. You think it can tell us something?"

"Maybe. The systems are often computerized, which makes it easier to identify faults in the system. Call and make sure yours worked properly all weekend. The company should be able to tell you if the system was armed Saturday night." He raised his hands in a placating motion as she started to protest. "Now I'm not sayin' you didn't, but a call should let us know if the system was armed or tampered with. That could lead us to other important information."

"All right." She had to have set the alarm Saturday. If she hadn't...she didn't know what she'd tell John-John. "I'll get the contact information from the office."

"Sure. But don't touch anything while you get it."

Cheryl's eyes widened, and she realized for the first time that Esther wasn't at the front counter. They'd walked out of the office together, but now Esther wasn't around. Had she returned to the office? Surely she knew better than to touch anything.

"Esther?" Cheryl called out, scanning the store.

There was no answer.

"Esther!" she called louder.

"Back here!" The voice came from the office.

Chief Twitchell's eyes grew big, and his posture stiffened into his authoritative stance. "Cheryl Cooper, tell me you do not have Esther cleaning in there."

"I didn't ask her to organize the space. I sure hope she's not…but it's second nature to the girl."

He shook his head and strode toward the office. "Esther Miller, come on out of there before you destroy any more evidence."

When Esther slid past the chief, her kapp was askew and her eyes downcast. "I did not mean to make trouble. It's just that once I got started organizing that filing cabinet it was hard to stop, especially when no customers have arrived yet. I, uh, just went in there to organize a few files. I just hate standing around, ain't so?" She turned to Cheryl with a pleading gaze, hoping for forgiveness.

The chief released a low moan that sounded like a growl. "The best-meanin' folks never do mean to cause trouble, but it doesn't keep that from happening." He gestured toward the store displays. "Why don't you two rearrange the dolls?"

Esther looked up at him, her petite frame leaning toward him. "I did that on Saturday. The display looks fine."

"Then find something else to fix. Just stay away from the office and my crime scene. If you two keep interferin', I may not be able to call it a crime scene."

Cheryl pulled out the phone book from under the counter to find the number for the security company. No way she was taking one step toward the office when he was in a mood like this. She'd have to be careful what she said until he was back in investigator mode. "But if the coins were stolen, it *is* a crime."

"Not if all the evidence has been trampled. Even if you didn't mean to mess up the crime scene, it seems you've done a fine job of that." He narrowed his gaze at Esther and then back to Cheryl. "Let me guess, you two have already touched every surface and opened every cabinet and drawer in there lookin' for the coins that were obviously missing?"

Cheryl glanced to Esther and winced, but neither said a word.

"Now if you'll let me, I'm goin' to see what I can learn in your office while you call the security company."

"Yes, sir." She thought of the notes they'd found in the safe. "Before you go, I should tell you that Esther and I found a V-mail and note in the safe."

"V-mail?"

"Mail that was sent to and from troops during World War II. We found three in the jars with the coins. Then there was this fourth that was left in the safe."

"And you're sure you didn't have it before?"

"No. I mean, yes, I am sure. It must have been left by whoever took the coins." Cheryl led the way to her office, gingerly walked in, and pointed into the safe. "There. Those are the papers."

The chief put on a pair of gloves and then pulled the papers from the safe. "Who else has touched them?"

"As far as I know just Esther and me."

"All right." He looked around the small office and sighed. "This doesn't look like a place that was robbed."

The desk surface was clean, and as the chief opened cupboards, Cheryl realized Esther had been doing more than just organizing a few files. Her shoulders slumped. Any information or clues that might have been left by the thief would be long gone, organized into oblivion by her overly helpful assistant.

"I'm sorry." The words whispered from her mouth. She cleared her throat. "I didn't realize Esther would come back in here."

"What's done is done." Chief Twitchell nodded to a box on the second shelf. "Can you hand me an envelope for these notes?"

She did as he requested then asked, "Can I read the notes?"

"When I'm done in here." He slid the notes in the envelope then shook his head. "It won't take long. Probably about the length of time it takes you to reach the security company."

Taking the hint, Cheryl returned to the phone book and made the call. When the chief joined her a few minutes later, she filled him in. "Someone will be here within the half hour."

"All right." He set the envelope down on the counter and pulled out the note. "Let's see what this says."

Don't bother looking for me. I've only taken what's rightfully mine. These coins are mine, not yours.

There was no signature. Nothing to indicate who had written the note. Even the block letters didn't give much to go on—it could be a man's or a woman's writing as far as Cheryl could tell.

Next he opened the V-mail and turned it so Cheryl could see it too. "Does the writing look like the others?"

Cheryl nodded and then pointed to the salutation. "He's also addressed it to Maam and Daed just like the other letters." It was a short letter, and she read it quickly. It just talked about how much he missed everyone and the importance of family.

"I'll look into analyzin' it. Can you make copies of the other three letters? I don't see why I need the originals."

"I can do that." As he started to refold the letter, she put a hand on his arm. "Could I take a photo of it to read? It might add to what I can learn from the other letters."

"Fine." After she snapped the photo with her phone, he refolded the letter, tucked it in the envelope, and then took off his gloves. Next, he pulled out one of his ever-ready pocket notebooks and opened it. "Tell me what you can."

She walked him through finding the coins inside the walls of one of the cottages. Then she relayed how Levi helped her move the coins to the office, their realization they wouldn't fit in the safe, and how they transferred the coins to baggies.

"What kind of baggies?"

"Just a second." She hurried to the office and brought out one. "They aren't that durable, so I'd be surprised if they could contain the weight of the coins for long." As he nodded for her to continue, she told him the rest. "That's it."

The door jangled, and a woman walked in the store. She wore a shirt with the security company's logo and headed straight toward them. Ben and Rueben watched her progress, eyes wide. Cheryl could only imagine what they were thinking of all this activity at the Swiss Miss.

"Chief Twitchell, I didn't expect to see you here."

"Morning, Lauren. We're hopin' you can help us out."

"Happy to if I can." She turned to Cheryl and shook her hand. "I'm Lauren with the security company. What can I do for you?"

Cheryl quickly filled her in on what had happened. "What we need to do is figure out if the alarm was set on Saturday, and then why it was released before this morning." *Please tell me I didn't forget to set it!*

"Sure, that won't be hard to do. Let me pull up your account information and check out the panel. It should take about fifteen minutes." Lauren nodded to them and then walked over to the panel. Ben scooted his chair closer to the checkers table so the medium-sized woman could squeeze through.

"Why don't you call me with the information once Lauren is done with her check? Better yet, I'll ask her to call me on her way out." Chief Twitchell picked up the envelope and then shook Cheryl's hand. "Let me know if anything else comes up."

"Thanks for coming so quickly. Guess I'd better try Johnson again." Cheryl settled on the stool behind the counter, wishing she could come up with anything else to do, but she knew the task wouldn't get easier by putting it off.

The front door opened again, and when Cheryl glanced up, she saw that it wasn't from Chief Twitchell leaving. Instead, it was a man who'd volunteered at the cottages. What was his name? She racked her mind, shifting through the list of volunteers. That was it. Brandt Sorenson. The tall man looked like a college offensive lineman and had the carpentry skills of a master. Fortunately for the cottages, he'd willingly donated his time to the project.

"Hey, Miss Cooper. John-John asked me to see if you had the assignment list for the volunteers. We're about all there—just looking for our game plan for the day."

She guessed he played football using metaphors like that. Did she dare tell him that she'd fumbled?

Cheryl pushed up her lips in what she hoped was a smile. In the rush and upset of the morning, she'd completely forgotten about the volunteer sheets. "I promise I'll have the list there by nine thirty. I just wanted to check over it one last time."

"I hate to tell you this, ma'am. But it's already ten."

Cheryl's mouth dropped open. She glanced at her watch, confirming what he'd said. How on earth had the time evaporated that fast? "Oh no. Let me go grab it from the office. If I can, I mean. Is it all right, Chief?"

The chief looked up from the book of poetry he'd picked up. "Anniversary is coming up, and I need some ideas. Sure, you can go ahead in the office. I've got all I need for now."

Brandt looked from her to the chief. "Is something the matter?"

Chief Twitchell set down the book and stepped closer to the large man. "Not really. Nothin' we can't handle just fine."

Brandt's gaze darted about the store, seemingly unable to land on any spot. He lumbered away from the chief then looked at Cheryl. "I've got to get back."

Without another word, he headed out the front door, leaving the volunteer list behind.

Chapter Eleven

W hat was that about?" Cheryl frowned as she watched the man hurry down the street.

The chief looked up from the display of Amish wisdom books, his gaze following the retreating figure. "Do you know much about him, Cheryl?"

"No. Just that he's volunteered to help at the cottages."

"Maybe he's one of those people who needs some coffee before his day really gets started."

Maybe. But Cheryl decided to learn more about him when she got to the volunteer work site. "I'd better take the volunteer schedule to the cottages. I'll have to tell Johnson about the robbery while I'm there." A heavy weight descended on her shoulders at the thought. She'd hoped that somehow the coins would miraculously reappear, but that had been a foolish wish.

Chief Twitchell carried a book to the counter and handed it to Esther. "I'll take this. I have a feelin' my wife will love it, and it gets me a start on anniversary presents." He turned toward Cheryl. "I'd be happy to give you a ride to the cottages. It would be good to see where the coins were found."

"Thank you." Cheryl hurried into her office and looked for the volunteer sheet. She was certain she'd put it on top of her desk against the wall. Where was it?

"Esther, did you organize my volunteer schedule?" She tried to keep her voice light, but she felt the pressure of being late. She hated the thought that the volunteers were waiting on her, though surely all of those construction folks could just dive in to the next thing that needed to be done. Why did they need her to tell them what to do? Oh yeah, because she'd volunteered to do the scheduling to make sure everything happened on time and in the right order.

Esther scurried into the office, opened a cupboard door, and pulled out a file folder. "Here you go."

The file bore Esther's distinctive script and was clearly labeled *Cottage Project*. The girl was amazing. "How did you have time to get organized to this level of detail?"

Esther shifted her feet and looked at the floor. "It was not anything. I used the file folders as I found things I knew you'd want to access." She opened the next cupboard to reveal random piles. "These I have not touched." An impish light came into her eyes. "I will tackle these piles as I have time today."

Cheryl shook her head and grinned. "Have at it. I can see I've missed not using your skills this way before." She opened the file and confirmed the schedule was inside. "I'm not sure how long I'll be, but call me if anything comes up."

"I have your number. The store will be fine."

Cheryl knew she was right. Esther was more than competent when it came to running the store. In fact, the girl was a whiz. She really freed Cheryl to do all the volunteer and other projects that came her way. "Thanks, Esther." She grabbed her purse from the office and patted Beau on the head. "I'll be back in a bit. Don't get into anything while I'm gone."

Beau swished his tail back and forth but didn't vocalize.

She walked to the front of the store. "All right, Chief. I'm ready."

A minute later he was opening the passenger door to his police cruiser. It felt so odd getting willingly into a police car. Not that she could imagine getting unwilling into one either! The car smelled of gun oil and boot polish. It also had a slightly stale smell. Unfortunately the pine tree air freshener didn't help.

As they turned off Main Street, a tour bus pulled into town. It looked like tourists filled it and could keep the Swiss Miss and other downtown businesses hopping all morning.

Cheryl resisted the urge to jump out of the vehicle and run back to the shop. Esther would provide the tourists with exemplary service, and Cheryl couldn't put off the need to have a conversation with John-John. It would be better to let him know before word somehow spread and he received it from someone else. Still, her breath hitched, and her heart raced as the chief approached the cul-de-sac.

Cheryl slid lower in the seat and sighed. "I really don't want to tell Johnson his coins are gone."

"Way I heard it, he's not convinced they're his anyway. He thinks he needs to find the owners. And if it's just mason jars of coins, they can't be that valuable."

"Almost as soon as I got to the Swiss Miss with the coins Saturday, an appraiser arrived demanding to see the coins. She sure thinks they have value."

Chief Twitchell shrugged. "Anything's possible, I guess, but I wouldn't worry too much, Cheryl. Unless you left the alarm off, there really wasn't anything you could have done to protect them."

And that was her fear at its heart. What if the security company called and said she hadn't set the alarm? She might not ever forgive herself for that oversight. The chief parked the vehicle in front of the center cottage.

He looked at Cheryl, kindness filling his eyes. "You might as well get this over with. It won't get easier the longer you build it up."

She puffed out a breath but couldn't quite get her lungs to inhale. "I know." She tried again. "All right. Let's see if we can find him." She climbed from the car and started toward the cottage. It only took asking a couple people to learn that John-John was in the cottage where the coins had been discovered. Maybe he was hoping to locate a few more. If she were him, Cheryl might be tempted to knock down all the walls in that cottage to make sure there weren't more coins hidden inside.

She walked through the open door into the living space. Drywall leaned against the main wall, waiting for the demolition to stop so the rebuilding could begin. Muffled voices filtered from one of the back rooms, so Cheryl walked deeper into the house. From the main room, there was a small hallway that led to three small bedrooms and a full bathroom. Branching off of that was a short hallway that led to the kitchen and laundry room. From there, a door opened into the small garage. John-John stood in front of the garage door conversing with a couple volunteers. Cheryl was surprised to see the intern standing right behind his shoulder.

Sadie had a clipboard in hand and jotted something down while she nodded her head.

Why was she standing so close and acting so important?

Sadie nodded again and took another series of notes. Wasn't she just the intern? Then why was she acting so serious, intent, and part of the team?

Cheryl bit back the impulse to say something. She was just out of sorts because of all that had happened at the shop. She didn't want to tell Johnson about the robbery, but she had to. She cleared her throat, and four heads popped up from glancing at the sheet on Sadie's clipboard. Cheryl swallowed and held up the volunteer schedule. "John-John, I have the schedule for you."

"That's great. We were just trying to create one after Brandt mentioned you didn't have it."

"He was in such a hurry, I didn't get to grab it for him. Sorry I'm late with it."

Johnson stepped away from the others and studied her, his blue eyes colored with concern. "Is everything all right? I hope you aren't mad that I haven't made it over to get the coins yet."

"Actually, I needed to talk to you about the coins."

"I'd be happy to come get them now. Just let me get everybody into their assigned jobs so the work can start again."

"It's more serious than that." Cheryl stopped as a lump filled her throat. Her face felt flushed, and for a moment she thought she was going to cry. It was even harder than she'd imagined to tell him she'd let him down.

"Unless someone died, it's not as bad as you've imagined."

She took a step back toward the living area. "Would you come over here?" He followed her, and she stood near the piled drywall.

Cheryl took in a deep breath and released it slowly. "Someone broke into the store—sometime between when I left the coins on Saturday and when I got back there this morning. That's why I was late getting the volunteer schedule to you. I've been working with the police and the security company."

"Okay." Johnson cocked his head and put his hands on his hips as he studied her. "Did they damage the Swiss Miss?"

"No."

"You weren't hurt?"

"No, it's nothing like that." She sighed as her shoulders slumped. "John-John, whoever it was stole the coins and left a note that the coins were theirs and not to bother them."

"Did they sign the note?"

"No."

"Then how does telling us the coins are theirs help anything?"

"It doesn't. I guess it's meant to tell us to not hunt for them, but I can't do that. Volunteers found them here in this cottage. A cottage you own. They should be your property. And if this person thinks they aren't, then they should lay out why and let a court or some third party decide. Just taking them and telling us not to look for them . . . well, that's just wrong."

"Maybe." John-John took off his Cincinnati Reds ball cap and scratched behind his ear. "Or maybe this is just God's way of answering whose coins they are."

Cheryl's jaw dropped open. Surely he couldn't believe that. Was he really this casual about a theft? After all, the coins could be more valuable than any of them could guess.

She lifted her chin. "The person probably left the note just to throw us off. Until we investigate, we won't know if anyone else has a claim that's better than yours." As she'd spoken, her posture stiffened at the rightness of her words. She looked at the drywall, and her lower lip quivered. Drywall that might not be hung because there wouldn't be funds. "I'm so sorry I let you down."

"I don't see how you can take responsibility for that." He leaned a shoulder against the wall. "You were doing me a favor. It would have been a lot easier to get the coins if I'd left them here. At least they had to break into a safe there. I'm sure Chief Twitchell will figure it out."

At his name, the chief walked over and joined them.

Sadie, too, entered the living space. Her ponytail swayed as she walked. "I couldn't help but overhear. These houses are so small." She turned to John-John. "Is there anything I can do to help? I could talk to the police or help search. Maybe Miss Cooper just misplaced them."

Cheryl's spine stiffened at the thought. "I assure you we did not misplace those bags and bags of coins that were in the mason jars. They're sort of hard to miss."

"I didn't mean to suggest you couldn't *see* them. I . . . I was just trying to help." Sadie looked down at her clipboard and bit her lower lip. "I'll take this to the other cottages."

"Chief, would it help to give you some photos of the coins?" John-John pulled out his phone. "I took some photos of them Saturday night before Cheryl took them to her shop."

"That would be great. Then I'll have a better idea of the possible value. It won't be exact, but it will give us a startin' point."

"I can walk my phone over to the drugstore right now. Have the photos to you in an hour or two."

Sadie raised her hand. "I can do that for you. Then you don't have to leave."

John-John grinned. "That would be great. I feel pretty behind already."

Cheryl held her stomach as her shoulders curled in. Sadie was being so nice, yet part of Cheryl wanted to protest that she should be the one to help John-John. Was she worried about Sadie taking her place? As the thought crossed her mind, she pushed it away. That was ridiculous!

Yet, as John-John handed her his phone and pointed to the photos he wanted printed, Cheryl felt unsettled. "Johnson, I'd be happy to do that for you. I'm headed back into town anyway."

"No, this is good. Sadie's here to help me, and you have your own store to get back to. You can't spend all your time helping me out."

"I'm happy to do it." Sadie bounced on her toes then looked at the chief. "Should I bring the photos straight to you?"

"That would be fine. Thanks."

"Sounds awesome. I'll be back as soon as they're printed." Sadie hurried out of the room with John-John's phone clutched in her hand.

As she walked away, Cheryl felt bad about getting upset. Still, something about Sadie didn't add up. The girl was almost too helpful and too...*everywhere* all of a sudden. What was her real motivation for being so available?

Chapter Twelve

Silence settled on the kitchen until John-John held up the work list. "Thanks for bringing this by. We'll figure out something on the coins. Hard to miss what wasn't really mine."

Cheryl swallowed the lump in her throat. It then settled in her stomach as a weight. "Can you tell me anything about Sadie?"

"Why? She's interning here."

"I know." How could Cheryl explain what bothered her without sounding like a crazy woman? "I'm just curious."

Now it was John-John's turn to shrug. "Not sure what to say. She came and asked for an internship. I couldn't really turn away free help."

Chief Twitchell nodded. "That's the truth." He placed the small notebook and the pencil back in his front shirt pocket. "Well, it's been nice to see what you're up to here. It's shaping up real nice. If I find out anything about the coins, I'll be sure to let you know." The chief slapped on his hat and after nodding toward everyone sauntered out the door. A minute later he stuck his head back in the room. "You need a ride back to the Swiss Miss, Cheryl?"

"No, the walk will be good for me. Thanks for checking." After the chief left again, she turned back to John-John. "Where's Sadie from?"

His eyebrows lifted, and he released a sigh. "Now, Cheryl..."

"I'd think with the people you're helping, you'd want to know she's not a threat to any of them, that's all..."

"Sadie? A threat?" John-John's stance tensed. His shoulders stiffened, and his jaw tightened. He looked down at her. "Don't be crazy."

"You can never be too safe."

"You can be too paranoid though." He crossed his arms over his chest. "She's not up to anything."

An Amish man, Samuel Swartzentruber Cheryl thought, strode into the room, a tool belt secured around his waist. "Mr. Williamson, you have a job for me today?"

"Sure, Samuel. Glad of the help. If you'll excuse me, Cheryl." And with that, Johnson disappeared out the door toward another cottage. Cheryl didn't understand how he could be so unconcerned about the loss of the coins. He needed money to finish the project, and it seemed to her that their find had been an answer. Didn't the loss bother him?

Cheryl decided to look around the rest of the cottage while she was here, just to see if there were any other clues. She wandered out of the kitchen toward the bedrooms. When she entered one, she gasped. Holes had been punched in each wall of the room, large enough to reach a hand through. Maybe John-John had asked the volunteers to check the rooms for hidden treasures. Wouldn't he have mentioned that? Maybe not.

Whoever had bashed the walls did it with gusto. The drywall contained a fair assortment of punch outs about every four feet—just close enough that a long arm could reach in and probably stretch to about the area of the next hole. And with a flashlight, someone might see enough to verify whether more jars were in the walls.

After leaving the bedrooms, Cheryl went back to the kitchen where two Amish men were replacing a window. She smiled at them and waited a moment until they stopped what they were doing. "Were either of you here Saturday and working in this cottage?"

"Ja." One of them stood. "I was here. Is there a problem?"

"No. I'm just curious about something. Since Johnson just left, I thought you might be able to help me. There's something in the bedrooms that I wanted to ask you about."

"Sure." He brushed off his dark work pants and gestured to the doorway. "After you."

They walked into a back bedroom, and both men gasped.

The first man paused in his steps in shock. "What in the world?"

The second man nearly ran into the first. He craned his neck to look around his friend toward the damage. "That's brand-new Sheetrock! Or at least it was. Who would do that?"

Cheryl pointed at the holes. "So these weren't here Saturday when you stopped work?"

The man frowned and moved closer. He fingered the rough edge around one hole. "No, ma'am. That's such a shame. We had so many volunteers who worked on this room. Sheetrock is not cheap either."

"It's not just this bedroom. It's all of them."

The man's eyes widened. "All of them? Who would do this?" he repeated. "Why?"

"I was wondering the same thing…" She didn't tell him she guessed that whoever did this was looking for more jars of coins. She didn't want to worry them or make John-John think she was stirring up worries among his workers. "So Johnson didn't ask you or anyone else to do this after we found the jars of coins?"

The man adjusted his hat. "No. I would remember that."

"Thank you." She forced a smile as the tension in her stomach grew. "I won't keep you from what you were doing, but can I ask one more thing?"

The man nodded.

"Can you tell Johnson about these holes?" Cheryl leaned closer. "And maybe encourage him to call the chief?"

"Ja, of course. I would be glad to find him, though I fear he will be distraught." The man clicked his tongue. "So much work that needs to be redone."

And time he was taking away from his family and other work, she guessed.

As the man turned to leave, Cheryl placed a hand on his arm. "Thank you for what you're doing to help."

He glanced at her hand, and she quickly withdrew it. "It is a pleasure to serve those Gott sets in my path. It is a small way to thank Him for all He has given me."

Cheryl knew what he meant. That was why she liked working on projects like this—liked helping people. As she followed him down the hallway and then turned to leave the cottage, a thought ricocheted around her mind. *That's exactly why I find it so hard to say no.* There were so many ways to thank God for all He'd done.

Cheryl pulled her cell phone from her pocket and checked the time. It was later than she thought, nearly lunchtime. The morning hours were wasting as she hung around here. Her to-do list ticked through her mind, and the pressure intensified. Glancing at the holes one last time, Cheryl ignored her mounting questions and forced herself to hurry from the cottage. Maybe Naomi would learn something at her sewing frolic. Until then, Cheryl needed to get back to the Swiss Miss and serve the customers. She might even have time to place a couple orders for graduation gifts. Seeing Chief Twitchell with the book of Amish wisdom had reinforced her thought that she could create sample graduation gifts by bundling the books with other items. Yes, there was still a store to run even with all the questions surrounding the coins.

The walk back to the Swiss Miss passed quickly. Cheryl tried to enjoy the sunshine on her face, but with her mind swirling with the mystery of the disappearing coins—and how to best position the store to sell graduation and wedding gifts—she felt drained rather than refreshed.

Beau met her in the aisle by the Amish dolls. His meow pulled her thoughts back to the moment as he twisted in between her legs. Then she looked at the counter and saw Esther slumped on the stool.

"Good heavens, are you all right?"

"Weary, but fine. This batch of tourists wanted all of your preserves." A small smile graced her face. "I need to tell Maam to bring in more or you'll be out. I had to bring in everything from the storeroom."

"That's great! More income for your family and more happy customers for the Swiss Miss."

"Ja, but it was hard to stock, answer questions, and ring up orders." Esther twisted her lips as if worried her words sounded too much like a complaint. She sat straighter. "But do not worry. I did it—it all worked out. You caught me sitting for the first time all morning. I just needed a moment to catch my breath."

A pinch of guilt grabbed Cheryl. "I shouldn't have left you here alone so long. How about you grab lunch, and I'll cover the store."

"It is too early. I do not want to leave you..."

"Don't worry about me. You've worked so hard." She gazed around the store. There were only a couple customers perusing the store's unique collection of Amish gifts. "I've got this covered, just like you covered the store for me. Thank you for watching the store so well."

Esther straightened her skewed kapp and grabbed her purse from the cubby beneath the counter. "I will eat quickly."

The rest of the day flew as Cheryl helped customers, reorganized the shelves and displays, and did a quick inventory.

Esther also helped her create a display of sample graduation gifts and another with sample bridal bundles. Esther found some white tulle in the storeroom that made the bridal display look even more special. The gifts seemed to float on a tulle ocean. Yet even as she worked, Cheryl couldn't get the coins off her mind. Had the Amish man alerted Johnson? Had Chief Twitchell come up with any leads? Were there any suspicious people hanging around the cottages? Was Naomi learning anything new about the jars at the sewing frolic?

"I'll see if I can find some white flowers we can turn into a bouquet," Cheryl said, pulling her thoughts back to the task at hand. "I remember seeing a box of silk flowers in the attic. Maybe Aunt Mitzi had kept them for times like this?" The flowers would be the perfect finishing touch for the table.

The bell on the door jingled, and Cheryl quickly glanced up hoping it was someone coming to bring news of the coins, but it was yet another customer. Cheryl took two steps toward the back room and then paused, turning back to the young Amish woman. "Esther, when does your maam usually finish with her sewing frolics?"

Esther wiped a line of sweat from her forehead. "It varies based on who needs to talk and what the latest news is around the community." She chuckled. "Maam always says these are more therapy than anything else. The quilting and sewing keep hands busy while the women chat."

It wasn't the answer Cheryl wanted. She looked at the clock, realizing there must have been a lot of therapy needed today.

"After work let me give you a ride home, and then I can see if your mom learned anything."

Esther fiddled with her kapp strings, and Cheryl noticed humor in her gaze. "Yes, ma'am."

The last hour of work passed quickly, and soon Cheryl was closing up the shop, readying to go.

Cheryl picked up her purse to leave when the phone in the office rang. She turned to Esther. "Just a minute." She hurried into the office. "The Swiss Miss, Cheryl speaking."

"Hi, Cheryl. This is Lauren with Ohio Security."

Cheryl sucked in a breath. "Did you learn anything about the system?"

"Yes, it looks like the code may have been entered, but there was a power fault later. The data is actually pretty confused, which is unusual. Typically I can get into the system and get a pretty clear idea of what happened, but not this time. I'm sorry. I'll keep digging, but I can tell you that right now it does look like you started to arm the system on Saturday at about five thirty. After that, the system is confused until you got to the store at eight thirty Monday morning and entered your number again."

"Okay. Let me know if you learn anything else."

"Will do, and I've already let Chief Twitchell know. I'll ask him to set up extra patrols around the store too, although I doubt whoever entered your store will try again. They already got what they wanted."

"I appreciate that." After she hung up, Cheryl stood there another minute. So she had started to arm the system, but it was still unclear whether she'd actually followed through. And no matter how many times she replayed that night's events in her mind, she couldn't figure it out either.

Cheryl sighed but then shook it off. There was nothing she could do about it now. Instead, she should find Naomi and pray her friend had more success asking questions at the frolic.

The drive out to the Millers' was pleasant. The fields were beginning to show signs of coming to life. Small green stalks of crops poked out of the soil, hinting at future fields of corn or beans. Esther said little, but it was a comfortable silence of women who knew and enjoyed each other's company.

Cheryl again thanked God for the way He had brought the Millers into her life. She couldn't run the store without Esther's help, and Naomi had become such a dear friend. Then there was Levi. Her stomach twisted a bit at the thought he might be at the farm. She felt so conflicted around him. He offered his friendship freely, yet at times she felt the spark that there could be more between them. She stepped away from the thought as she turned into the long driveway leading to the Millers' home.

She had to leave her hopes and fears of what could happen with Levi in God's hands. God was the only One who knew what He had planned for them, no matter what her heart hoped.

As Cheryl parked the car, Levi stepped from the barn and shaded his eyes. Sweat dampened his neckline, and he pulled a handkerchief from his pocket and wiped his brow, offering her a smile. He was so ruggedly handsome and both strong and gentle— all of which were appealing. Cheryl sucked in a small breath.

No matter the fact she'd just turned over *their* future into God's hands, her emotions caused heat to move through her limbs.

The fact that Levi remained unmarried continued to surprise her, but she needed to quit pining after a man who was a good friend and nothing more. Especially when there was so much about this mystery she needed to concentrate on.

Levi strode across the yard toward her car. Before she could move, he opened the door. "How are you today?"

"I've had better days."

His blue eyes were hooded with concern. "Anything I can do?"

"Is Naomi home?"

"Not yet. She should be soon. The frolics end in time to feed the hungry men." He patted his flat stomach and made a pitiful face. "If you stay long enough, you'll hear a roar that is loud enough to scare small children."

Cheryl laughed as she got out of the car and followed him toward the house. Esther climbed from the car and headed toward the phone shed, most likely to check the day's messages.

Levi slowed his steps and glanced over at her. Then he looked at the house as if questioning if they should go inside or wait outside for Naomi to arrive. It was no question for Cheryl. The afternoon was too beautiful and the warm breeze just perfect, carrying on it the scent of earth and new life. Seeing the small bench that sat in the shade of the large maple tree in the Millers' side yard, she hurried there and sat. Levi followed and sat beside her.

"Oh, Levi. Have you heard the terrible news?"

"I am not sure. I have not heard anything too terrible today, except the cows might have been mooing a little more loudly." He cocked an eyebrow. "I believe they think the grass on the next pasture over is greener." His gaze lowered to hers. "But that is not it, is it?"

"No. I wish." She sighed. "Someone stole the coins over the weekend. They somehow got into my shop and took the coins. I thought with the safe and the security system it would be the safest place for them, but it didn't work that way at all." Her voice rose with the anxiety.

Levi stood and removed his hat. "I cannot believe it. It is horrible, Cheryl. You are all right?"

"I'm fine—a little stressed over the thought of someone being in my store—but I feel so responsible."

"You did all you could. You were just trying to do a good deed. You were helping a friend."

"But he trusted me with his treasure."

Levi sat down beside her again. "Things are just things . . . that is what my grandfather always told me. People matter. You said you were distraught over someone being in your store?"

She nodded and clasped her hands on her lap. "What if . . . if they come back?"

"I do not think they would. They got what they wanted, right?"

She lowered her gaze to her lap. "Yes, unfortunately."

Levi sighed. It felt good to know that he cared—that he was concerned about her, not just the coins.

"How can I help?" he asked.

How like Levi, or any of the Millers, to offer help rather than passively listening. Cheryl considered his offer. What *did* she need most? And what could Levi help with while still keeping his many responsibilities fulfilled?

"Would you mind taking over the volunteer schedule for the cottages? If it's too much, just say the word." He opened his mouth, but Cheryl hurried on before he could speak. "I really want to find the coins and get them back to Johnson. They were stolen on my watch, and I want to make sure they are found."

"Are you sure it is your job—finding the coins?"

"Yes. This is something I can do to fix what happened." Yet even as she said the words, she could hear her mother's voice in her head. *Cheryl, you are too busy and too overcommitted. You need to take a break. You need to take time for yourself.* But at least now she was asking for help. Surely that meant something.

They sat together another ten minutes, talking about the security system and the safe and wondering who would be knowledgeable enough to bypass both. Esther emerged from the phone shed and sauntered over to them.

"Cheryl, Maam left a message a bit ago. One of the younger ladies, Hattie, went into labor while at the sewing frolic. Maam helped to drive her buggy home and is watching Hattie's five little ones until her sister can arrive from Charm. She asked me to make dinner for Daed and the boys."

Cheryl smiled at how Esther called her older brothers "boys," especially since Levi was now in his thirties.

"You're welcome to stay," Esther added.

As much as Cheryl was enjoying the conversation with Levi, weariness was clear on Esther's face. She'd already imposed on the young woman enough today.

"Oh, no thank you." Cheryl stood. "I have a lot to do at home, and I'm hoping to connect with Aunt Mitzi tonight. She has some information about a World War II soldier she knew, and it might be a good lead."

"Be careful, will you?" Levi reached a hand to touch her arm but then paused.

"Of course. And I'll talk to Naomi tomorrow. I'm sure if she did find information about the jars, it was overshadowed by the baby coming."

"I will tell Maam you stopped by."

"Thank you, Levi. I appreciate that."

I appreciate so much about you, she added to herself. She especially liked the protective look in his eyes—if only she didn't have to feel as if she were in danger to see it.

Chapter Thirteen

Cheryl opened up the search engine on her computer. She typed in a simple phrase: *V-mail World War II*. She scanned through numerous Web pages and discovered that V-mail, or Victory mail, was the primary method for sending correspondence during the second war. It saved the cost of sending mail as letters were censored, copied to film, and then printed back on to paper. One hundred and fifty thousand one-page letters could fit in a single mail sack.

"It saved space, allowing more vital items to be shipped," she said to Beau who slept at her side. The cat opened one eye, obviously not impressed.

"All right, if that doesn't interest you, what about this? V-mail also cut down on espionage since photocopying foiled invisible ink."

Beau yawned, and Cheryl turned back to her task at hand. She flipped the V-mail letters over in her hand. It seemed strange that whoever wrote the letters didn't sign his name. He did mention farming and names of family members. Sugarcreek wasn't a big town. Surely someone knew who could have written the letters.

Cheryl still had an inner nudge the author was Amish, or at least was before he joined the military. Was it someone who turned his back on the church? Was that why he received no letters in return? She pulled out her notebook, preparing to write her questions on her list when a familiar chime sounded. Seeing that Aunt Mitzi was calling, she sat up straighter and smiled. Cheryl had hoped to connect by e-mail, but this was even better. Her aunt was fifteen hours ahead, and it meant she was interrupting her day to contact Cheryl. Had she thought of something—something that couldn't wait?

Cheryl clicked the green button to answer the call. A moment later, her aunt's face appeared. Aunt Mitzi wore a red bandanna knotted around her head, reminiscent of Rosie the Riveter. Perhaps her aunt had World War II on her mind too?

Cheryl flipped on the lamp next to the sofa so her aunt could see her better. "Hello, Aunt Mitzi."

The smile on Mitzi's face immediately turned into a scowl. "Cheryl, you look tired."

"Do I?" She feigned a yawn. "It's getting close to bedtime."

"It's more than that." Mitzi shook her finger. "Don't try to fool me. Something is wrong."

"I never could hide the truth from you." Cheryl sighed and then told Mitzi everything—about the stolen coins, how she and Esther mistakenly ruined the evidence, and the holes in the walls in the cottage. Mitzi's mouth grew rounder with astonishment as each moment passed.

"What about the letters? Were they stolen too?"

Cheryl lifted them up so her aunt could see them. "No. The letters are fine."

"Oh, good." The picture started to get scratchy, and Cheryl hoped the connection would stay.

"Oh, good? Do you know something about them?"

"Well, I thought about it last night when I went to bed. When Ralph and I were first married, I earned extra money cleaning houses. One of the houses appeared more like an Amish home, even though an *Englisch* couple lived there. The couple was always nice. She was an artist, I believe, and he... I can't remember for sure. Maybe he was a dentist or a doctor. Anyway, I was looking for cleaning supplies once, and I found some items from World War II. One day I was trying to make conversation and asked the man about the war... "

The picture flickered, and Cheryl held her breath. "Please, please don't quit now."

A few seconds later, Mitzi's image returned.

"Was he Amish?" the question blurted out.

"Actually, yes. I remember I wasn't surprised. Even though he wore ordinary clothes and drove a car, there was just something about him that made me think he was."

Cheryl reached down and stroked Beau as her excitement built. "And did he tell you anything about the war or about his family growing up? Did they live in the cottages?"

Mitzi laughed and leaned closer. "Let me see what I can remember. That was a long time ago. I do remember he was drafted and decided to join. I'm not sure if he realized how it would impact his family. Maybe he hoped they'd accept his choice since he was going to help people."

"Let me guess. That wasn't the case."

"No. I don't remember him talking about his family much. But there was one thing he liked to talk about—Papua New Guinea." Mitzi sighed. "He talked about his friends and tropical sickness. He mentioned the battles, but not much. Mostly he talked about the jungle and the bays. There were swamps and no roads. They marched down dirt trails and were met by native people. I remember thinking about that jungle fighting and wondering if those natives really understood what was happening. My own relationship with God was growing during that time, and I wondered if they even knew about God. Were they afraid of the fighting? Did they have any hope to cling to? Those thoughts never quite left me."

Cheryl hung on Mitzi's words, and for a moment it was as if she was seeing her aunt in a new light.

"And when you decided you wanted to be a missionary..."

Mitzi smiled. "That was the first place I thought of. I remembered my prayers as a young woman for the people there. I'd prayed God would send someone to them willing to walk those dirt trails into those jungles to share the truth." She chuckled. "I had no idea at the time I was praying for myself."

Tears rimmed Cheryl's eyes, and her chest felt warm and full. She never would have heard this story if she hadn't seen the coins and the letters. It amazed her that God had put her near that cottage when workers discovered the treasure. And she felt honored to be the first to read the letters that had remained hidden for so long.

"That's amazing." Cheryl blew out a breath. "Do you think it was your friend who wrote those letters?"

Mitzi nodded. "I really do. From what you read, it just makes sense. He served in World War II, but he wasn't welcomed by his family when he returned. He was a wonderful Christian man, but always a bit displaced because he never reintegrated with the Amish. I remember not long after I cleaned for them, they moved—I think it was somewhere in state, but I can't be sure."

"And do you remember his name?"

Mitzi shook her head. "I wish I did. Everyone just called him Pinky."

"Pinky?"

"Yes, he had bright red hair, but his wife told me that his older brother had already claimed the nickname Red. I wish I could remember more."

"Aunt Mitzi, you've done so much." Cheryl's stomach growled, and she remembered she hadn't eaten dinner. "This is a big help. I'm sure there aren't too many men who once lived in Sugarcreek with bright red hair who left the Amish and served in World War II."

Mitzi chuckled. "I bet you're right." She glanced at her watch. "But I best be going. I have to grab some lunch while I can, and you need to get your supper."

Cheryl narrowed her gaze. "How did you know?"

"Your computer has a microphone, remember? I believe that was your stomach growling. Either that or you're watching garbage truck videos on the television."

"Ha ha." Cheryl patted her stomach. "I am hungry. But I'm also feeling better after talking to you. I can't wait to tell Naomi tomorrow. And I'll let you know if I discover anything."

Mitzi glanced at her watch again, but she didn't say good-bye. Instead, she tilted her head and leaned closer to her computer screen. "I'm glad my information helped you, Cheryl, but are you taking care of yourself? Like I said before, you look a little…weary tonight."

Cheryl patted her cheek. "What a sweet way to tell me that I look horrible."

She grimaced. "It's not that, but I think you should rest more. I should have warned you—in addition to the store, the community has a way of sucking you in. And"—she winked—"running you ragged. I speak from experience. Promise me you'll take better care of yourself. Sleep in, get a manicure, and get away for the weekend."

Cheryl nodded and smiled. "Yes, Aunt."

"Yes to which one?"

"What?"

"You said yes, so which are you going to do?"

"Uh…" Cheryl wasn't expecting the question. "Uh, sleep in?"

"Tomorrow?"

"Yes, tomorrow."

"Wonderful. I'll check on that next time we talk."

"Yes, Aunt."

She signed off with her aunt and then turned off her computer and headed to the kitchen. She eyed a head of lettuce and found both a tomato and some cheese. There was lunch meat still too, and she boiled an egg, making herself a simple Cobb salad. It took care of the hunger, but she also craved some fresh bread with butter and maybe a slice of homemade cake for dessert. As she finished off the last of her salad, she wondered what Esther had made. No doubt the young woman's simple meal would put hers to shame.

Wondering if Naomi was home yet and eager to tell her what she'd learned from Aunt Mitzi, Cheryl glanced at the clock and then decided it wasn't too late to call. She dialed her phone and then waited for it to ring. After the third ring, someone answered. Cheryl was surprised. She usually had to leave a message.

"Hello?"

"Esther, this is Cheryl. I was just checking to see if your maam made it home all right. And if she did if she had a few minutes to talk."

"Ja, she made it home, but I believe she already went to bed. She asked me to call you though. I'd just made it to the phone shed when the phone rang. Maam wanted to know if you could take her and a friend to the doctor's office tomorrow."

"Doctor? Is everyone all right? There wasn't a problem with the labor was there?"

"Labor? I don't understand…" Esther's voice trailed off.

"Yes, the woman from the sewing frolic. Didn't she go into labor today?"

"Oh no!" Laughter poured from Esther's lips. "I haven't heard any more about that. It's our neighbor, Fannie. She fell. My maam wanted to know if you could possibly give her a ride to the doctor tomorrow before the Swiss Miss opens. Fannie called her Mennonite cousin to ask for help, but she hasn't heard back."

"Oh. Well..." Cheryl thought of her conversation with her aunt and her promise to sleep in. Had Momma talked to Aunt Mitzi? She didn't think so, but if both of them had come up with the same conclusion about her, then her weariness should be obvious. It seemed silly now, but she needed to rest. She *was* tired. Then again, Naomi's neighbor was more important than her sleep.

"Of course I can help...if it turns out Fannie's cousin can't help. Can you call the cousin again first? And if you still need me, let me know."

"Ja. Of course."

Esther said a quick good-bye, and then Cheryl picked up the letters. She considered reading them once more, checking to see if there were any more clues, but it no longer sounded interesting. If her mother and aunt were right—and she needed more rest—then why did she feel so awful every time she said no or tried to push the responsibility on someone else?

CHAPTER FOURTEEN

Tuesday morning Cheryl loaded Beau in his carrier and grabbed her purse. She'd slept, and she did feel better. It was amazing how an extra hour of sleep made the day seem even brighter.

The sky hinted at the possibility of rain, gray clouds skittering in quick bursts along the sky, blue poking through the gaps. The forecast hinted at a clear afternoon, but the sky seemed to disagree. She picked up her pace as she walked the blocks to the store. As she neared downtown, her steps slowed.

"Been eating more than your usual portion of kibble, Beau?" She switched him to the other arm and flexed the first to release the tightness. Beau shifted in the carrier but didn't bother to meow. Apparently he couldn't be disturbed, but she'd have to cut back on his treats if he was feeling this heavy.

She slowed as she saw John-John in a heated discussion with Sadie. She slowed her steps to give them some privacy but couldn't avoid hearing their words.

What had happened?

Tension reverberated off of them like waves from a shore.

She stepped in the direction of the voices that were a low but angry murmur. Then she hesitated. She didn't want to interfere. Not when they clearly had something to discuss.

"I don't understand how this happened. What did you do to my pictures?" John-John's posture stiffened, and his jaw clenched. Cheryl couldn't remember ever having seen him so intense.

Cheryl slowed even more, shifting the cat carrier back to her other arm. Maybe she should let the dispute run its course before she talked to him.

"But I didn't do anything." Sadie's stance was the opposite of John-John's. Where he was tight and stiff, she'd curled in on herself. "I promise I did exactly what the lady at the drugstore told me to do. I plugged in your phone and told the machine to print the copies."

"Then why didn't we have the photos yesterday when I sent you?"

"Because the machine didn't work. So she told me to leave the card and she'd make them." She held up an envelope. "This is all she gave me now."

Was this about the photos of the coins? Cheryl edged a step closer.

"But I took dozens of photos of those coins. If you really did, then I should have more than one out-of-focus shot." The last words were practically yelled, and Cheryl cringed. This wasn't like John-John. Why was he so upset?

"I don't understand why you would do this, Sadie."

"It wasn't me. Why would I do anything to mess with your silly coins?" Her volume matched his, and a moment later Sadie flew by, her blonde Barbie doll ponytail brushing side to side. She didn't even glance at Cheryl as she hurried past.

Cheryl closed the distance to Johnson. He paced in front of the storefront, mumbling under his breath as he waved the envelope back and forth.

"What good is one unfocused picture? There's nothing we can use."

"John-John?" Cheryl reached out to get his attention, slowly as if he were a distracted dog that might snap at her.

"I just can't believe it." The man snapped to a stop when he noticed her. "All those photos I took, and they're gone. That just doesn't happen."

She had to agree. He'd snapped a bunch in the couple minutes he'd had his phone out on Saturday. "Surely there are a few."

"Yep. One. One lousy photo out of all of them. Of all the lousy luck, that one is out of focus."

"That's ironic."

"Not sure that's the word I'd use for it." His spine slumped, and some of the fire went out of his eyes. "Maybe it just reinforces that I'm not supposed to focus on those coins. There's been nothing but trouble since they showed up."

"We can still find them."

"I'm washing my hands of them. It's the only thing I can do." He wiggled as if shrugging off his thoughts. "There's too much to do back at the cottages to waste any more time or effort on those coins. But that's not why you're here. What can I do for you, Miss Cheryl?"

Her heart hurt for him as he forced a smile. "Nothing. I was on my way to the Swiss Miss." She turned to continue on then shifted back toward him. "Did Sadie develop the photos at the drugstore?"

"Yes." He rubbed a hand over his face. "I've never had anything like this happen before. Have you?"

Cheryl shook her head. "No." But she made a note to check with the drugstore and see if they'd really had problems with their machine or if this was unique to John-John's photos. Maybe a distraction would help. "Is Levi working out?"

"With the scheduling? Yes, he's been great. Right here when I need him with the info I need."

Cheryl felt a small stab. If only she'd been so diligent. "I'm glad he's a help to you."

"Me too. Well, I'd better get back to it. The cottages aren't getting painted and fixed on their own."

Cheryl watched him walk the way she had come. As soon as she knew he was focused elsewhere, she slipped into the drugstore. She still had a few minutes until the Swiss Miss opened, and she walked with quickened steps. It only took a minute to walk past the aisles of cosmetics and hair products to find the photo corner. A couple machine stations sat next to a counter. A bell waited on the glass top, so she hit it. Beau meowed his displeasure at the sound.

A hand waved from a door behind the counter. "I'll be right with ya."

"No problem." While Cheryl waited, she unzipped a small opening in the carrier and rubbed Beau's ears. He purred his pleasure. As a woman walked out of the back room, Cheryl quickly withdrew her hand and rezipped the carrier.

"What can I help you with, hon?" The lady was likely in her mid-fifties. Her fuchsia lipstick struck a sharp contrast against her red shirt, which clashed equally with her out-of-a-bottle auburn hair.

"I needed to get some photos printed, but I heard your machine was down."

"No, ma'am. Our machine is just fine."

Cheryl frowned. "Maybe I heard my friend wrong. She said when she brought the photos yesterday, the machine was broken. Then she didn't get all of them back."

The woman planted her hands on her hips, and those fuchsia lips turned upside down. "These machines have been working fine all week. I wasn't here yesterday, but they worked fine. Your friend is mistaken or you are."

"Thanks." Cheryl turned to leave. "Time to get to work."

"What about your photos?"

"I'll have to bring them another day."

During the rest of the walk to the Swiss Miss, Cheryl's thoughts flipped through what she'd just learned. Sadie must be lying about the machines, or the woman working at the counter was misinformed. Why would the lady at the drugstore have any reason to lie about the machine? She wouldn't as far as Cheryl could see.

As she reached the Swiss Miss, her heart smiled at the cheery white paint with blue shutters. Then her smile drooped when she saw Chief Twitchell leaning against the store. "Hello, Chief."

"Cheryl." He pushed from the wall. "Did you hear about the trouble at the cottages?"

"No, and I just saw Johnson fifteen minutes ago."

"He may not have discovered the problem then. Sounds like someone got in and demolished some more walls in one of the other cottages too. Freshly finished walls too."

"Oh no." All that hard work undone with the swing of a sledgehammer. "What can I do?"

"Why don't you come out there with me? I'm guessin' whoever did this was lookin' for more coins."

Cheryl looked into the store. She noticed that Esther was already inside readying everything for the day. "Let me go ask."

"Esther? I've already told her that I was going to ask you. She said not to worry about her."

"Yes, just like yesterday." Cheryl sighed. She hoped that today wouldn't be as busy as yesterday, but what choice did she have? The chief himself was asking for her help.

Cheryl put Beau in the store, gave a quick wave to Esther, and then joined the chief. In a few minutes they pulled up to the cottages. The piles of covered supplies that had filled one section of the cul-de-sac were diminishing and taking up less space each time she visited the site. Amish and Englisch workers mixed with the common purpose of helping John-John turn his vision into reality.

As she stood there, the sun warming her face as birds sang their twittering songs, she could imagine the peace that would envelop the families that would be sheltered inside the cottages. What a gift to be part of making that sanctuary for them. If the work continued at this pace, then she should begin designing the flower gardens that would add color to the outside of the homes. Maybe they should add a vegetable garden too. The only problem was that if the destruction continued, then who knew when the cottages would get done? Things were going backward not forward as they should.

The new incidence of demolition was disturbing. It felt like someone was determined to keep the cottages from being finished and becoming homes for the women and children who needed the sanctuary.

Chief Twitchell asked the first worker he saw, an Amish man with his straw hat pulled down to shade his eyes, if he knew where to find Johnson. A minute later Cheryl followed the chief to the cottage next to the one where the coins were found. As soon as she entered she could feel the tension that coated the rooms.

Ragged holes had been pounded into walls a soft robin's egg blue. In other places chunks had been ripped out.

"Oh no." The words sighed from Cheryl.

John-John stood slumped in front of one of the most heavily damaged walls. "I'm not sure I have the money to repair this cottage again." He held up a sheet of paper. "Chief Twitchell, you'll want this."

The chief pulled a pair of gloves from his pocket and slipped them on his hands. "What's this?"

"We found this jammed on a nail. Guess the person who did all this left it."

Cheryl stepped closer to the chief and read over his shoulder. In large block letters that looked to have been written in Sharpie someone had penned, *This is my property. I'm the rightful heir, and if you continue with your plans here, I'll make sure not a single stick of wood in any of these cottages is left.*

She read it again. The sense of hate was so strong she could practically feel it rise from the sheet. It looked like regular copier paper, nothing special or distinguishing about it.

"If they're the heir, why don't they just tell us?" The question escaped before she'd really thought about it.

John-John shook his head. "I don't know. The title search didn't reveal any owners we could find. We tried, but the property's been abandoned for at least fifteen years."

"I wonder if the property taxes weren't paid as they should have been." Cheryl had heard that government bodies could take property from owners if they failed to pay their taxes. If it had been fifteen years, that could have certainly happened.

"A tax sale would have happened years ago." Chief Twitchell confirmed her suspicions. "Whoever thinks they're the heir is likely too late. Showin' up now probably won't change a thing."

"Someone needs to tell them before they destroy more of our hard work." A flash of temper flared as red raced up John-John's neck.

"I can send someone out here to try to get fingerprints, but I'm not sure it's going to do much good. How many people have worked in this cottage?"

John-John shrugged. "I'm not sure. We have a schedule and assignments, but people go where they want and do the work where it's needed. They're volunteers."

"I understand." Chief Twitchell pulled off his hat and rubbed a hand over his hair. "What would you like me to do?"

"Besides finding this person?"

"That's understood."

John-John nodded. "I guess do what you need to do in order to find the culprit."

"I'll grab my camera and get someone else out here to take photos. I need everyone to leave this cottage, and I'll need a list of the folks you know have been here. We'll fingerprint them for elimination prints." He gave Johnson an intense look. "You might think about which of your volunteers could be behind this."

"None of them would be. They're all good people who want to help."

Cheryl nodded. "I can vouch for that. I recruited many of them. They just want to help create a safe place for families."

The chief shook his head. "I don't agree. I've discovered that crooks like to stay close. Someone knew enough to know which cottage the coins were found in. Only someone who'd worked here would know that detail, right?"

"But they could tell someone else."

"It wouldn't make much difference when these homes don't have numbers on them yet. They all look alike from the outside. Nothing to distinguish them."

John-John shifted his feet and looked at the ground. "Sir, I know you're the crime expert, but I hate to think that anyone who has been helping here would do these things."

"I understand, but you need to. If we don't consider every possibility, we may not find the right person."

When the chief left to get his camera and call in help, Cheryl stepped closer to John-John. "I'm so sorry."

"I don't understand. Why is all of this happening? Did I miss God on this? I thought it was so clear He wanted me to take this project."

"He may very well want you to. That doesn't mean we don't experience opposition. We'll get this figured out." And until they did, she was going to pray for God's protection. Families needed these homes.

"We have to get this finished. Children need a place where they can roam and play. This would be so much better for them than the shelters." John-John's passion reignited the fire inside Cheryl.

This project was too important to let anything slow it down. As Chief Twitchell walked back and started systematically shooting pictures of the demolition, she stood in the doorway out of his way. There wasn't anything that she could see to go on, so she told everyone good-bye and headed to the shop. If things weren't too busy, she could do some investigating in the slow times at the shop. There was much she could dig into from Aunt Mitzi's story.

Esther had the shop open when Cheryl arrived. Beau ignored her, instead choosing to shower attention on a little girl bent over petting him. Cheryl headed straight to the office and booted up the computer. She'd barely opened the Internet search engine when Esther appeared in the doorway.

"Someone from the security company is here."

Cheryl looked up from the computer with a frown. "Why?"

"I don't know." Esther shrugged and headed back to the front.

Better go see what this was about.

A man with the security company's shirt came over. "I'm here to recheck the system."

"Why? Lauren was already here."

"We just want to make sure she didn't miss anything."

The answer didn't make sense to Cheryl. "Why not come over with her or right after?"

"This isn't a high priority. In all likelihood you forgot to set the system properly. I'll be in and out in fifteen minutes."

Cheryl stood at the counter and watched him the whole time he worked. It didn't look to her like he did much other than open the panel and hit a couple buttons. Then he got out a tablet of some sort and clicked around on it for a few minutes.

He returned to her with a cocky grin. "Just as I expected. You didn't fully engage the system. What we call 'operator error.' Next time make sure you hit Enter after you punch in the code and you'll be good."

"Thanks." She shook her head as the arrogant man left.

Esther giggled. "That was helpful?"

"Not at all." Something didn't seem right about him coming so long after the event. Maybe she'd call the company to confirm. But right now she had more important things to do. Things like discovering who was causing all the damage at the cottages while also relocating the coins. That had to be her priority.

Speaking of which, it was time to fill Chief Twitchell in on the coin photos. Was Sadie behind it all? Cheryl wouldn't be surprised if she were.

CHAPTER FIFTEEN

After a few minutes of waiting, Chief Twitchell came on the line.

"Chief Twitchell."

"Hi. This is Cheryl."

"Didn't I just see you at the cottages?"

"Guess it didn't take long for you to finish there."

"No. Wish I could do more for them, but we're looking into it." He sighed, and she could imagine him rubbing a hand down his face as he did when he was tired. "What can I do for you now?"

"A quick question. Did Johnson bring the coin photos by for you?"

A gruff harrumph came across. "No. He claims somethin' happened to them."

"I heard him and Sadie, the intern, arguing about the photos while I walked to work." She paused, reevaluating whether she should fill him in or not. Would he think she was just jumping to conclusions too? "I didn't mean to overhear, but their voices were pretty loud. Sadie claimed the photo printer at the drugstore wasn't working right. I went into the drugstore and talked to the lady working at the photo counter. She said the machines are working just fine. The clerk didn't know about problems."

"Likely a simple mistake happened. I'll make a note and put it in the file with the rest of the odd things happening up at the cottages. Anything else?"

"I was just wondering if you discovered anything about the V-mail letters. Do you think they are important to the case?"

"I read through the copies you made and the one original that I took, and I didn't see anything important. Do you want to come by and pick up this last original?"

"Sure. How about as soon as the tour buses leave?"

"I'll look for you then."

The rest of the morning flew by as Cheryl worked in tandem with Esther to help the tourists who stopped to shop. The two flowed back and forth between the cash register and the shop floor. Cheryl appreciated how well Esther anticipated her thoughts. Working together for months had its benefits when you had a colleague who was eager to serve with a ready smile that welcomed all who came.

Today's hot items seemed to be the homemade jellies and breads, though quite a few people bought hand-crafted items like the pot holders and place mats. A few people bought candy and chocolate, but the jelly and jam table was almost depleted when the last tourist exited the shop, hurrying to the buses with bags slung over each arm.

"I'm going to get this table restocked." Cheryl adjusted one last jar before she headed to the storeroom. The shelf with the extra jellies was getting as bare as a picked-over sales rack on Black Friday. "Time to reorder"—she glanced over the table—"everything!"

Once she had brought the remaining jars up front, she touched base with Esther. The young woman stood at another table reorganizing the display of Amish pull toys and dolls.

"Do you think I could come to your farm tonight to get more jam?"

Esther looked up even as she kept tidying the area. "Sure, but I can also bring them to you in the morning. No need to make an extra trip."

"Oh, if you don't mind, that would be a tremendous help!" Cheryl would love the chance to see Naomi...and possibly Levi. She really ought to touch base and make sure he was still fine with the volunteer schedule. It was such an overwhelming undertaking when she had it that she hoped it wasn't too much for him. Even so, she had so much to do already...

"As soon as I get home, I will let Maam know to prepare a box for me to bring with me tomorrow."

"Thanks. I need to run something over to Chief Twitchell, and then I'll be back. Shouldn't be gone more than fifteen minutes." She grabbed her purse and confirmed that the letters were in the side pocket of the purple bag. She'd already lost the coins, and she was extra protective of the letters now. The large leather flower on the side always made her smile and think of the springiest of days.

A wrinkle formed between Esther's eyes. "Why do you have the letters in your purse?"

"With all the odd things happening around here, it seems safer keeping them close at hand."

"I guess. Get on with you now." Esther waved her off with a shaky smile as Cheryl headed out the door with her purse slung over her shoulder.

It only took a couple of minutes for Cheryl to walk the two blocks to the police station. The one-story, brick building had white gingerbread trim on the roof and a large picture window with decorative shutters. As she entered, a wide counter provided a barrier between the tiny lobby with a few old, vinyl chairs and a couple offices in the back. Before she could say hello to Delores Delgado at the desk, Chief Twitchell waved her into his office.

Cheryl sidled around the counter.

Chief Twitchell handed her the V-mail, still in the envelope she had provided.

She took it from his hand and tucked it into her purse. "So you didn't find anything special about the letters?"

"I'm not sure what you want me to see, Cheryl. These look like lightly censored letters from a soldier to his family back home."

"So why were they in the jars with all the coins?"

"We may never know."

"There has to be a connection. But I can't make out enough from the letters to get any real indication who wrote them. The signature is a blurred scrawl."

Chief Twitchell chuckled. "I think you're being generous. This handwriting is bad enough to make a doctor proud. Thanks for letting me read them, but they don't tell us anything useful."

Cheryl sighed, but knew he was right. They were the clues that refused to release their secrets. All the censor blackouts didn't help, but she'd still harbored hope he would have seen something she missed.

"I think this is the work of a professional crook." He studied her carefully, his gaze searching her face. "Cheryl, these could very well be his way of trying to send us in the wrong direction."

"But how could a professional know about the coins so quickly?" She was going to say more but paused.

"The grapevine around Sugarcreek is healthy and strong, I'm afraid. Also, we didn't know about the coins, but somebody did. Those coins didn't magically jump into jars and then between the walls. For some reason, they were put there years ago. Somebody knew they existed, but they might not have known where. So maybe the moment the jars were found and word circulated, the thief knew where to go."

"Thank you for your time. I'll get back to the store now."

He held up his hand. "Before you leave, there's somethin' else I need to tell you. Why don't you take a seat."

Cheryl eased on to the edge of the ancient olive-green vinyl chair in front of his desk. "This doesn't sound good."

"I wouldn't worry too much, but you need to know that I got a call first thing this morning that there was a strange car parked on your street overnight. One of your neighbors walked their dog after eleven and noticed it with someone sitting inside. Then when they let their pooch out this morning at six, the car was still there with someone in it." He leaned across the desk. "They tried to take a photo with their phone, but whoever was in the car took off before they could get a shot."

"Okay. So we don't know why they were there or if they were there for me or someone else."

"True. I'm going to have my officers take some extra patrols on your street over the next few days. Chances are it wasn't anything, but I'll feel better keeping an extra eye out. With the cottages just a couple blocks away, I want to make sure nothing else happens there."

Tightness clenched down in Cheryl's chest. She tried to ignore it, but it built until it felt hard to swallow too. Surely the chief wasn't saying what she thought he was saying. "But there's no reason I should be concerned that the person was watching my house, right?"

The chief looked over her shoulder a moment as if choosing his words carefully. "Sugarcreek is a safe place, Cheryl. You know that after your months in our community. At the same time I can't guarantee anything."

"All right." She nibbled on her thumbnail. "Uh, thanks for letting me know. I'll definitely be more alert tonight." What else could she do? The fact a car had parked on the street did not mean that it was focused on her. There were many other homes on her street, even a couple businesses, not to mention the cottages. Or it could have simply been someone who needed a place to rest and had been noticed by a super attentive neighbor. "Thanks for looking at the letters."

"Sure. Be careful."

She offered a small salute, smiled, and then left his office. "Yes, sir."

As she walked the short distance back to the Swiss Miss, she ran through all that had happened since the coins had been discovered on Saturday. She needed to do something to learn if the coins had any value. She called John-John. "Can you text me that photo of the coin you do have?"

"It's a terrible photo."

"That's okay. I'd just like to see if there's anything I can learn from it." She should have taken a closer look when he'd offered it to her, but he'd been so distressed she'd simply wanted to help. Now she knew the best way to help was to discover more about the coins. There was a reason someone had decided to steal them and now to continue to wreak havoc at the cottages. Maybe if she learned more about the coins, she could back into who had owned them and use that knowledge to back into who might think they owned them now. It had to work.

"All right. I'll snap a picture and get it over to you."

As she entered the store, her phone dinged that she'd gotten a text. She pulled it up and saw a grainy image of a couple coins. Several customers stood at various places in the store looking at items. She slipped her phone back in her pocket. After she helped Esther with their guests, then she'd examine the photo in detail.

More tourists walked into the store, some fanning themselves with random pieces of paper.

"It's turning into a warm one out there." A woman wearing a big, floppy straw hat and purple muumuu waved her paper briskly in front of red cheeks. "I'd think I'd jumped into Hades if I didn't know better."

Cheryl cocked her head and raised an eyebrow. It hadn't been hot when she'd come inside. In fact, it had felt pleasant with the light breeze running across her face as she'd walked.

The woman's friend elbowed her with a grin. "I think it's your internal furnace, Letty."

"Maybe so." The women continued their chatter as they examined the candles before moving to the wooden toys.

The afternoon sped by in a flurry of helping customers find the perfect items to add to their homes.

As the afternoon wound down, she worked alongside Esther putting the store back in order. By the time they were finished, Cheryl felt sweat squiggling down the small of her back.

She settled a stool back into its row with matching chairs. "I think we're done."

Esther wiped her hands on her apron. "Then may I head home?"

"Of course. Thank you for all you've done today."

The young woman grinned as she slipped off her Swiss Miss apron and replaced it with her clean white one. "It is my job. I like it so well, and I want to do whatever you need so you keep me around."

Cheryl squeezed the girl in a one-armed hug. "I appreciate you. Tell your mom hi. Okay?"

"Yes, ma'am." Esther reached into her apron pocket and pulled out an envelope. "She wanted me to give you this. And, oh, I almost forgot... She said if you didn't have plans you're welcome for dinner."

"Thanks for the note, but I'd better say no to dinner." Even though she wanted to say yes, Cheryl had a date with her bills and checkbook. She could put it off until later if she really wanted, but when? Besides, she knew her mom wouldn't be happy about her doing too much. Maybe she did need more time alone, more time to rest. Cheryl followed her friend to the door and turned the sign to Closed. "See you tomorrow."

Beau wound around the tables toward her, tail held high as if he surveyed his kingdom. In a way that's exactly what the Swiss Miss was. His place away from home where everyone doted on him. He was king of the castle and the store.

"I wonder what Naomi has for me, Beau." She also wondered what she was missing for dinner. Anything Naomi made would be a huge improvement over the microwave meal she'd heat.

He looked at her with a placid expression which indicated he didn't really care. Maybe this was information on the jars and what Naomi had learned at her frolic. Cheryl hoped so as she ran a finger under the envelope's edge.

Chapter Sixteen

One piece of paper rested inside the envelope, Naomi's clear, ordered script flowing across the page.

Dear Cheryl,

The ladies and I examined the jars while we were at the frolic.

I had hoped to come see you and update you myself, but the days have been full. In case I cannot get away today, I want you to have this information. Maybe it will help your search.

The old mason jar reminds some of our older members of the ones their maams used when they were children. There was tape residue on the side of the jar, and they remember some of the jars having a label taped to them. That made us think they must have been used in town during the 1930s and 1940s.

One of the women insisted jars just like this were used by a pharmacist in Sugarcreek. I am not sure how to confirm that, but maybe the library has some information that dates that far. I am sure you will know. One woman believed the name on the store may have been Jacobsen.

I will visit one or two of the ladies at their homes. Maybe a night or two to think about the jars will loosen additional memories.

I hope this helps, my friend.

Naomi's careful signature followed, and Cheryl refolded the note and slid it back inside the envelope. She slid the envelope next to the V-mail letters and then collected Beau. "Time to go home, boy."

He purred a quick rumble then squirmed as if to be put down. She tightened her hold as she walked to the office and then slid him in his carrier. She grabbed one of the mason jars that Naomi had left and added it to the collection in her purse. Maybe tonight she could dig into the jars based on what Naomi had learned. In a moment she set the alarm and then locked up the store. The light breeze complemented the song of birds filling the air. A few cars drove by, and she waved at a couple people she recognized. The evening felt perfect, the kind that would be ideal for eating her supper on the back porch.

She hummed a worship song as she covered the blocks home. Her phone rang as she turned on to the street leading home. As she tugged her phone out of her bag, she scanned the street for any car that looked out of place. "Hello?"

"Hi, honey." Her mom's voice covered her in a glaze of condemnation. Would Momma ask how she'd been doing on creating white space in her life? Cheryl tried to brush off the concern as she noted a white Impala she'd never seen before.

"How are things in Seattle?"

"Busy but good. Your father started a new sermon series, and it's going to be a good one. People responded well Sunday." Cheryl kept her talking about the series while she walked up the sidewalk to Aunt Mitzi's cottage. "But I called to see how you are."

Shoot, that hadn't worked as well as she'd hoped. "Good. Things are good."

Silence answered that response.

"Really, Momma, everything's fine."

"How are you coming on freeing up your calendar?"

Cheryl bit her lower lip as Beau's carrier slid from her grip while she tried to unlock the front door. He meowed his displeasure, and she slid him inside. If she juggled her life as well as she'd just juggled the cat, keys, and phone, she was doomed. "I'm trying."

"That's a start. What are you doing?"

"Right now? I'm walking in Aunt Mitzi's door. We had a good day at the store, but it feels great to be home."

"Any plans for tonight?"

"I think I'll eat supper on the patio. It's such a beautiful night."

"That sounds like some great self-care. Who have you told no to this week?"

"Probably as many people as you have, Momma." She hadn't meant to let the words slip out with such a harsh tone, but her momma had never been the best at saying no.

"Cheryl, I just want to keep you from making the same mistakes I did. If you can learn now to take better care of yourself, you'll be in a much better position when you're my age. That's what every mother wants. For her children to learn from her life."

"Mom, I've tried hard to say no to things, but all I feel is isolated." She sighed as she sank on to the living room couch. "It can get lonely at night, and sometimes it's nice to say yes so I can be with other people."

"I hadn't thought about it that way. I thought Sugarcreek was beginning to feel like home."

"It is." She told her mom a couple stories about the people she'd seen that day and how many she recognized. "But it's still lonely. I come home at night, and it's just me." Beau meowed, and she laughed. "Well, and Beau. Can't forget him. But it's still not the same as having a roommate or lots of friends to hang out with. Besides, I like helping people."

Momma was silent before changing the direction of the conversation. Fifteen minutes later when the call ended, Cheryl was caught up with the events and happenings at the Seattle church. It sounded like the church was in the middle of a mini baby boom with the occasional wedding thrown into the mix.

Cheryl slipped her cell phone back into her pocket and then picked up Beau. "I love my mom, Beau, but sometimes I wonder if she really understands me." Beau granted her an obligatory purr before wriggling free. He settled next to her on the couch and watched her with eyes that seemed wise and knowing.

"How can I make her understand that I get joy from helping people?"

He cocked his head and meowed.

"Well, that's true. Sometimes it is overwhelming, but it doesn't mean I should cloister myself here after work. If this was all my life was, I would feel very sad."

He nudged her arm and licked it with his sandpaper tongue.

"I'm glad I have you, boy." She pulled her notebook over and opened to a clean page. She'd been so busy at the shop that she hadn't found time to research during the day. Cheryl decided the bills could wait. Now was as good a time as any to add what little she'd learned to her list.

Chief Twitchell didn't think the letters offered much in the way of information, but she didn't agree. The letters wouldn't have been with the coins if they weren't important to somebody. Why the jars had been hidden in the walls was still a key question. Once she recovered the coins, their value might make it clear, but if they'd been walled in during World War II, the owners at that time might have remained leery of using the banks after the collapse and Depression.

Why leave the jars there?

Maybe over time the jars had simply been forgotten. The war ended, life continued, and as the months passed, the coins simply weren't important.

And why not get bills instead of coins? The coins probably held value better—maybe even increased in value . . . if the appraiser had been correct. But paper money would take up much less space.

She pulled up the photo that John-John had e-mailed her. He was right. It was grainy. She dragged her fingers along the image to make it bigger, but it became so pixelated, she couldn't discern any helpful details. Maybe the image of the face was Thomas Jefferson. Maybe it was a nickel. It was a really bad image of a coin. She squinted at the image and then shrunk it. Maybe it was a quarter. The jar in the background looked like it was filled with a mishmash of coins. It certainly had seemed that way as she and Levi had filled the baggies with coins. There hadn't been a predominance of one kind over another. Instead it had been a mix of quarters, dimes, nickels, and some pennies.

Could coins from the World War II era have grown in value over the years to the extent it would give them significant enough value to entice someone to break into her shop?

She grabbed her bulging purse and laptop and resettled on the couch. Maybe the appraiser could give her a better idea of what to expect. After she removed the jar from her bag, she tugged Suzanne Marshall's business card from the side pocket she'd slipped it in. The card didn't list a Web site for Suzanne, so Cheryl opened an Internet browser and typed in the woman's name. A minute later she was looking at a page of links, mostly to newspaper articles about different auctions and acquisitions. However, she couldn't find a Web site for the woman. Next she called Suzanne. The phone rang several times before rolling to voice mail.

"I'm sorry I can't take your call right now, but I'm out of town for business. Leave a message, and I'll be glad to get back to you as soon as I can."

Hmm. Out of town still? Cheryl left a brief message requesting a return call then did a search for coin appraisers in the area. The list was small. There must not be much demand for such appraisals.

She noted a couple options and jotted the names and phone numbers in her notebook. It was probably too late, but she'd go ahead and call anyway. At a minimum she could leave a message. And that was exactly what she ended up doing. All of the businesses were closed, so she left messages asking for return calls.

Next she pulled out the V-mail letters and reread them.

One thing was very clear. Whoever had written them was very familiar with the Amish if he wasn't actually Amish. The Pennsylvania Dutch phrases wouldn't be in there otherwise. She also thought the fact that he was a medic could relate to conscientious objector status. She knew enough about the Amish to know that they wouldn't voluntarily serve in a fighting role. It went completely against their pacifist ways. But serving as a medic? She'd heard that was possible, though it might depend on the local group. And what if the person was still in their *rumspringa* when they were drafted? Could they take on an alternate role during that?

A clumping on the porch drew her head up.

Was someone out there?

Chapter Seventeen

Clomp. Clop.

A shiver skittered down Cheryl's spine. "Did you invite anyone over, Beau?"

He ignored her as something clattered against a window.

Cheryl swallowed then pushed to her feet, the jar rolling to the floor, but fortunately not shattering. "I guess I'd better see what's out there."

The white Impala slashed through her mind. Could whoever was in it be related to the events of the prior night Chief Twitchell had warned her about? Or had his warning sent her imagination into hyperdrive? She crept on tiptoe toward the front window, wondering as she did if it wouldn't be wiser to go hide in her room. Still, she had to know who could be out there. Maybe it was simply the wind blowing through branches and she could laugh at how jumpy she'd been. Or maybe she should throw an overnight bag together and go stay at the Millers' farm or a hotel.

"Now you are being ridiculous, Cheryl." Hearing her whispered words did nothing to calm the crazy beating of her heart as another thump resonated. She jumped and scurried back to the living room. She grabbed her cell phone and dialed the police department. In a moment she felt a little silly as the dispatcher picked up. "This is Cheryl Cooper. Could you send someone to check my house? I'm pretty sure someone is on my front porch."

"A cruiser is just a few minutes away. I'll send them your way now."

The dispatcher kept chatting with her, and Cheryl could feel her shoulders relax.

"Have you heard anything else?"

"No, ma'am." Cheryl stepped back into the hallway. "Maybe it was just my imagination."

"The cruiser should be driving by soon. We'll check it out and make sure you can sleep well tonight. In about five minutes, Officer Spencer will knock on your door. Don't open it until you've confirmed that the person on your porch is in uniform."

"Thank you."

"No problem. Chief Twitchell told us to make sure we kept you safe tonight."

Heat flashed up Cheryl's cheeks. She didn't necessarily want to be the police department's special project, though she appreciated the extra concern. True to the dispatcher's word, it was only a few more minutes before she heard the steady clomp of boots headed to her door. She headed that direction as she heard a knock on the door.

"Officer Spencer with the Sugarcreek police. Everything all right, Ms. Cooper?"

Cheryl cracked open the door. "Can I see your ID, please?"

The officer pointed to his badge. "Chief Twitchell has me patrolling past here twice an hour tonight. I haven't seen anyone around your house in any of those times."

Cheryl swallowed as she looked up at the burly guy. He looked like he spent most of his time off in a gym pumping iron. If he was watching her house, she should feel safe. "Maybe I overreacted, but I heard a steady clomping on the porch about ten minutes ago."

The officer stepped back and scanned the porch then turned and examined the walk and dirt around the porch. "Could be, but whoever it was, he's gone now. I've checked the perimeter and didn't see anything to indicate a person's been around. If anyone was here, he left. Anything else I can do for you?" With his hands propped on his hips, the man was downright intimidating.

"Thank you, I'll be fine. I appreciate your coming so quickly." She eased the door shut and then leaned against it. The thought of going to sleep in her bed after this was nerve-racking. She knew it shouldn't be. The officer had done his job and made sure she was secure. The problem was she didn't feel that way. She felt wary and on edge. She picked Beau up and rubbed his silky fur. "What do I have that the thief would want? Huh?"

Nothing came to mind. The letters weren't much, and word hadn't gotten out that she had the heavily censored V-mail, so she didn't think the thief would know to look for them. "Tea, that's what I need."

Fifteen minutes later when she'd brewed a cup of herbal tea, she settled at the kitchen table but didn't feel any less jittery. She bowed her head. *Lord, will You calm my heart? I know You don't want me to be afraid like this.* She opened her eyes and took a deep breath that she blew out slowly. Then she opened her Bible and read a couple psalms. As she read, she could sense the truth that God was her protector soak into her soul. After a few more minutes, she felt peace to her core and knew she'd be able to fall asleep.

The next morning, Cheryl stirred slowly when her alarm rang. Part of her wanted desperately to roll over, pull the covers over her head, and try to claim more sleep. She'd slept, but it had been fitful, the kind that wasn't fully restorative. She forced herself to get up, and in twenty minutes, her hair spiking in its uncontrolled manner, she was in her car headed to the Miller farm. It might be too early to head to the Swiss Miss, but the Miller place would be full of activity.

As she reached the field that would hold the Millers' corn maze, a freshly painted sign advertised buggy rides and hayrides. The crisp blue of the lettering against the sunny yellow matched the personality of the family—bright and cheery. Next she approached the covered bridge, the creek bubbling underneath with all the spring rain. At the end of the bridge she saw the welcoming white farmhouse with the inviting wraparound porch. In the pasture, several horses poked their heads over the fence as if curious why she'd invaded the farmyard so early in the morning. The barn doors stood open, and one buggy was already pulled out as if ready for a quick drive to town. Cheryl parked the car and wiped her hands on her capris. She shouldn't be nervous since Naomi was her dearest friend in Sugarcreek, but she feared she may have been rude in not accepting her friend's invitation twice.

As she opened the car door, Naomi stepped onto the front porch, wiping her hands on her white apron. Then Cheryl's friend raised her hand to shield her eyes as she looked at Cheryl.

"Is all well?"

Cheryl walked to the porch. "Yes. I just wanted to come tell you something I learned about myself last night."

Naomi nodded to the rocking chairs. "I have a few minutes before I need to pull muffins from the oven. Let us enjoy the beauty of this morning."

"Perfect." Cheryl settled on a rocker, the seat padded with a soft cushion. She breathed deeply, letting the peace of the place settle over her.

Naomi's concerned gaze met hers. "Are you sure all is well?"

"Yes." She took another breath then told Naomi about her mom's concerns. "It was so ironic to hear her telling me to be careful about overscheduling. She's usually one of the first to say yes to every request."

"Maybe she wants you to live a different life."

"That's what she said too." Cheryl set the chair to rocking back and forth on the wooden porch. "And I appreciate her concern. But as I sat in Aunt Mitzi's home by myself last night, I learned something important."

Naomi nodded, as if encouraging her to continue.

"I like helping people. I miss being around people when I'm in the silence at home. Spending dinner with your family last night would have made me feel part of something bigger than me. Instead, I had a terrible microwave dinner because it wasn't worth the effort to cook for one."

"Speaking of cooking, I should check the muffins." Naomi pushed to her feet then turned to Cheryl. "Come in and share a cup of *kaffee* with me. I want to hear more about your revelation."

Cheryl followed her friend into the home's roomy kitchen. The kitchen was the heart of the home with its huge wooden table in the middle of the room. Against the wall was a long wooden sideboard that would be loaded with food during a meal. A pot of coffee percolated on one of the burners of the old-fashioned gas range. Naomi grabbed two mugs from one of the wooden cabinets then filled the mugs with the fresh coffee. After setting them on the table, she checked the muffins and pulled them from the oven. Next she grabbed cream and sugar.

"Now tell me more about your epiphany."

"I've thought about it, and what is right for my mom—during this season of her life—isn't necessarily right for me. She told me that I need to stop helping people so much. My mom urged me to take time for myself more often." She held up a hand as Naomi began to speak. "I'm not saying I shouldn't be mindful about what I agree to do. At the same time, I shouldn't just stop because my mother suggested I'm too busy. I need to ask God what He wants me to do and adjust my schedule accordingly."

Naomi took a sip of her coffee. "That sounds reasonable to me. He will show you what you should do." She set her mug down and studied Cheryl with thoughtful eyes. "I've learned that when I pour out love to others from the love that Gott fills me with, that is when I most get to see Him at work. There is something special about working with Him to touch the world."

The words settled over Cheryl like a cloak. The rightness of them struck her deeply. "That's exactly it. I won't pretend I make the right choices every time. Yet I know there are times when I'm doing something as a way to serve others that I almost feel His smile."

"Exactly." Naomi reached over and patted Cheryl's hand. "Your heart is sensitive to His. He will show *you* what to do and what to leave for others to do."

After they chatted over their mugs of coffee, Cheryl glanced at her watch. "I need to head to the shop in a minute to open it for the locals. Before I leave, do you have the jar you took to the frolic?"

"I do." Naomi stood and retrieved the jar from the sideboard. "Do you need it?"

"I just wanted to look at it." Cheryl turned it over in her hands but saw nothing that marked it as different or unique from the one she'd brought home from the store. "If only these jars could speak..."

Naomi cocked her head and looked at Cheryl with an odd expression. "Why would you want that?"

"I would love to know what the jar witnessed all those years ago before it was plastered inside a wall." She set the jar down and scooted it across the table toward Naomi. "It still doesn't make any sense why someone would do this. There's a layer to the story that we don't know yet, and when we figure it out, I bet we'll know who the money belonged to originally."

"Do you want to take Esther to the store with you this morning?"

"She can stay with you." Cheryl ran her hands over the jar. "If I can sneak away to check the deeds for the cottages this afternoon, that will be enough. And I should be able to do that when she comes in."

"All right. Let me know how else I can help."

"I will." Cheryl hugged her friend and headed toward her car, pausing just outside the door. As she looked up, she noticed Levi working in a field. He had so much work to do on the farm yet had been willing to take the burden of the volunteer schedule for the cottages for her. "How does Levi have time to help me with the cottages while doing all he is needed for here?"

Naomi smiled as she watched her stepson. "He loves to help those he cares about. It does not seem like a burden to him then."

Cheryl sensed a double meaning in Naomi's words. Did Levi care about her? Really care? Then again, maybe she was making too much of simple words.

As Levi looked up from his work and a lazy smile graced his face, she couldn't resist grinning back. And praying that she was wrong after all.

Simple words could be the most profound.

Chapter Eighteen

Cheryl knew if she spent time with Levi Miller it would be easy to lose track of the time until the Swiss Miss opened, but as she saw Levi wipe his brow and then walk her direction, she couldn't make herself get in the car and drive away.

Levi ambled toward her, his grin widening as he approached. "What brings you to our farm so early?"

"I needed to speak with your mom." She resisted the temptation to reach over and brush stray hay from his shirt. "Is everything going well with the schedule?"

"For the cottages?" He shifted until his feet looked planted in the dirt and his fists stuck to his hips. "Ja, I have a handle on it. You act as if it were a complication."

"I guess it felt that way to me."

"A very good reason you handed it to me. I do not mind and can handle the work."

Cheryl felt heat rise up her neck. "I appreciate it." She turned toward her car. "Well, I should head to the Swiss Miss."

His gaze remained locked on hers. As it did, her thoughts began to spiral. Was it possible their friendship would move beyond friends to something more...to life mates? She jerked slightly at the thought. Was it even possible, or had she read too many romance novels? Ones where nothing stood between two people who were in love? Her religion made a large barrier to their friendship ever developing into something more. Could she become Amish? Would that be allowed if she even wanted to make that huge leap? She could just imagine her parents' reaction if the word got back to their large church that the pastor's daughter had left the faith for another denomination.

"Are you all right?" Levi leaned across the fence, and his hand twitched as if he'd wanted to check her forehead for a fever but restrained himself.

Cheryl jerked her attention to him and away from her wayward thoughts. "Yeah, I'm fine." She took a step toward her car. It was time to get out of this conversation before she verbalized her thoughts and questions. That was a surefire way to make Levi run the other direction. "Well, I'll see you later."

He nodded, and she strode toward her car. As she pulled on the door, Naomi ran toward her with a covered basket in hand.

"May I ask a favor, Cheryl?"

Cheryl paused mid squat as she'd started to slide into the car. "Sure."

"Do you have time to drive me to a friend's home? I would like to share some of these muffins with Fannie Borntrager. She cannot do much right now since her arthritis flared up with the spring rains, and I would like to cheer her."

Cheryl glanced at her watch. She still had about an hour before the locals—Rueben and Ben in particular—would expect her to open her shop. "I can do that."

Her mother's voice telling her to build white space filled her mind, but Cheryl brushed the thought away. This was not a burden, but an opportunity to serve Naomi and her friend. Surely this was exactly the kind of thing that Jesus had meant when He talked about serving the least of these.

Naomi directed her through a couple of turns, and before reaching Sugarcreek they pulled into a short drive off the highway. The small home looked like it had been a *dawdy haus* at some point. The yard was neat, even if the beds did have their share of weeds. The paint looked fresh and the home well maintained. Naomi hurried from the car.

"I will let Fannie know that I am here with a friend. I am not sure she receives many visitors, so this will be a treat for her."

Cheryl nodded and followed slowly from her car. By the time she reached the front door, Naomi was inside the cottage. She waved for Cheryl to join her.

The sitting room was dim, with the curtains still drawn to the world. Naomi set the basket on a coffee table as she introduced Cheryl. "Fannie, this is my friend Cheryl. You may have heard me speak of her. She is here running the Swiss Miss for her aunt Mitzi who is serving God in the Pacific."

Fannie turned her face toward Cheryl, watery blue eyes examining her carefully. "Your aunt is a nice woman. Loves the Lord."

Cheryl nodded as she stepped forward. "It's a pleasure to meet you, Mrs. Borntrager."

Fannie patted the quilt that covered her lap. "My old knees and fingers are not as nimble and spry as they used to be. Otherwise

I would stand to greet you. Please have a seat. Any friend of Naomi's is a friend to me."

"I shall prepare tea." Naomi hurried to the small kitchen—it was simple with a small table, two chairs, a gap-powered refrigerator, sink, and stove. "Fannie, Cheryl is in the middle of a mystery, and I thought you might be able to help."

"Oh?" Fannie slowly shifted her body toward Cheryl, a gray curl falling in her face at the effort. "Like in the books? I have read all of the Miss Marple mysteries at least four times." She glanced down at her hands. "There is little I can do right now, and reading helps."

Cheryl smiled as she wondered what Naomi was doing. Her friend hadn't mentioned any kind of help Fannie could provide in the short car ride. Of course, that could have something to do with the need to give directions to Cheryl as she drove.

Naomi found three delicate china cups and set them on the table. "Cheryl found some V-mail in jars, and she wants to know who wrote them."

"That was a long time ago." Fannie rubbed an arthritic hand across her forehead. "Let me see them. Maybe I will know something as my dear friend hopes."

Cheryl dug the envelope with the letters from her purse and handed them to Fannie. "I think the author was Amish, maybe from here since the letters were found in Sugarcreek."

"With the mason jars?"

Cheryl's eyebrows rose, and Fannie smiled. "I may be homebound, but that does not mean I do not hear what happens in town. Naomi is not the only one who graces me with visits." She took the envelope but fumbled trying to open it. With a sigh, she handed it to Cheryl. "Would you mind?"

Cheryl eased the letters out and laid them in front of Fannie on the table. Fannie opened and read first one and then another. She made clucking sounds as she read but said nothing until she had finished the last.

"I see why you think an Amish boy wrote these." She ran a finger over the writing. "You are right." She slid the papers over to Cheryl. "This boy did what he knew he must... against his parents' wishes. It broke their heart and his."

Cheryl's breath hiccupped. "Do you know him?"

"Yes, if I am right, and I am certain I am. He grew up Amish but left the faith after the war."

Cheryl sucked in a breath. "Do you think the war caused him to give up on God?"

"Oh no. He still followed Gott, just not in our way." She tapped the top letter. "The war conflicted him. It did that for many of our young boys. But we know fighting is not what Gott would have us do. He doubted after all he saw as a medic."

"How do you know this man?"

A soft smile lit up Fannie's wan face. She shifted slightly and then settled back against the chair. "His sister was one of my dearest friends growing up. She and I did everything together as soon as our chores were complete and we were no longer needed at home." She gazed past Cheryl and out the window as if seeing them as young women. "The war was hard on all of us. I was only a young girl. Thirteen when the war ended. But we read the newspapers and talked about the events at our school." She swallowed and pulled her gaze back to Cheryl. "An Englisch friend told me how at the high school they would read the names of any of their boys who had died in the battles. Can you imagine? Starting the school day that way?"

Cheryl could see the scene in her mind's eye. What a heartbreaking way to learn a friend or acquaintance had given the ultimate sacrifice. "Can you tell me his name?"

"Frank Raber, but his friends liked to call him Pinky because of his red hair. His sister was Wanda, but she died ten years ago. Not long after Frank did." A cat wandered into the room, stopped to sniff Cheryl, then arched his back and hopped into Fannie's lap.

Cheryl ran what Fannie had said through her mind. Could this be the same Pinky her aunt had mentioned? The thought caused her heart to race. She could feel the pieces of the story begin to fall into place.

Fannie stroked her cat with a soft smile. "The family has seen much tragedy, the kind that makes you wonder how one family can bear so much." She rubbed the kitty's ears, her eyes taking on a distant look. "That boy had to go when his number was called, but instead of joining the conscientious objectors, he became a medic. He sent every paycheck home. I am not sure he kept one during all the years of his service."

"How long did he serve?"

"At least two years, maybe three. His parents refused to use the money. He sent every penny home to help them recover from the Depression. But they were too stubborn. They insisted it represented blood money, something they could never condone."

Butterflies danced in Cheryl's stomach, and she clung to the woman's words. So many answers balled up in this sweet woman. Still, she had a hard time believing a good Amish family would treat their son that way. Cheryl tried to imagine Seth and Naomi treating Levi like that. She couldn't imagine it. Especially when it wasn't his choice. "He was drafted. That means he couldn't say no."

"Not the way they looked at it. His choice was to become a conscientious objector. The government had made allowances for men like him who had a faith that required pacifism. But he would not do that. He was too proud of his country, he said. Wanda wept when he left. His parents...they kept their chins up, but I know it broke their hearts."

"He sent the checks home, but what did they do with them? They didn't keep them as checks. Why turn them into coins?"

Naomi freshened everyone's cups and then joined them at the table. "You may not realize this, Cheryl, but the Amish were as hard hit as the rest of the country during the Depression. Paper money was not seen as safe. Its value could change too much. Instead, coins made of metals that held their value were a better choice. My grandparents talked about it once or twice. After the

Depression, many Amish were reluctant to return to the banks around Sugarcreek."

Fannie nodded. "It took some longer than it took others. Frank's family lost a lot in a bank run. So when it was time to do something with this money they refused to spend, they must have cashed the checks and stored the proceeds in the jars. Wanda never mentioned the jars to me, so I don't think she knew."

"How interesting." Cheryl took a drink of her cooling tea. "Was Frank's family into farming?"

"His father was until he died. By the war, Frank's mom had remarried. His stepfather was a cabinet maker and worked hard to provide for his family, but it was not simple. They needed the money Frank sent, but they were stubborn."

"What he intended as a blessing, they couldn't accept."

"Yes." Fannie pushed her cup back. "After the war, he never quite felt a part of the community again. The war had changed him. And he wanted to do something more than farm or make cabinets. His father had been a doctor of sorts, helping those around the community, so Frank decided to take what he learned as a medic and go to medical school. That was the final break with his family."

The story cast a shadow over the table. Cheryl swallowed around the sudden lump in her throat. "How sad that he couldn't have both."

"Life is full of choices." Naomi swirled what was left in her cup. "Unfortunately for Frank, his choices caused a breach with his family and community."

Had Cheryl's choices led to the same? If she wasn't careful, could she too end up with broken relationships? She gave her head a little shake to clear the thoughts. "But why hide the coins in the wall and not tell anyone where they were?"

Naomi sighed. "And that, my dear, is a question I think we would all like to answer." She offered a sad smile. "I have a feeling the crook knew. He stays one step ahead of us in this whole thing."

Chapter Nineteen

Steps sounded on the front porch, interrupting the conversation. Fannie straightened and then glanced at the clock. "That must be Irving. He finishes his morning chores about this time. I am surprised he did not come earlier when you first arrived."

Cheryl glanced at her watch. Time was running out. She needed to open the Swiss Miss in less than thirty minutes and needed to get a new display up before she looked for the deeds of the cottage. Fortunately, all she needed to do was unlock the door and turn on the lights. If Esther had a car and a phone, she'd call her employee and ask her to go in early. Instead, Cheryl needed to learn all she could and then head to the store.

The back door opened, and a burly man stepped into the kitchen. He took off his hat and put it on a hook beside the door then nodded at the women. "Morning."

"There is kaffee on the back of the stove, Irving."

He grabbed a cup and filled it with the dark brew. "Anything to eat?"

"Sure. I sliced some bread, and it is on a plate beside the refrigerator." Fannie made a motion like she would push to her feet, but he waved her back.

"I will get it. It is enough that you prepared it." After he collected the plate and mug, he nodded to the women again. "I will leave you to your visiting."

Naomi held up a hand. "You may help us. Fannie was telling us some of Frank Raber's story."

His forehead wrinkled as he studied them. "Why would you discuss him?"

"We found some letters that Fannie thinks he may have written home during World War II."

Irving set down the plate and nodded for her to continue.

"There are holes in his story. You were a few years behind him. Maybe you can help us understand him."

"As long as it is not gossip."

Cheryl spread her hands wide on the table, seeking answers before he changed his mind about talking. "We found something that may be his, but we can't be sure. Knowing more of his story may help us return something to his family."

"If it will put your mind at ease."

"Thank you." Naomi sat forward and propped her elbows on the table. "On Saturday, workers discovered mason jars filled with coins inside the walls at the cottages. We are trying to learn who the money belonged to so it can be returned or donated to the work at the cottages."

"What makes you think the letters are Frank's?"

Fannie explained while Cheryl showed him the letters. It took him a long time to read the letters, and Cheryl could feel the ticking of the clock. She was running out of time but didn't want to leave if Irving could help her understand Frank.

"I agree with my wife that these could be Frank's. He was almost ten years older than me. A man we young boys aspired to follow until he left and never really returned." He stroked his long white beard that fell to his second button. "He sent home every check. His mother and stepfather could have stored the coins in those jars. They built their small cottage about then. It was a new area. Built at the end of the war. It was filled with kids the minute they moved in, but Mr. Johansen's work did not provide enough to maintain the family and the farm, so they let the farm go. In those days there was no extra."

Fannie nodded. "Such a hard time."

"Why not use the money to save the farm?" It didn't make sense to Cheryl that an Amish family would let family land go when that was such a big part of their identity. "Frank was likely sending it to them with that expectation."

"Expectation? Maybe. He was a good kid. But his stepfather was a stubborn man, bordered on hard. He insisted on doing things on his own. I wonder if Frank even knew they didn't spend the money. I doubt it."

Cheryl leaned forward. "Why?"

"Because they were killed in a horse and buggy accident a few months before Frank came home. He came home to a passel of siblings in their rumspringas and a desire to go to medical school. He stayed in the Amish community just until his last sister married."

"What happened then?"

Irving shrugged as he blew on his coffee. "The man left for medical school and never really returned. Sure, he lived just outside

Sugarcreek, but he abandoned his Amish faith. That meant his siblings had to choose."

"They stayed." Fannie settled against her chair back. "Broke Wanda's heart."

"Is any of his family still in town?" If they were, wrapping up this mystery would be easy.

Irving and Fannie exchanged glances, looks that communicated even more than words. Cheryl wanted that with someone, to have that deep knowing of another that removed the necessity for words.

"Leonard Raber is still around. He is Frank's nephew and actually owned the cottages until he got behind on his taxes. He bought them over time and thought they would pay his way for life. I hated to see him lose them at the tax sale." Irving took a bite of the bread. "This is good, Wife."

"Thank you."

"There have been two or three owners since Leonard lost the cottages. Then your friend purchased them. I hope his project goes well. It's a worthy use for the homes."

"I agree." Cheryl resisted the urge to tell him all about the women and children she had met who would benefit from the shelter the cottages would offer. "Did Frank have any children?" If he had, the coins might belong to them since their father had earned the salary turned into coins.

"His older daughter lives in Columbus last I heard."

Fannie nodded. "That is right. She has been there a number of years. I have not heard anything about his younger girl."

"Neither have I," Naomi added. "It is like she disappeared or moved to another country."

"There has only been silence about her for many years." Irving took the last bite of his bread and then brushed off the crumbs. "I must return to work."

"Thank you for your time. I think I have enough to run some Internet searches and find both women." She stood and shook Irving's hand. She planned to shake Fannie's until the woman pulled her close for a hug.

"Good luck with your search. And be sure to tell me the end. I would like to know if it ends as well as the Miss Marple stories."

"I will." Cheryl followed Naomi outside and soon reversed course to the Miller farm. If she kept moving, she would only be a few minutes late opening the Swiss Miss. "Thanks for taking me to meet Fannie."

"My pleasure. I had a sense she could help us. I did not know how much though."

"She and Irving were wonderful helps. I should be able to find Frank's daughters and do more research on Frank himself."

"His nephew, Leonard, is still a member of our community. I am afraid he is not the best with money. His wife works full-time at Yoder's, but she seems to be the one with the steady employment. Leonard, he always has big ideas but not such big effort."

Cheryl smiled at the thought. Sounded like a man with great ideas, but little will or way to follow through on those dreams. "Does he attend your church services?"

"He says he is Amish, but rarely attends. I think with him it is more cultural than heart level." Naomi stared out the window at the passing scenery. "Being Amish is safe. It is what he knows. But I do not think he has let it go past his mind."

Cheryl sighed. "It's easy to do that with religion."

"Yes, but it is supposed to be faith." She wrinkled her nose and looked at Cheryl. "He is a reminder that none of us is perfect."

After she dropped Naomi with more thanks, Cheryl drove back to Sugarcreek, her thoughts troubled.

Could Leonard be the rightful heir to the coins, or would it be Frank's daughters? If it was Leonard, would he use the money well, or would it merely fuel his dreams for a season?

She prayed John-John would get the riches when they were recovered. He needed them and would use them for the good of others. She wasn't so certain that Leonard would, though maybe others weren't seeing him in a proper light. Maybe the man could use the money well too.

Still, she couldn't shake the certainty that John-John would use the money more wisely in a way that would bless many.

If she located Frank's daughters, would she remove the find from John-John's reach?

The thought depressed her as she pulled into her usual parking spot near the Swiss Miss. Ben and Rueben leaned against the plate-glass windows, staring at her.

Rueben pushed away. "What took you so long?"

"Running late this morning, Miss Cheryl?" Ben's words were polite, but his gaze was inquisitive.

At the moment she wished she hadn't learned all that she had because now she'd have to act on that information. And that action could harm a friend.

By revealing the possibility of a true heir to Chief Twitchell, John-John would lose the coins even if they were found. More than that, all those families he'd hoped to serve wouldn't have a warm, safe place to go.

CHAPTER TWENTY

The morning settled into a routine that was the usual rhythm of the Swiss Miss. Ben and Rueben set up their usual checker game, a few soft words floating from that direction. Cheryl smiled at the slight softening in their relationship. Several other locals ran in for a jar of jelly, a bag of sweets, or a wall quilt that would make the perfect gift. Through it all, Cheryl smiled and interacted with her customers and friends, yet her thoughts never strayed far from what she had learned from Fannie and Irving.

If Frank Raber was indeed the author of the letters and the one who sent his paychecks home, then his story was one of brokenness and pain. The war had changed him and altered his family.

The thought pained her.

She'd do some online research later to see what layers she could add to the snapshot she'd received. There had to be more that could help her identify who might have a claim to the coins.

The bell over the door jangled, and Naomi entered the store with Esther and a picnic basket. "I have brought you lunch."

"Isn't it too early for that?" Cheryl glanced at her watch. "Oh, I didn't realize it was already eleven thirty. I guess the tour bus must be running late."

Esther slipped on her apron. "I heard it had a flat but should arrive in about an hour."

"Maybe after the tourists leave, we can go meet Leonard." And she still had to get to the county recorder to check the deeds. Maybe there were online records she could start with.

"Ja. I can stay in town until three." Naomi handed the picnic basket to Cheryl. "You eat while Esther and I care for the shop."

Cheryl slipped into the office, the basket in hand. Knowing Naomi, it would be filled with delectable treats. The kind of goodies that had Cheryl's mouth watering. After she set the basket on the small desk, she opened it and pulled out a chicken salad sandwich, thinly sliced apple, carrot sticks, and two homemade chocolate chip cookies that still felt warm. She quickly prayed over the food and then dug in. While she ate, her gaze glanced around the smallish space. Why hadn't they found any clues about who had broken in? Nobody could be that careful—except in the movies or books. In real life, people made mistakes.

After she took her last bite of the sandwich—the homemade sourdough bread was amazing—she sank to the floor. There had to be something here. Something that would give her a clue to unravel.

All she found in her search were dust bunnies. She sneezed then wiped her hands on her khakis and stood. She grabbed a slice of apple and then examined the safe. She'd used it reluctantly each night since the theft, but she didn't feel nearly as secure that what she'd placed would still rest in it the following morning. Just like she wasn't convinced the alarm system would work each night.

Nothing about the safe seemed out of place or unusual. Instead, it looked like a small safe a business would use to protect small amounts of cash and important papers.

Cheryl opened the safe and then grabbed the stack of papers inside. She went through them, one by one, searching for something, anything. A clue.

She was almost to the bottom when she stopped. A sheet of paper, faded with age and fragile as the V-mail letters she had in her purse, rested in the stack. She carefully opened it. The handwriting matched that of the other V-mail, and the message was similar. The writer missed home. He still battled sickness, and in this letter he spoke of heartache too.

Sometimes at night I fall asleep to the sounds of children crying. They don't understand this war. They're fearful of us. They don't understand we're here to protect them.

What caught her attention though was the scrawling signature at the end. If she squinted until her eyes practically crossed, she could interpret the scribble as a rough *F* followed by a line. Above it was a scribble that might just be *Your faithful son.*

She sat back in the office chair. Had his parents believed he was faithful? Or had their doubts reached him across the Pacific Ocean?

Maybe when she and Naomi talked to Leonard Raber later that afternoon, she'd hear the answers to that and other questions. She certainly hoped so. It wouldn't necessarily tell her who had broken into her store and stolen the coins, but it might give her more background than she had now. Every piece of information would help, especially if it led her to people who might be Frank's heirs. That would bring resolution for John-John and simplify the decision about what to do with the coins if—no, *when*—she recovered them.

Before she slipped back into the store, she ran an Internet search for the cottage deed. With a few clicks, she was in an online database entering her credit card information. Five minutes later, an e-mail report on the deed history of the property landed in her inbox.

Naomi entered the office. "Everything all right?"

Cheryl hit Print on the report. "Look at this. I found a deed report." She scanned the still warm pages. Much of it was legal gibberish to her, but as she reached the third page, she found what she hoped. Leonard Raber's name and below his, his father's. "Here's the proof that the cabins were owned by the Rabers during the war. Those coins could very well be from Frank's military pay."

"That is good news."

Yes, it was. Not unexpected, but now Cheryl knew the cottage was the Rabers'. A spike of hope hit her heart. This meant the money might just be able to go to John-John and his ministry.

She spent the next hour helping customers find unique items for gifts and personal enjoyment. She loved this part of her job. When the store calmed down around two, Cheryl and Naomi got into Cheryl's car. "I found Leonard's address in the church directory."

Naomi clicked her seatbelt in place. "It is not far. Just a few miles out of town."

When the GPS got confused, Naomi directed Cheryl. Before long, they pulled in front of a small home in the middle of a field. A shed behind it provided shelter for a few chickens, but Cheryl saw no other animals. The home was painted a dingy white, and a few purple petunias valiantly grew on either side of paver stones that formed a walkway to the front door.

The door opened and a man with no hair except for a beard that reached to his belt stepped outside. His pants were patched on the knee, but his shirt was clean and reasonably white. There was no hint of welcome to his face or stance.

Cheryl swallowed and looked at Naomi. "Are we safe?"

"Ja, he is gruff, but life has not gone as he expected."

Cheryl opened the car door and slowly stepped outside. She used the door as a bit of a shield, unsure he wouldn't hurl something at her despite Naomi's assurances he was harmless. "Mr. Raber?"

"What do you want?"

"I'm Cheryl Cooper, and I'd like a few minutes of your time."

"Who's with you?"

"It is me, Leonard. Naomi Miller. I hope you are well."

He shoved his hands through his suspenders and rocked on his heels. "I will be better when I know why you drove here."

Cheryl puffed out a breath. "We had a few questions about your uncle Frank."

His shoulders rounded, and his eyebrows drew together. "Why? He has been gone fifteen years."

"Do you mind if we come in?" Naomi's voice was calm, clear, determined. "It will be more pleasant to talk inside."

He shrugged then turned inside. "Clara, we have company." A faint voice murmured a reply. "Come in. Mind we were not expecting you."

"Of course." Naomi swept ahead of Cheryl up the path. "We will not take much time, I assure you."

It took Cheryl's eyes a moment to adjust to the dim interior. The windows were covered with quilts that did little to let in light. Two cats perched on the back of a couch that had seen better days. Stacks of old newspapers littered one wall of the room. A young man sat on an oversized chair, hunched over a lit-up tablet. He didn't tear his gaze from the device as Cheryl and Naomi entered.

An older woman with kind but droopy eyes walked into the room, wiping her hands on a stained apron. "Come in, come in. This is such a surprise. I put the kaffee on, so I can offer that in a few minutes."

Cheryl hesitated to burden her. If only they could have called ahead. "Please don't trouble yourself."

"No problem." She quirked her head as she studied them. "What brings you here?"

"Let us go into the kitchen." Leonard led the way, Clara wringing her hands behind him.

"It is not ready for guests, Husband."

"It is fine. They did not come to inspect your housekeeping skills." He glanced over his shoulder and winked. "Good thing too. The kitchen is lived in."

Cheryl smiled at his sudden good humor even as she glanced around and decided the whole home—at least what she had seen—was very lived in.

Clara busily pulled dirty lunch dishes off the table and stacked them in the sink that was already filled with dishes. "I was occupied with other matters this afternoon. I hope you will overlook the mess."

Naomi reached over and stilled Clara's frantic efforts. "We do not care how your home looks. Truly it is unimportant."

"Danki." She fanned her pink cheeks. "I have aspirations for keeping house one way." She looked around the small kitchen. "Clearly the goal is not easily met. Please have a seat."

Cheryl sank on to a chair and then cringed when her khakis stuck to the seat. "I wondered if you could tell me about Frank."

Leonard frowned, and any remnants of his earlier good humor evaporated in an instant. "Why do you ask about him?"

"I have some V-mail letters that may be his."

"V-mail? What is that?"

"Letters sent between soldiers and their loved ones during World War II. I believe we've successfully traced them to your uncle, but hope you can confirm it."

Leonard sighed. "Do you have the letters?"

"Yes." Cheryl tugged the envelope from her purse and handed it to him. "Do you recognize the handwriting?" That would be the easiest way to identify the author.

"Clara, what do you think?" Leonard held a letter toward his wife. "It looks like his scrawl, ja?"

"Ja."

Leonard handed the letter back to Cheryl. "Why does this matter? Are you simply curious?"

"Where we found the letters makes this interesting."

The coffee bubbled in its pot, and Clara pulled it off the stove. She poured some into mugs for each of them. "Why?"

"We found the letters over the weekend at the cottages in town that are under renovation." Cheryl paused as bright color crawled up Leonard's neck. "It may mean the coins were his."

"If you found them in the cottages, they are mine. Those cottages were robbed from me. There is no need to allow someone to take the coins as well."

The conversation stilled as a young man in Amish dress but without the beard walked through the room, his head close to a tablet that sounded as though he was playing some sort of YouTube video. He didn't bother to look up or say anything as he headed to the fridge. Cheryl marveled at the way he seemed to know exactly where he was going and avoided colliding with anything.

"Stephen!" Leonard stood with a low roar. "You must stop this."

"It's okay, Daed." The sarcasm in the young man's words nearly scorched her ears. "I am on my rumspringa, remember?"

"You must still be respectful while you live in my house."

Clara stood and placed her body between her son and husband. "Please." She glanced between the two as she held her hands up. "May we have peace while we have guests?"

Stephen shrugged without really glancing at Naomi or Cheryl. "Don't worry, Maam. I'm leaving." He grabbed an apple from the counter and left in the same languid manner he had entered.

"The disrespect!" Leonard sputtered as he stared after his son. "What did I do to deserve such a son?"

Cheryl looked down at her hands and shifted on the sticky seat. That wasn't the kind of question she would answer even if she could.

Clara placed a hand on her husband's arm. "Let us sit and continue the conversation." She sighed and swiped at her eyes. "I apologize for our son. He is taking his rumspringa too seriously." She collapsed on to the edge of a wooden chair and then tugged her husband's sleeve. When he joined them with a huff, she turned back to Cheryl and Naomi with a small smile. "What coins do you mean?"

Naomi stepped into the conversation. "They were stolen from the Swiss Miss where they were taken for safekeeping. The cottages were too insecure, and the banks closed at the time. We hoped you might know who would want them."

Leonard stared at her, jaw slack as if he couldn't quite believe what Naomi had said. "Do you mean you think I was involved?"

"Of course not." Naomi patted her hands in a placating motion. "I thought since you'd owned the cottages for a time, you would know their history better than we do."

"I grew up in one of those cottages. They were a mess when we moved in and a mess when I moved out. I do not think my grandfather understood what a job it would be to keep them. He never liked to work."

Naomi caught Cheryl's eye, and Cheryl nodded. Maybe Leonard's reputation of inability to keep a job was inherited.

"Did they do any major renovations while you lived there?" Cheryl leaned forward as she waited for his answer.

"I do not remember. The cottages were not nice, but they were not terrible either. They were good enough." He shrugged. "But that does not explain the coins. Why do you think I know about them?"

"Because they were found at the cottages."

He nearly leapt from his seat. "Then they may belong to me. I demand the money be returned to me."

"They're gone. That's why we're here." Cheryl counted to ten quickly before continuing. "If you didn't see them while you lived there and controlled the cottages, maybe they weren't placed there until after you left."

Naomi nodded. "It is important to know if your grandparents improved the cottages."

"They might have thought they did, but they were essentially worthless at the tax sale. A lifetime of ownership gone in mere months. And nothing I could do to stop the travesty."

Clara patted his hand. "It is all right, Husband." She turned to the ladies with an apologetic smile. "Leonard still mourns the loss of his heritage."

"How did you come to own them?"

"Inherited them from my father when he died. He inherited them from my grandfather."

"Didn't he and your grandmother die during World War II?"

"Ja." The word was bullet-quick and hard. Almost as hard as his eyes as he watched her.

Cheryl fought the urge to lean back, placing more space between them. "So you owned the cottages for many years?"

"Not as many as my father, but enough. Then those sharks in the town hall kept upping the taxes, and I couldn't afford to pay. A man shouldn't lose his property over a few thousand dollars, but I did."

His mouth curled in a scowl as he turned to Cheryl. "You did not know what you were getting into when you came asking about Frank Raber, did you? There is more to those cottages than anyone knows."

Chapter Twenty-One

Clara patted Leonard's hand and whispered something in his ear, but it did nothing to lower the red that was crawling up his throat and into his face.

He bolted to his feet and pointed to the door. "I think it is time for you to go. I will tell the police I expect the coins to be returned immediately." Without another word, he turned and stormed out the back door.

"I am so sorry." Clara placed her hands in her lap as her shoulders hunched. "He feels everything intensely." She stood to her feet with stiff and weary motions. "I must return to my work if you do not mind."

Cheryl stood and grabbed her purse. "Thank you for your time."

Naomi stood and then approached the other woman. She murmured a few quiet words, and Clara wiped a tear before she turned away.

Cheryl and Naomi were quiet as they exited the home and then got into Cheryl's car.

It was only as the car turned on to the highway leading back to Sugarcreek that Cheryl exhaled. "That was *interesting*." Maybe the word wasn't strong enough. "He certainly has strong thoughts on the coins, but he didn't tell us whether the construction happened while his grandparents were alive."

"He may not have paid attention or remembered." Naomi stared out the window at the passing fields. "It is like the corn over there. We only notice it when something is wrong. If his grandfather was always tinkering with something, then he may not have noticed yet another home improvement project." She turned back to Cheryl. "The thing that bothers me is they died before Frank returned home. The coins could have been placed before the parents' death, but we may never know for certain."

Cheryl slowed as she reached the outskirts of town. "I would think seeing jars of coins would make an impression on a kid no matter how old they were. If his father knew about them, surely he would have said something. The fact Leonard was evasive with our questions doesn't mean he didn't know something." She rubbed a temple. "This puzzle isn't getting easier to solve. I want to find those coins so John-John and his ministry can benefit. But what if they go to Leonard? Or I never find them?"

"Gott will give us wisdom. He has helped you many times before. He will again," Naomi said. Cheryl felt Naomi studying her as she turned the car into her parking spot. "You should come to the farm tonight. Join us for supper. Stay the night. I know you did not sleep well last night."

"That's true. I heard every little sound." Cheryl turned off the car and gathered her things. "I don't want to impose though. You have a large family and have already helped me so much today. I know Leonard wouldn't have spoken to me if I had shown up alone."

"He may have surprised you, but I am glad to be a friendly face and helpful hand. Come. There is always enough food. The Lord always provides more than we need."

"Thank you." Cheryl soaked in the warmth of Naomi's friendship and caring. "I'll come after the shop closes and I get Beau settled at the house."

"We will eat at six o'clock and enjoy fellowship after." She smiled conspiratorially over the car's hood. "Maybe we will solve this puzzle while we are at it."

"I hope so." It would feel so good to make any progress. "Who would be a good person in town who understands the history of its unique antiques?"

"Like the mason jars?"

"Yes. I know they looked familiar to some of your friends, but there must be a way to learn more. A local expert could fill in the details."

"I will think about it. The jars are distinctive because of the labels."

"Yes. I'll call the local historical museum. Maybe someone on staff knows. But if not, I need another thread to pull." They entered the Swiss Miss to the bell announcing their arrival.

Esther sat at the counter with a smile. "Was your trip successful?"

"It depends." Cheryl forced down disappointment on the little they had to show for their time. "Leonard let us know he expects the coins when we find them. It felt like he believed I had them stolen so he couldn't claim them."

Esther leaned forward on the old counter, eyes alight with interest. "Did he know of the coins *and* the theft?"

"It did not seem he was familiar with them." Naomi tugged on one of her daughter's kapp strings. "Now that Cheryl is here, collect your things. We must go home and prepare for our company."

"Who is coming?"

"I am." Cheryl stepped behind the counter and stashed her purse in a cubby. "The shop looks great. Go ahead with your mother, and I'll see you in a couple hours."

After her friends left, Cheryl took a quick tour of the shop. It really did look great. Esther must have worked hard to get it organized after all the tourists had been through. Cheryl knew all too well how they could disrupt the order in the store as they hunted for the perfect purchase. She didn't mind because they usually left with bags full of purchases. Yet it did get tiresome to constantly repeat the process of getting the store back to rights. The balance of the afternoon was quiet with only a customer or two wandering in each hour. As soon as she could, she closed the shop and headed home.

The idea of spending the evening as a part of the Miller family filled an empty place. Tonight would rejuvenate her soul as she bantered with the kids and enjoyed the warmth that filled the Millers' home.

When she headed to the door to leave, Beau followed on her heels. He tried to sneak out as she opened the door that led to the garage. "No, Beau. You have to stay here." She edged him back inside. "The farm is no place for a city cat like you."

He hissed at her as she eased the door shut. She peeked in the door's window. He stood underneath it staring up at her. She shook her head and laughed. "You scamp."

Cheryl hitched her overnight bag over her shoulder and walked to the car. In a few minutes she'd driven out of town and breathed deeply of the spring air that rolled in through her open windows. The sun had begun its slow descent to the horizon as it played across the tops of the trees in the old windbreaks that separated the fields. A tractor worked its way across a field, and in another a horse chewed on hay while a foal balancing on spindly legs frolicked nearby. Peace flowed into her as she turned on to the road that led to the covered bridge and then the Millers' farm.

The moment her car parked in front of the farmhouse, the porch filled with Millers to greet her. Caleb, Eli, Elizabeth, and Esther welcomed her heartily and then ushered her inside, where the dinner table sagged beneath the bowls of green beans and mashed potatoes, a platter of roast and carrots, and a basket heaped with fresh bread. The conversation bounced from person to person with lots of laughter, teasing, and good-natured ribbing. Cheryl had to stifle disappointment that Levi wasn't at the table. At the same time, she realized she needed to be careful because she hadn't realized how much she had expected him to be there. Her gaze strayed occasionally to where he normally sat, but then she shook herself and engaged with the Millers who were at the table.

It was only after the simple dessert of homemade cookies and coffee that the table cleared of all but Naomi, Seth, and Cheryl. Their conversation meandered around the town and into stories Naomi and Seth knew about the businesses in town. Before long their focus turned to those businesses that had existed since World War II.

"Sugarcreek is really unchanged." Cheryl tried to imagine Columbus looking the same today as it had sixty-five years earlier.

"It is true." Naomi slid the plate of cookies toward Cheryl. "You should have another. That is one thing I like about this community. It is stable and consistent. I shop at many of the same stores my mother did. Possibly her mother before her."

"Take the bank. It has been a constant factor since the Depression. I have heard that past bank presidents helped to ensure the community as a whole survived that hard time." Seth leaned back in the chair and hitched his thumbs through his suspenders. "Do I remember that the bank was robbed during the war?"

"Really?" Cheryl pushed the cookie platter back toward the middle of the table. The last thing she needed was another one of Naomi's delicious creations.

Naomi tilted her chin as she looked at the ceiling. "Maybe, Husband. It was well before I was alive. But I may have heard the story."

"If so, then that could be the source of the coins." Cheryl didn't know whether to whoop or sag. Would John-John have a better claim to the coins if they were Frank Raber's or if they were stolen from a bank at least sixty years ago? She had to think the bank would have a stronger claim.

"Maybe you can search on your Internet and pull up the story. If not, the librarian can find the story. Events like that do not happen often here. That is probably why it continues to be talked about."

Cheryl nodded. If there had been a bank robbery without recovery of the stolen goods, that could explain the coins. They chatted a bit longer, and then Cheryl helped Naomi clean up the remaining dessert dishes. "I'll head to town early and see what I can find out."

Naomi nodded. "Maybe Esther can open the store for you. That will give you more time, ain't so?"

"Yes. That would be great if she's willing and you don't need her."

"This is more important. There will be other times I need her here more than tomorrow."

The screen door slammed, and Esther hurried inside. "Maam, there is an interesting message on the machine."

"So?" Naomi shrugged. "What would you like me to do?"

"Come listen." Esther tugged her mother toward the door. "You come too, Cheryl. It may have something to do with the coins."

Who would have called the Millers with information rather than calling Cheryl or the police? It seemed off, but as Cheryl glanced at her phone, she realized she'd let the battery run down. That might explain the lack of call to her. It only took a minute to get across the farmyard and to the small phone shanty where it sat a bit off the road. *Shack* was a fitting word for the building. It was sturdy, made of wood, but small and rough. The Millers did not spend much time at the shanty, merely keeping the phone for the ease of their business ventures.

Twilight had fallen as the three women neared the shack. Esther entered, followed by Naomi, while Cheryl stood in the doorway.

"The message is short, but odd." Esther pressed the button on the old machine. A moment later a static-laced woman's voice chattered into the room.

"Mrs. Miller, this is Suzanne. I need more information on the coins from the cottages. I'm at a coin show today, and someone is selling lots of old coins. It's someone I've never seen before. Makes me wonder. Call me when you can." The woman rattled off a number then the machine clicked to a stop.

"Could you play it again? And could I borrow the notepad?" Naomi handed Cheryl the paper and pen while Esther replayed the message. "So Suzanne called because she's seen some old coins at a show." Cheryl rubbed her forehead. If only they had good photos of the coins and John-John's card hadn't failed. "I'm not sure how to describe this out-of-focus coin. It's too blurry for anyone to identify."

"It is all right, Cheryl."

"I should call her back, but my phone died."

"Use our phone." The ladies shuffled around until Esther and Naomi had made room for Cheryl next to the phone.

She dialed the number that Suzanne had left in her message and then waited for the woman to answer.

"This is Suzanne."

"Hi, Suzanne. This is Cheryl Cooper. We got your message about the coins."

"Yes? Can you speak louder?"

Cheryl repeated her words. "What can you tell me about the coins you're seeing?"

"They're old. But that's not unique at this coin show. The Berlin shows usually attract some quality dealers. What's odd is the person who's selling the coins."

"Oh."

"Yes..." Static interrupted the call. "...young and disinterested. He doesn't seem to know much about coins either." More static filtered on the call. "...sitting there like he doesn't have any interest in the coins."

"That's unusual?"

"Depends on the seller. Some will get right in your space, they are so eager to make a sale. But it's like he's not really trying to sell them. He's just sitting there."

"What kind of coins does he have?"

"A couple steel pennies. A handful of silver nickels from the early forties. And some silver quarters also from the thirties and forties. None are that valuable alone. Put them together, and there could be significant value."

"Oh?"

"In the thousands of dollars."

Cheryl could imagine how John-John would use that at the cottages. "Any chance you can get a picture of him? Maybe talk to him?"

She waited for an answer then looked at the phone. Nothing but dead air.

"I'd better call Chief Twitchell." Cheryl dialed his number and sighed as he picked up.

"Twitchell here."

"Chief, this is Cheryl. The Millers got a call from Suzanne Marshall about some coins she was seeing at the Berlin coin show. She thinks they might be from the stolen coins, but we got cut off." She filled him in on what little else she'd learned from Suzanne.

"*Hmm.* I'll track her down. Sounds like there are few enough details that she's not really helpin'. I'll check while I'm followin' up on her call."

After Cheryl thanked the chief and hung up, she turned to Naomi and Esther. "Well, he doesn't think much of what she said, but he's going to follow up." She rubbed her eyes. "Esther, would you be willing to come into the Swiss Miss for me first thing? I could give you a ride to town."

"If Maam does not need me."

Naomi shook her head as she smiled at her daughter. "I will be fine. Cheryl needs your help more tomorrow."

"Thank you. I'll plan to spend the morning at the library seeing what I can learn."

CHAPTER TWENTY-TWO

Cheryl woke up to the aroma of fresh bread baking and the smell of sizzling bacon.

"And coffee." She sighed, taking an extra sniff.

She turned over and snuggled the soft pillow under her cheek. She pulled up the quilt, telling herself she needed to rest for five more minutes. The quilt smelled of sunshine and the spring breeze, and she guessed it had hung on Naomi's clothesline just days before. She was sure she'd never slept better. For one night she'd forgotten about the missing coins, the interesting jars, decades old bank robberies, and even the cottages. Instead, she'd rested in a quiet peace.

But now the day started, and the sun streamed through the windows. Cheryl was ready to attack the day and its fresh investigation trails.

She stretched and then pushed off the quilt. If she got moving, she'd have time to swing by the house for her phone charger and Beau before taking Esther to the store. Beau would not be happy about spending the night alone, but spending time with the Millers had filled up part of her soul. It was just the type of rest she needed.

Her mother was right that she needed to work on a better balance in her life, but the way she felt this morning reinforced that walking away from time with the people she loved wasn't the answer.

Cheryl showered and dressed by the light of a high window in the bathroom. She entered the kitchen and saw Naomi sitting at the long dining room table.

Her enthusiasm buoyed when she looked around. Levi was already gone. She stifled a sigh as she sat for the hearty breakfast of oatmeal, bacon, fruit, and coffee cake. Three loaves of white bread sat cooling on the counter.

Cheryl forced a smile, but Naomi seemed to notice anyway. She sent Cheryl a sympathetic smile. "It is a busy time on the farm. Levi and Seth are busy from sunup to sundown. It does get lonely in the house at times. It will get better."

"I'm sure it will." She decorated her oatmeal with raisins and brown sugar before turning back to Naomi. "I certainly understand what it means to be busy."

"Doing the Lord's work will always exhaust us, ain't so? But I'd rather be busy doing Gottes work than idle and left to my own devices. Like my mother always quoted, 'Idle hands are the devil's workshop.'" Naomi reached across the table and patted Cheryl's hand. "You're doing a *goot* thing, Cheryl, caring for others and helping them out. Look what you have discovered about the letters and coins already. John-John is overwhelmed with so many things right now, but know your hard work is not being overlooked."

"Thank you, Naomi. That means so much."

Thirty minutes later, the breakfast dishes were washed and Naomi had loaded up a box of more preserves for Cheryl to take to the store. A worship CD played softly as Cheryl drove Esther into town. Instead of her usual round of banter, the young woman was quiet. Her dark brown eyes were troubled as she played with her kapp strings. Cheryl let the silence drag for a while before she felt like she had to fill it.

"Are you sure you don't mind working extra today?"

Esther startled and looked at Cheryl. "*Ne*. I enjoy helping in the shop."

"Then is something bothering you? You seem extra quiet today."

"I am thinking about much." She shrugged and twisted the kapp string. "It is hard to always know how to be a friend."

Cheryl nodded but stayed quiet. Whatever was on her young friend's mind was disturbing her deeply. She pulled into her driveway and parked the car. Still Esther was silent. "Would you like to come in while I get my phone charger and Beau?"

"I think I will wait if it is all right."

"Absolutely. I won't be a minute." Cheryl hurried from the car, sending a prayer up for Esther. Whatever was bothering her had her in a deep place. "Beau, I'm home."

Not a sound greeted her. She hurried to the kitchen counter and unplugged her phone charger. Then she walked through the house. Finally she found him on the guest room bed. "So you abandoned my bed last night? I see how it is." She rubbed under his chin as she picked him up. "It's time to get you and Esther to the Swiss Miss. Do me a favor, okay? Keep Esther company and make her smile if you can." He reached up and batted her chin as if to say he would. "Thanks, Beau. I think she needs a little extra attention today."

In a few minutes, Cheryl dropped Esther and Beau at the shop then continued down the street to the library. Sugarcreek had a nice library considering the town's size, but it didn't have half the books a branch would have in Columbus. Fortunately, interlibrary loan worked well in getting books the library didn't carry. At the same time Pam, the librarian, had an eye for the kind of books that Cheryl liked. It hadn't taken more than a couple visits before Pam was reserving books for Cheryl she just knew Cheryl would love.

The cheerful woman sat behind the circulation desk running books through the computer. She looked up and grinned at Cheryl. "I hoped I'd see you soon. What can I do for you?"

"Two things. First, I'm trying to find out information about the jars some coins were held in. Second, I need to pull up some old newspapers to see if I can find articles about a bank robbery that may have occurred in town during World War II. Seth and Naomi remember hearing about it when they were younger, but they didn't have much information."

"Are the jars the ones that held the coins from the cottages?"

Cheryl nodded, no longer surprised that seemingly everyone in town knew about what had been found in those walls.

"I might be able to help with that. I know I can get you set up with the microfiche of the newspapers. Do you know anything more about the exact time period?"

Cheryl shook her head. "I wish I did."

"Well, let's get you started. I have a few places I can check as well." Pam dropped her reading glasses on the chain around her neck then ran her fingers through her short gray hair. "We'll start in the local section. There are some great resources dating back to the turn of the century."

The petite librarian led the way through the stacks to a small corner that had two microfiche stations as well as a row of industrial gray filing cabinets. She patted the fourth. "This one will have the newspaper rolls you're looking for. I'll pull a few business directories from that area and scan those—when I'm not helping patrons, that is." She smiled and wrinkled her nose. "I still have to make sure books get checked out."

"I appreciate the help."

"No problem. It will be fun to help you dig. Librarians live for finding details." Pam set up Cheryl with a canister of microfiche fed through the machine, and then she paused beside her. "What do you know about the jars?"

Cheryl pulled out her phone and pulled up a photo. "This is what they look like. Kind of a milky green but flat. We have discovered a couple with tape remnants and a few others had fragments of notes with German writing on them. A few of the ladies in Naomi's frolic are convinced they are from this area."

"I'll check our antiques section for books on glassware. They may be in there, or I'll find something similar. Mason jars weren't always the clear ones we expect today. You'd be amazed what shows up in those books." Pam startled as someone knocked on the front desk. "Better get back to the checkout desk. Let me know if you need anything else."

An hour later Cheryl had learned a lot about her new hometown during World War II, but she hadn't uncovered anything about a robbery. At least it hadn't occurred prior to 1943. She stretched her arms as she leaned back in the chair. It wasn't the most comfortable chair she'd sat in. She stifled a yawn and then glanced at her phone. Almost eleven already? She'd need to work faster through the microfiche, or she'd never find the robbery—if one had even occurred.

Half an hour later Cheryl startled when her phone vibrated. Sliding it on, she raised it to her ear. "Yes?"

"Cheryl, the store is swamped. Can you come help?"

Cheryl glanced around to make sure no one had noticed she was on the phone then whispered, "I'll be right there."

She collected her notes and the couple of photocopied pages she'd made then went to the circulation desk. Pam was flipping through a thick blue book.

"Did you find what you need, Cheryl?"

"Well, I made it from 1940 through June 1943, but haven't found anything about a robbery."

Pam slipped her glasses from her nose. "Sounds like you're effectively eliminating months and years."

"True. How about you?"

"I'm pretty sure they are mason jars, but I'll keep digging. I'm like a dog with a bone. Hard to distract once I'm on the hunt."

Cheryl grinned as she wondered why she hadn't sought Pam's help before. "I appreciate it."

"I'll call the moment I find anything."

When Cheryl got outside, the sky was overcast with thick clouds weighing down the horizon. As she inhaled, she noted the unique scent that indicated rain could be on the way, so she picked up her pace and hurried the short distance back to the Swiss Miss. When she entered the store, several customers were stacked at the counter, each carrying a few items. Another handful were circulating through the store examining all kinds of merchandise, including the refrigerated cheese display. As Cheryl walked by, she noted the cheese offerings were getting slim. Time to place a fresh order.

Cheryl slipped behind the counter and pulled on one of the aprons Naomi had made for the store. She slid her phone into one of the heart-shaped pockets. "Need any help here, Esther?"

The young woman looked up with a slightly dazed expression. "I have the register covered. But I have not had the opportunity to help the latest customers."

"On it." Cheryl moved toward an older lady standing near the quilts. Her hands gripped a walker. Cheryl smiled as she realized how much she was enjoying being back in the store, in the routine that filled her time at the Swiss Miss. Esther made it very easy to shift around, though she'd need to make sure the young woman got some time off after Cheryl found the coins. Esther looked frazzled, and that wasn't normal for her.

"Is there any quilt you're particularly interested in?"

The woman didn't turn from the quilts as she stared at them. Her hair was gray and thin, and the top of her head came to Cheryl's chin. "They're all so beautiful I can't begin to pick a favorite." Her voice quivered with age.

"It is hard. Are you looking for yourself or for a gift?"

"It's for my granddaughter and her fiancé. They're getting married in a few weeks, and I want a gift that can have lasting meaning." Her gray curls bounced as she pivoted toward Cheryl. "It's a hard decision. And the quilts are pricey."

"It's because of all the hours lovingly poured into each stitch. None of these are mass-produced. They are crafted at quilting frolics and in the evenings after the day's work is done."

"They are certainly beautiful."

"Well, if you have any questions or need any help, let me know. That one"—Cheryl pointed to a quilt of green and purple triangles on a cream background—"is popular for newlyweds."

A half hour later while Cheryl was helping another customer, the older woman shuffled up and stood to the side. When Cheryl finished explaining why the Amish dolls did not have faces, she turned to the woman. "Did you pick one?"

"I think I have." She led Cheryl to the display with slow steps. "I like the one you pointed out, and purple has always been my granddaughter's favorite color."

In no time Esther had helped Cheryl gift wrap the quilt.

Cheryl took the oversized box from Esther and turned to the woman. "Can I carry this to your car for you? It's an awkward size."

The woman puffed out a breath, and her bangs ruffled above her forehead. "Thank you. I wasn't sure how I was going to manage."

"Are you from the area?"

The woman shuffled down the aisle in front of Cheryl. Cheryl hurried ahead and held the door open with one hand while holding the quilt in the other.

"Yes, lived here my whole life, but I don't shop much. It's too much work for me, especially with a bad knee. This wedding is the perfect excuse to get out to my favorite shops. Where's Mitzi?"

"She's off in Papua New Guinea. Following a dream."

The woman stopped on the sidewalk. "So she did it? She talked about the country for years."

"Yes, ma'am."

The woman smiled. "Mitzi and I were in one of the same Bible studies years ago. I always liked that young woman."

Cheryl enjoyed hearing her aunt called a young woman. She shifted the box as she followed the woman down the block. "Are you going to need help getting this out at home?"

The woman popped the trunk, and Cheryl eased the box inside. "I'll try to find a neighbor or someone to help me."

"Why don't I come with you? Esther can watch the shop without trouble as long as you live in town."

"Are you sure? That would be such a help and take a worry off my mind."

"Absolutely. Let me just run inside and alert her." When she got back, the woman was waiting in the driver's seat.

"My name is Lucy Twain."

"Cheryl. And happy to help." It didn't take long to reach the woman's home and another minute to carry the box inside. The home was decorated with wonderful vintage signs on almost every available space in the living room. "These are amazing!"

Cheryl focused on one of the signs. *Does your head ache? Are you in pain? Chandlers head ache and anti-pain buttons. Buy it! Try it!*

"Thank you. My father owned the soda fountain in town for a number of years. We had wonderful signs there, and I couldn't bear to part with them. It was attached to the old pharmacy. Della, the pharmacist's daughter, and I had good times going back and forth between the two shops."

The pharmacist's daughter? Cheryl's heartbeat quickened slightly, and she looked closer at the signs. They looked old, but the most exciting part was that this woman had known the pharmacist's daughter. Maybe she knew something about the old jars too.

"It sounds like you two young girls had fun. I bet she enjoyed visiting the soda fountain even more. When was this?"

"Oh my. Must have been the forties. Way before you were around." A soft smile tilted her fuchsia lips. "I haven't seen her in ages even though she still lives in town too."

"Do you think she'd have a few minutes to meet with me? I'm trying to figure out the history of some old jars I have. One of the ladies from Naomi's quilting circle said that she believed they were from the pharmacy in town."

"Let me call her and see. This is a great excuse to catch up." The woman tottered to her kitchen and grabbed the phone. Cheryl hadn't seen a cord that long in ages. In a few minutes she turned around with a happy lilt. "She's home and would love to meet you. I can take you right now."

"I need to get back to the shop. Would you mind asking if I could come over after the Swiss Miss closes?"

Lucy relayed the message then responded. "She says that's fine. Just bring her a few pieces of that marvelous candy."

"Delighted to. Thank you for your help."

"Thank you, young lady. Tell your aunt Mitzi hello."

Cheryl let herself out as Lucy kept chatting with her friend. It didn't take long to walk back to the store, and it felt good to spend time in the fresh air. She sent Esther home with many thanks as soon as she returned. "Would you ask your maam if she would like to make the trip with me to visit the pharmacist's daughter? I will swing by your house about seven to see if it works."

"I will ask her." Esther played with one of her kapp strings. "She can probably call to let you know so you will not make a needless trip."

"All right. Thanks again for all your help today."

Esther smiled and then hurried out of the store almost as if she were afraid Cheryl would somehow call her back.

Cheryl spent the next minutes setting a few displays to rights. The phone rang, and she hurried over to the counter.

"Swiss Miss. How can I help you?"

"Cheryl, this is Chief Twitchell. A quick update on Suzanne. I couldn't reach her. She's already movin' on to another coin show in Chicago. She's not answerin' her cell either. I checked with a couple other dealers at the show. No one else remembers seein' anyone out of the ordinary."

"I wonder if Suzanne was doing all that as a distraction? If she'd really been concerned, she should have called me rather than the Millers." She sighed. "Thanks for the update."

"Let me know if you hear anything else."

"Will do." Cheryl mulled over the facts all afternoon. Why would Suzanne call and leave that message and then leave the area? It didn't make sense unless she was trying to throw them off her trail. The thing was, Cheryl hadn't been on Suzanne's trail. She'd just wanted to ask her opinion on the coins and whether she'd seen enough to have any indication of their value.

"All right, Beau. Let's go." She collected her cat and slid a jar into her purse then headed to the door with her purse and keys. As she inserted the key in the lock, she stopped.

Pam stood in front of the door ready to knock.

"Come in."

"I promise this won't take long. I found these articles about the bank robbery." She handed a small sheaf to Cheryl. "This has to be the one you were talking about. There weren't any others in Sugarcreek during the war that I could find. The good news is all the money was returned."

She flipped through the pile. "I suppose that's good news."

Pam's eyebrows folded in. "You suppose?"

Cheryl chuckled. "It is good news for the bank, but I was hoping it would help me find more answers to where those coins came from."

Pam patted Cheryl's hand. "You'll figure it out. You always do. You have a good instinct and ask the right questions. I'll help whenever you need me."

"Thank you, Pam. I'll remember that."

Cheryl then ushered her out and locked the door behind them. As she walked home, she considered the fact that the coins were not stolen from the bank was good for John-John. Unfortunately, it was another research dead end. She needed a breakthrough. Maybe it would come when she visited the pharmacist's daughter.

CHAPTER TWENTY-THREE

Cheryl scanned Pam's articles as she ate a quick supper. The librarian was right. In May 1944, a couple of men in their midtwenties had broken into the local bank in the middle of the night. The thieves had used dynamite to blow the door off the safe and then hurried away with two duffle bags each filled with currency. It had taken the police several days to track them down, but after a week they were in custody.

She read the articles through a second time more slowly, but all that struck her was the fact that the thieves had stolen paper money while leaving rolls of coins behind. She leaned back against the chair's back. She could understand the thieves' logic. Coins were heavy and duffle bags filled with them would be too burdensome to haul any distance. Currency still had weight, but not as much as coins. Even that was found two days later in a field outside Sugarcreek.

Another dead end.

Which led her right back to *who* took the coins this time. Who would want them? Could it be Leonard? He could consider himself an "heir." He'd acted surprised to learn about them, yet at the same moment he had leapt to the conclusion he was owed them. Deciding if he really was would be a battle after the coins were found.

Could Suzanne Marshall have stolen them and now sold them at coin shows around the region? If so, what could Cheryl do to stop her? Best to leave that investigation to the police.

Who else might have a claim to the coins?

She should track down Frank's daughters. Maybe they could tell her definitively whether the writing was their father's. Leonard hadn't given her a chance to dig deeper concerning his uncle. But a daughter would surely know her father's handwriting and be able to determine once and for all if Frank was the author.

"One thing at a time, Cheryl," she mumbled and then wiped her mouth with her napkin. "One thing at a time."

She'd clean up the kitchen, and then she'd visit the pharmacist's daughter. Only after that would she see if she could find Frank's daughters. Surely someone around town knew their names. If nothing else, she could visit Leonard and Clara again. Too bad she hadn't gotten more information from him the first time.

Her phone rang, and she answered. "This is Cheryl."

"Cheryl, I'd like to go with you tonight if you don't mind picking me up." Naomi sounded slightly out of breath as if she'd hurried to the phone shanty.

"I can be there in half an hour."

"I will be ready. Thank you."

Naomi was waiting in one of the porch rocking chairs when Cheryl pulled into the yard. Cheryl looked around then stopped herself from turning all the way around to scan the fields. She shouldn't care whether she saw Levi or not, but she did. It had been a couple days, and she missed interacting with him.

"He is in the barn working." Understanding brightened Naomi's eyes as she entered the car. "A piece of equipment broke today, and he is helping Seth repair it."

"I'm sure Seth appreciates the help." She put the car into gear and bit her lip. "I hope you don't believe I mean anything by our... friendship. I just enjoy seeing him, that's all."

"It would not matter if you did. Levi is a goot man. He will make someone a goot husband."

Cheryl was grateful for the dusk. She prayed it hid the color climbing her neck and cheeks. "He *is* a good man." She took a deep breath and backed the car around so she could leave. "Do you know anything about Della—the pharmacist's daughter?"

Naomi was silent a minute then shook her head. "No. I am not familiar with her. She is not of the community, and I have not had the opportunity to interact with her." She grinned. "I am here merely as your partner in crime."

A giggle erupted from Cheryl. "Partner in crime, huh? Don't let Chief Twitchell hear you say that."

"Ja, he might not be amused."

The fifteen-minute drive to Della Dolan's home was filled with conversation. Along the drive, Cheryl noted the crops in the fields were growing but needed some rain to truly take off. In a few months, the corn would be in and knee high. Right now the winter wheat was growing, but the beans didn't look well. She shook her head. "I think I've been in Sugarcreek long enough to wash some of the city girl off me."

"Why?"

"I'm noticing the crops and how they look."

Naomi laughed with Cheryl, and then they plotted how they hoped the meeting would go.

"I grabbed one of the jars and have it in my bag. I hope Della recognizes it."

"I grabbed mine as well." Naomi patted her oversized bag. "If she does not recognize them, someone will. We will keep asking."

Cheryl nodded but had to admit she didn't want to keep asking. She wanted to find answers.

Her phone rang as she pulled in front of Della's home. She double-checked the address then answered the call. "Hello."

"Hey, Cheryl. This is John-John."

"How are things going?"

"Well, we have the volunteers, but I'm about out of funds for supplies." He blew out a breath that seemed heavy with care. "How am I going to do this, Cheryl? Without more money, these cottages will stand half-finished and empty. Was I crazy to think we could do this?"

"No." His sadness weighed on her. "I'm trying to find the coins."

"But that won't necessarily solve things. Not if someone else has a claim to them. And how much money can the coins actually be worth?"

"Suzanne Marshall seemed to think they're valuable."

"But we don't know." He sighed again. "Well, I'd better start praying. I'd hate to waste everybody's time if God isn't in this."

"Don't give up, John-John."

"I won't, but I can't continue unless I'm sure God is in this." He clicked off with a soft good-bye.

"That was Mr. Williamson?"

Cheryl nodded.

"Sounds like he transferred his burden to you."

"Only I think he kept it too." Cheryl rubbed her forehead and then dug out her purse. "Here's praying Mrs. Dolan knows something that can help us."

The sidewalk to the small front porch was lined with purple and yellow pansies. The bungalow was showing the first signs of wear with a bit of peeling paint around the window frames. Otherwise, the white siding and red windows looked bright and clean. Naomi followed her to the front door and waited as Cheryl knocked.

A moment later she heard a faint voice say, "Coming."

Slow minutes passed before the door opened. A small woman with shining blue eyes and white perfectly coiffed hair stood before them. "Which one of you is Cheryl Cooper?"

Cheryl raised her hand, feeling a bit like she was back in second grade for the first time. "And this is my friend Naomi Miller."

"Of course. Naomi of the famous jams." She stepped back from the door. "Do come in. I made some fresh lemonade if either of you would like a glass. Nothing quite as refreshing, is there?"

"I would love some." Cheryl followed her into the small front room, and Naomi murmured that she would like a glass too. Two loveseats faced each other in front of a fireplace. End tables shaped like elephants sat next to the undersized couches. Books lined every surface, including the built-in bookshelves on each side of the fireplace. "Your home is charming."

"I love it. It's been home for fifty years. Can't imagine living anywhere else. I tell my kids I'll only leave my home when I'm dead. No going into a 'rest' home for me. Just give me a minute to get the drinks." In a couple minutes, Della was back with a tray containing three glasses. "Please have a seat." They did as she handed out the lemonade. "Lucy tells me you may have some questions for me."

"Thank you for seeing us."

"I may not talk to Lucy often, but if she thinks I should talk to you, I'm happy to do so."

Cheryl quickly filled her in on what she was looking for as she pulled the jar from her bag. "You see, the coins we found were stored in a bunch of jars just like this one. A couple people thought they might have been used by the pharmacy back in the thirties and forties. Does it look familiar to you?"

Della took the jar and slowly studied it. "My father had dozens of these jars. Regular mason jars until he used them." She pulled on reading glasses and pulled the jar to her nose, running a finger along the remnants of the label. "See these words here?" She pointed to some letters that didn't spell anything in English. "This says *Kalium Chloride*. That's potassium chloride in German."

Naomi reached into her bag. "I wonder if the one I brought has German words as well." She turned it over. "Look...Kalium *Nitraat*."

Della accepted the jar. "That would be potassium nitrate, I believe. My father often got items and then labeled them in

German so he could easily read them in a hurry. He was a first-generation immigrant. His spoken English was very good. It took his reading longer to develop."

"Do you know what he did with the jars when he finished with them?"

"Now you're stirring up memories that have been stuck in this brain longer than time itself." Della closed her eyes and rocked back against the couch. "If I remember correctly—it has been a long time, you know—there was an Amish man who would take the jars periodically. He and my father spoke German to each other, which was odd because this was during the war and many people frowned on all things German. It was safer not to use the language.

"In fact, my parents tried very hard during the war to hide they were German. It was safer that way. Much safer."

The tension in the older woman's face pained Cheryl. "What do you mean?"

"Sugarcreek is not the big city, so there weren't attacks, but many would not do business with someone who was German or Japanese. It was very sad. It hurt many businesses. The community was too small to alienate anyone. My father did all he could to help people forget where he was from…except for this one Amish man. They seemed to enjoy speaking to each other in German."

"And he bought the mason jars?"

"Bought them or my father gave the jars to him. I'm not sure which."

"Do you remember the Amish man's name?"

"I'm not sure. He had dark hair and a thin frame. Average height. He had a small farm at the time and a handful of small houses on the outskirts of town." She shook her head. "He never seemed to quite find his footing after his stepson enlisted rather than take conscientious objector status."

Cheryl and Naomi looked at each other and said in unison, "Frank Raber."

"I think that was the name of his stepson—but everyone called him Pinky. The Amish man walked around like his stepson's service was an eternal shame to him instead of something to be proud of." She shook her head. "I've never understood why the stepfather couldn't be proud of that young man. He made so much of himself when he came home. Became a doctor. Yes, that's right. I think he'd been a medic in the war and wanted to continue that work in the area. We desperately needed a good doc in those days."

Naomi picked up one of the jars and studied it. "I wonder where your father got the jars. Surely he didn't have that much medicine flowing through his pharmacy."

"Oh, my father saved everything. My guess is he'd saved them for a while until they overflowed in his storeroom." Della shrugged. "My mother got on him to clean out that old storeroom. He'd get rid of just enough to have walking space."

Della and Naomi started in, talking about people they knew in common, and Cheryl let her mind wander, considering what they'd just learned.

If the jars had gone to Frank's stepfather, it confirmed that the letters and coins were likely his. He used the jars from the pharmacy to put coins in. Now she needed to find Frank's girls while she kept looking for the coins. While it felt great to have a better understanding of where the money had come from, she felt no closer to locating the stolen coins. Without those coins, she couldn't quickly help John-John. And his call made finding them more important than ever.

CHAPTER TWENTY-FOUR

As she and Naomi left Della's home, Cheryl was more determined than ever to track down Frank Raber's children. At the same time she puzzled over how to locate Suzanne Marshall and see if she had the coins. It was unlikely she could outright ask the woman, but she had to try something. She felt renewed urgency after John-John's call. What he was doing was important, and she wanted to help him succeed with the cottages.

On Friday morning, Ben and Rueben arrived for their game of checkers as she unlocked the Swiss Miss. It didn't take them long to get embroiled in an intense game. As Cheryl watched, she couldn't help shaking her head. Seemed checkers would get routine after a while. Only so many ways the game could play out, yet it provided the brothers with an important forum for rebuilding their relationship. She had enjoyed watching their silent games slowly evolve into games with quiet conversation interspersed with patient silence.

After their game wrapped up, Ben approached Cheryl. "Are you all right today?"

"I'm okay. Just trying to figure out who the coins belonged to." She sighed. "I think they might have been Frank Raber's."

"Frank was a good man." His lips tipped up just a bit. "Our stories had similar layers. He just did a better job following his heart."

"Sounds like he did what he loved."

"He did." He patted her arm. "I'll leave now. See you later."

The tour bus crowd filtered in as the brothers left. Cheryl helped a couple women pick out small wall-sized quilts, and her senses piqued when Sadie slipped into the store. John-John's intern wandered around the shop as if she were a bit dazed or overwhelmed. As soon as her customers were taken care of, Cheryl made her way toward the young woman.

"Is there something I can help you with, Sadie?"

The young woman turned in a slow circle as if taking in everything in the shop. "I don't even know where to begin. You have so many wonderful things here."

"Thank you. My aunt worked hard to build the shop, and I've added a few things to her regular stock. Is there anything in particular you're looking for?"

"Mother's Day is in a couple days, and I don't have anything yet. I doubt I can get it mailed to my mom in time, but I'd like to at least get it postmarked before Sunday."

"Sure." Cheryl knew how hard it was to find the right gift for Mom. "What does your mom like to do?"

"Read, but I don't see many books in here."

"That's true." Cheryl walked over to the display of Amish wisdom books. "These probably aren't quite right. Have you tried the Christian bookstore in town?"

"No." Sadie sighed, and her shoulders rounded. "It's a hard year. I'm not even sure I should get her something, or if it would be better to let the day evaporate without notice."

"Why would you do that?" Cheryl straightened a book. "My mom always comments on the cards and gifts I send."

"I guess I'm really concerned about my best friend, Jessica's, mom. Jessica disappeared after her boyfriend threatened her." A tear trickled down Sadie's cheek, and she swiped it away. "I thought he was abusive, but I didn't do anything. Now it may be too late."

"Oh, Sadie." Cheryl took her hand and led the young woman to the stools behind the counter. "Is there anything I can do?"

"Pray?" She snorted. "Not that it's done much good so far. Jessica's disappearance is why I'm here in Sugarcreek this summer. I convinced myself that if I helped battered women—by helping with the cottages—I'd find her. How crazy is that?"

"It does seem like a long shot." Cheryl handed her a Kleenex box. "Why would she come here?"

"That's just it. She probably wouldn't. But I found a card on her desk with the information for the shelter in Millersburg. They directed me to John-John, saying he needed help so his cottages could be used for women. I thought helping him would give me a chance to find Jessica." Sadie blew her nose and then wiped her cheeks. "I just want her to be okay."

"I'm so sorry."

Sadie looked across the store. "I really thought Jessica would have returned or I would have found her by now. I haven't been a very good best friend for her."

"She knows you care." Cheryl reached over and squeezed her hand. "She'll call when she's ready."

"I just know Mother's Day will be a hard day for Jessica's mom."

"It will. Can I pray with you?" Without waiting for Sadie to say anything, Cheryl took the young woman's hand and bowed her head. "Father, I'm so glad You know everything. You know where Jessica is. I ask You to send people to help her. Bring her home safely, and please comfort her family and friends."

"Amen." Sadie sniffled and then squeezed Cheryl's hand. "Thank you."

Then, like a gentle crumbling, the wall that Cheryl had built up in her heart concerning Sadie crumbled piece by piece. Yes, the young woman didn't fit in, and there was a reason for that. She'd just come to Sugarcreek to find a friend.

"Thank you for telling me about your friend." The bell over the front door jangled, and Cheryl glanced up. An elderly Amish lady walked inside the store. "I'll keep praying for her."

"I'll have another look around for a gift." Sadie pushed off the stool and straightened her back as she moved across the floor. Then she turned back and smiled. "Thank you, Cheryl." Nobody would know she'd been crying just a few short minutes before.

As Cheryl approached the older woman, she decided to remove Sadie from her list of suspects. She couldn't be the thief unless she was an amazing actress. No, those tears were as real as any Cheryl had ever seen.

The flow of customers slowed to a trickle, enough so that Cheryl pulled out the newspaper. It had been a while since she'd had the luxury of reading it cover to cover. It used to be one of her favorite things to do when she was a preteen staying with Aunt Mitzi. The simple stories of neighbors and friends had drawn her in. It had been so different than her life with her parents. Maybe God had been planting the seeds of her move to Sugarcreek even then.

When Cheryl reached the legal notices, she skimmed over them until she saw a name she recognized. *Brandt Sorenson?* She thought about the other day when he'd come to get the volunteer list from her. He'd acted completely normal until Cheryl had mentioned the missing coins. Then the contractor had hightailed it out of there. His actions had seemed a little curious at the time, but she hadn't thought much of it. But this...seeing this legal notice made her pause. It was a collection notice. It appeared he owed a few thousand dollars to a local creditor.

Would that be enough to cause him to steal the coins?

It was certainly a sum larger than she had in the bank. Probably more than most people had lying around. That didn't necessarily mean he would steal money, but it did give him a motive to do so.

She picked up the shop's phone and dialed John-John. "Hello. Is Brandt Sorenson working with you today?"

John-John was quiet a moment. "Haven't seen him. I think he mentioned having appointments today, and I miss him being around but I don't blame him." He sighed. "You know I can't pay folks, which makes it tricky to expect them to come in every day."

"Sure. I just wondered."

"He's been in and out, but now that I think about it he mentioned going to visit family out of state. Getting a jump on his summer vacation I guess."

After she got off the phone with John-John, Cheryl sat at the front counter doodling a pattern as her thoughts raced. Beau walked over and hopped onto the other stool before bounding onto the counter. He marched toward her and plopped on her paper.

"Well, hello there." She rubbed the pencil along his back, and it arched. "Do you think I should call Chief Twitchell? I can't decide."

Beau's tail swished back and forth across the paper as he studied her.

"I thought so. I don't want to say something that could hurt Brandt, but it sure seems suspicious that he would just leave. It's too early for summer vacations, I think."

He meowed.

Cheryl smiled and rubbed his chin. "You're right. I'll call the chief now." A minute later she was on the phone updating Chief Twitchell on her thoughts. "Is there any way you can find Brandt Sorenson and learn more about his debts?"

"Sure, but it doesn't mean I can tell you."

"I understand. Thanks, Chief."

"Just remember to leave the bulk of the investigatin' to me, Cheryl."

"Yes, sir." After she hung up, Cheryl pulled out her phone and did a quick search for Frank Raber. Nothing came up on the search. At least nothing relevant. Cheryl squinted at the screen then set the phone down. "I'll have to wait until I can search on a computer, Beau. This screen is too small to try to read. Too hard on my eyes."

Cheryl refolded the paper and then straightened the store. When everything was back in place, Cheryl placed Beau in his carrier and collected her things. She was looking forward to getting home and launching into her research on her laptop. Just when she was about to turn off the lights, the store phone rang and she answered it.

"Cheryl, this is Lauren with the security company."

"What can I do for you?"

"I've been bothered since I stopped out at your shop to check on the alarm. Remember how I said it wasn't easy to figure out? Well...I wasn't satisfied with that. As you know, I sent one of our guys out to check the system. I was really hoping we'd find an answer other than the fact that it wasn't properly armed."

Cheryl started pacing, nervous energy bubbling inside her along with a hope that the repairman's findings were wrong. "Please tell me it was set."

"Unfortunately, I'm afraid I can't say that. We've combed the records and checked the system. We simply can't find anything to indicate the alarm was set Saturday evening. Instead it shows it being set that Friday night and again on Monday night." The only redeeming quality of the moment was that Lauren didn't seem excited to convey her news. "I'm sorry, but I'm pretty certain the alarm wasn't used Saturday night."

Cheryl rubbed the back of her neck as Lauren's words sank in. That meant the theft was her fault. If she'd set the alarm, the thief would have at least been slowed down. Instead, she'd basically left an invitation for someone to come waltzing in and take what they liked.

She puffed out a breath and tried to shake the thought. Even if she hadn't set the alarm, what about the other safety precautions? The thief still had to get inside the shop somehow. She *did* remember locking the door. Not that that mattered now. Not that that had stopped anything. All she cared about was the fact that but for her negligence, the coins would still be in the safe.

Instead, all the thief had to do was pick the back door lock and waltz into the office. Cracking the safe probably wasn't too hard either. If you could pick the lock, you could likely crack the safe as well. The safe wasn't very high tech or heavy duty. And it hadn't closed all the way with all those coins inside. The safe was meant to deter theft, not prevent it—she'd watched enough crime shows to realize that.

Breaking in to the store and the safe without being caught took knowledge and skill. Who from a simple, community-orientated place like Sugarcreek would have the right skill set to do that?

CHAPTER TWENTY-FIVE

The walk to her home felt very long. Cheryl's shoulders felt weighed down and her heart heavy as she wrestled with the real possibility that the safe and Swiss Miss had been vulnerable because she had not set the alarm. An alarm was absolutely no help if it wasn't armed.

A deep sigh welled from the core of her being, and she lifted her shoulders and let them fall. Beau shifted in his carrier as if he felt her disappointment. He pushed his nose against the mesh and into her fingers where she clenched the strap.

"I'll be okay, Beau." She would be okay once she found the coins. Cheryl was pretty sure that was the only thing that would ease her burden.

If Sadie had come to Sugarcreek looking for her friend, then she wasn't involved in the disappearing coins. Brandt might have been involved. His disappearance certainly seemed suspicious. But under those criteria, Suzanne Marshall's sudden trip out of town also felt forced. Did the woman really plan to go from one coin show to the next without coming home? It might be possible, yet it felt like a stretch that the trip would come so conveniently after the coin discovery and disappearance.

Then there was Leonard. What was Cheryl supposed to make of Frank's nephew?

Based on what she'd learned from the pharmacist's daughter, she was certain the jars had belonged to an Amish man who had communicated with the pharmacist in German.

As she walked up the sidewalk to her front door, Cheryl decided she had to find Frank Raber's daughters. That was the ideal way to determine whether the letters were his for once and for all. Everything certainly pointed that way, but she wanted certainty.

If the letters were Frank's and the coins were the proceeds from his paychecks, then it made her more certain Leonard was involved. Somehow. She just wasn't sure how yet. The man had been so on edge and abrupt that she couldn't scratch him off her list of possible suspects. The note left in the safe mentioned an "heir."

If the coins weren't the proceeds from Frank's paychecks, then she was back to a more fundamental question: where had the money come from? Cheryl would cross that bridge if she came to it.

She opened the door and released Beau from his carrier. He promptly flounced to the couch and plopped on top of her laptop. She hung up her purse and set the carrier in its place. She must not have moved quickly enough because he stood, turned a full circle, and then meowed at her.

"Not moving fast enough?"

He tipped his nose in the air and sat square in the center of the laptop.

"Any ideas what I should do with the laptop?"

Beau shook his head and twitched his ears. Cheryl laughed and then brushed him to the side.

"Don't worry. I have a few ideas." She opened the laptop, and as it booted to life she thought about where she could find the names of Frank's girls. It was unlikely that she could discover birth certificates without a lot more information and a subscription to a service like Ancestry.com. Maybe his obituary was online. If it was, it would likely include information about his children. She entered a couple searches but didn't have much luck finding her Frank Raber or any Frank Raber.

She sat back and thought about other searches she could do, but nothing seemed to work. Instead, she picked up her phone and called the library. If the library had hosted an evening event, then someone would be there. Otherwise, her search would stall until the morning. The phone rang a few times, and then someone answered.

"Sugarcreek Library, this is Pam."

Cheryl smiled. Just the person who could help her. "Pam, this is Cheryl. Do you have a moment to help with a research question?"

"Sure. Just give me a minute." After a minute of murmured conversation in the background, Pam was back. "How can I help?"

"I'm trying to find some information about Frank Raber and his family."

"You're not the first person to ask me that question."

"Really?" Cheryl stared at the laptop's screen with the results of her fruitless search. "He must have done something interesting to be so popular now."

"Suzanne Marshall called me yesterday for some information on his family. And then a young Amish man came in."

"Did he tell you his name?"

"Just that he was doing research on his family during his rumspringa. Wanted to know more about distant relatives."

"Interesting." The coins had triggered interest in a man who had faded into oblivion. At least the coins seemed the catalyst for the attention. "I'm specifically trying to find his children. I've tried to find his obituary. Thought it would be a great place to start, but I had no success."

"He died a couple years before the paper started putting everything online." Cheryl heard clicks like Pam was on a computer keyboard. "After Suzanne requested the information, I e-mailed it to her since she's out of town. I can forward it to you if you like."

"Perfect." Cheryl gave Pam her e-mail address. "Thank you for your help."

"My pleasure. Librarians love to help people locate information."

A few minutes after Cheryl hung up, an e-mail from Pam arrived in her inbox. When she clicked on the attachment, she found herself reading a fascinating bio that told the story of a man who had lived well in challenging times. His military service was highlighted as were his many contributions to the local community as a doctor. He had served the Make-a-Wish Foundation for years, helping to ensure that ill children had memory-making opportunities at challenging times in their lives. As she read, Cheryl wished she'd had the opportunity to meet the man.

There. At the very end of the recitation of his life, Cheryl found the list of his family. His wife had predeceased him, and his nephew Leonard lived in Sugarcreek. He was survived by his sister, Wanda, and two daughters. Linda Raber Haven lived in Columbus, Ohio, with her husband and three children. His youngest daughter Anna Raber Logan was listed as living in Indianapolis.

Cheryl smiled. Now she had information she could trace to Frank's daughters. With any luck she'd be talking to them no later than the next day.

Tension coiled in her stomach. She was getting close. She knew it. Soon she could give John-John an answer about the coins.

Her excitement dipped as she remembered this information wouldn't lead her to the coins. Beau curled on her lap, and she rubbed his back. "It's okay, boy. I'm not giving up. It's too important to track down those coins."

She did a quick search and found a phone number for Linda, but no matter how she entered the information, no number popped up for Anna. If she could connect with Linda, Cheryl would find Anna too. She only needed one daughter to confirm her suspicions about the letters and then the coins.

Beau moved to her cell phone and nudged it with his nose.

"Are you reading my mind? Time to call Linda." She dialed and listened to it ring. Eventually she left a message, telling Linda she'd love to talk to her about her father and items that might be his—specifically the letters. "Here's hoping she'll return my call."

Beau stood and stiffly walked off her lap and then hopped to the ground.

Cheryl laughed and packed up her laptop as she straightened the living room. She had the cottage in tip-top shape when her phone rang. An unknown number showed on the display when she reached it. "Hello?"

"Is this Cheryl Cooper?" After Cheryl responded, the woman's words continued. "My name is Linda Haven. You're trying to reach me, though I'm not sure why. You mentioned my father?"

"I'm so glad you called, Linda. Something was found— something of your father's that might interest you." Cheryl quickly explained finding the letters in the walls of a cottage that was being remodeled. She didn't mention the coins—not yet.

"So I was wondering if I could meet with you to see if these letters are indeed your father's."

Cheryl heard a sharp inhale.

"What a treasure if those are his." Linda sighed, and there was a hint of longing and sadness to her voice. "I've often wished he would have said more about his experiences during World War II, but he didn't. The only thing he indicated was that it was a painful time."

"It was for many veterans."

"Yes." Linda was silent for a minute. "I'd like to meet you tomorrow. Would that be okay? I'd be happy to come to you. I haven't been to Sugarcreek in ages, and this seems like the perfect excuse."

"Absolutely." Cheryl gave her directions to the Swiss Miss. "It's hard to miss. Just look for the white building with blue heart-shaped shutters."

"Thank you. I'm so excited to see these letters. If they're my father's…" She paused and exhaled another shuddering breath. "It would be such a gift. We were headed out of town on vacation tomorrow, but we can delay that. Thank you so much for finding me."

"I'm so glad I did."

"Until tomorrow."

Linda hung up, but Cheryl stood there another minute, trying to decipher the woman's words—the woman's tone. There had been something in the woman's voice, an undercurrent of sadness that didn't seem to match her excitement at learning about the letters. Cheryl said a quick prayer for Linda, then she made sure the letters were still in the baggie in her purse. She couldn't lose them too.

CHAPTER TWENTY-SIX

The next morning Rueben Vogel waited outside the Swiss Miss when Cheryl arrived.

Cheryl tilted her head and eyed him, her heartbeat quickening as she did. Rueben's brows were folded down, and she wondered what could be so urgent that he'd be waiting for her.

"Miss Cheryl."

"Hello, Rueben. You got an extra early start this morning."

"I heard something I wanted you to know."

Cheryl stopped and looked at the older man. He twisted an old hat in his hands, exposing what little white hair remained on his scalp. He shuffled his feet and reluctantly returned the hat to his head.

"Let me unlock the door, and we can have some coffee while you fill me in."

A few moments later, the two stood at the counter. "I have heard something." Rueben cleared his throat, but his voice was still gravelly when he spoke. "May be nothing more than a rumor. But I know how burdened you have been by the coins."

"I have." She couldn't deny how much she hated not knowing what had happened to them when they had been placed in her care for safekeeping.

"When I was at Yoder's Corner yesterday getting one of their cinnamon rolls, I heard something," he repeated again.

Cheryl focused on Rueben, even though the mention of cinnamon rolls made her want to grab her purse and go get one of those melt-in-your-mouth, gooey wonders. Nobody made cinnamon rolls like Yoder's. "Yes?"

"A couple of young men were sitting in a corner talking and yucking it up. One of them said something about getting a jar filled with treasure."

He had her full attention now. "Did you know him?"

"He looks like every other dark-haired Amish boy going through his rumspringa. More in the world than separate." Rueben sighed. "I am sorry Miss Cheryl, but I did not realize what his words could mean until after I had left. When I returned, he was gone. I could not help thinking his jar might be one of yours."

"Not mine, but John-John's." A spark settled inside Cheryl. This was what she'd needed—some simple indication the jars were still around. "Thank you for letting me know."

"It seems like it is not much help."

"It is something. That is very encouraging. I was beginning to think I was crazy to hope to find them. What do you remember of the young men? Anything you could think of would be helpful."

Rueben quickly sketched out a group of average-sounding Amish men. Hats shoved low on foreheads. No beards yet, so they were all unmarried. Black pants, solid-colored shirts, some suspenders.

But they had talked about a treasure found in jars.

That could only be the jars found at the cottages. And that gave her a surge of adrenaline. If someone was talking about them, then she could find them.

It was simply a matter of time and persistence.

And for John-John and his important work she would be persistent.

The bell over the door jingled, and a middle-aged woman walked in, uncertainty on her face as if she wasn't quite sure she'd found the right place. Cheryl sucked in a breath. She knew that all her research could pay off in the next few minutes. Was Frank Raber—this woman's father—the key to it all?

Hair frosted to almost white-blonde at the roots fell in a smooth bob around the woman's round face. A smile graced her lips but wobbled a moment as she spotted Rueben. She squared her shoulders and glided toward the counter, her maxi dress swishing around her feet.

"I'm looking for Cheryl Cooper."

Cheryl stepped around the counter and smiled at the woman. "I'm Cheryl. Are you Linda?"

"Yes. I thought you weren't open yet."

"I'm not, but Rueben had some news for me." She quickly introduced the two, then Rueben left with a tucked head and shy smile.

Cheryl strode to the coffeemaker and filled it with water. "Would you like to select a coffee before we talk?"

Linda followed her, and in a few moments both had steaming cups of coffee doctored with sugar and cream. Then Cheryl led the way to the checkers table, and they settled in.

"I have to admit you intrigued me last night." Linda blew on her coffee, but didn't take a sip. "Why do you think these letters might be from my father?"

Cheryl quickly summarized what she'd learned from Aunt Mitzi and Leonard Raber. "Your father inspired my aunt's love of Papua New Guinea. And Leonard seemed to confirm that your father was the one from the community who served." She purposefully kept his hostility to herself.

"My cousin Leonard seemed to hate my father. I never understood why." Linda took a sip and then grimaced. "Too hot." She blew again then looked at Cheryl. "My father was a complex man. He grew up Amish, but never fit in the box of the faith. He loved this town, all of its residents, and raised us in the church . . . just not the Amish one. I don't think Leonard ever forgave him for stepping away. Or understood that he didn't walk away, he just changed the address of where he worshipped. He always said that he could serve more people by gaining a little freedom in how he dressed and where he worshipped. It's complicated."

"Would you like to see the letters?"

"Yes." She sighed. "It's hard to believe they're his, but I'll know in an instant."

Cheryl walked back to the counter and grabbed the baggie with the letters from her purse. A moment later she handed them to Linda.

The woman wiped her hands on her turquoise dress before accepting the baggie. Her mouth worked, but no words escaped. Then she cleared her throat. "This is definitely his writing." She brushed a finger across the address block.

"You can open them."

"Thank you." A tear slipped down her cheek. "I miss him more today than when he first died."

The door opened, and Naomi slipped in. Her brown eyes sparkled with energy. She set a small napkin-lined basket on the checkers table. "I brought blueberry scones."

Cheryl stood and hugged her petite friend before introducing her to Linda. "Naomi is one of my dearest friends, and she's been helping me find information about your father. Now she's come at the perfect time." Cheryl smiled. "The coffee was missing something. Naomi is a masterful cook, unlike me. If I'd brought a treat to go with our coffee, it would have been inedible." While she grabbed a chair from the office for Naomi, her friend prepared a cup of coffee. A couple minutes later the three women were settled around the table with the still-warm scones in front of them.

Cheryl turned to Naomi. "Linda was telling me about her father."

Naomi broke off a bite-sized portion of the scone. "I have heard he was a wonderful man."

"I loved him deeply." Linda stirred her coffee, as if using the action as an excuse to collect her thoughts. "When he returned home from the war, he had decided he couldn't remain Amish—or at least that's what I've been told. His decision had harsh consequences on family relationships, but he knew God had called him to serve others through medicine. He'd learned much during the war, but wanted more. He used his GI Bill benefits to go to college and then medical school. When he graduated, he turned down offers in big cities because he wanted to return to this area and community." She took a sip and then shrugged. "He never said much about it, but I understood his family didn't make it easy for him."

Naomi nodded. "Breaking with the church is a difficult decision for all involved." A shadow of sadness passed over her face, and Cheryl wondered if she was thinking about her stepdaughter Sarah. Her departure had forever changed the Miller family.

"I never knew that side of my family. I eventually learned when I was seeing my cousin Leonard or his wife, but I would never have known it by the way they treated me." She shuddered as if trying to shake the memories free. Tears began to stream down her face, and Cheryl handed her a tissue. "Thank you." Her voice was broken.

Cheryl tapped the baggie filled with V-mail. "Would you like to read these letters?"

"Yes."

Cheryl nodded toward the counter. "Naomi and I will work over there while you do. If you need anything, just let us know."

"Thank you. He never talked much about his experience in the war. It will be a gift to read these."

Before Cheryl could walk away, Linda had tugged the baggie open.

"Oh, and if you'd like to take them with you...to read them in private...that's fine with me too."

The woman nodded her appreciation and then with a sigh pulled out the first envelope.

As Cheryl and Naomi walked to the counter, her Amish friend sighed. "Such brokenness."

"It reminds me so much of the Vogel brothers without the healing."

Naomi nodded. "It is a hard thing when a family member leaves. When you are Amish, it permeates all you do, all you are. When one leaves, it breaks that unity." She wiped her cheek, and Cheryl realized Naomi too was crying.

She felt a stillness inside. Would she ever be able to become Amish? Did she even want to? The thought felt so strange and foreign that she shoved it away. Yet at the same time, Levi's image slipped into her mind.

Naomi helped Cheryl ready the store for opening before leaving for another sewing frolic. When Cheryl went to the front to turn the sign from Closed to Open, Linda had slipped out. She'd taken the letters with her, and for a moment a twinge of anxiety filled Cheryl. Should she have let Linda take them? Would she return them? Cheryl resigned herself that even if she never saw them again, she'd made sure they'd been placed into the hands of Frank's daughter. She just hoped Chief Twitchell wouldn't be upset—the letters were evidence after all.

After the tour bus crowd had shopped, Chief Twitchell strode into the shop. He met Cheryl at the counter, his expression serious.

"Chief, is anything wrong?" Cheryl didn't think she'd mention Linda taking the letters—not yet. Not unless it was important.

"Just wantin' to update you on the coins." He rubbed a hand through his salt-and-pepper hair then leaned a hip against the counter. "Looks like Brandt Sorenson's left town after payin' all kinds of debts off. Haven't figured out how he managed that yet, but I will."

"Seems like that would take an influx of cash?"

"Yes. And that has me concerned. How does one get several thousands of dollars at once? There are legal ways, but I can think of a lot more illegal. Still, I've never had trouble with the man."

"There aren't many ways in Sugarcreek to make a lot of money quickly."

"Agreed."

The front door opened and Esther flew in, followed by Levi.

Esther hurried behind the counter and grabbed her apron. "Sorry I'm late, Cheryl."

Cheryl looked at the clock and startled at the time. "I didn't realize how late it was." She put a calming hand on Esther's shoulder. "It's been a slow day, so don't worry about it."

"Thank you." The girl hurried to the back as soon as she finished murmuring the words.

Levi strode to the counter and leaned an elbow on it. "Hello, Cheryl, Chief Twitchell. Is my maam here?"

Cheryl shook her head. "She was headed to a frolic of some sort."

"Oh, that is correct? Guess I forgot." He stood in front of the counter and looked between the two. "Why the long faces?"

"Chief Twitchell just told me Brandt Sorenson has left town."

"Sure has. He talked to me yesterday about joining him on a new job. Guess he will work for a tanker in the Gulf of Mexico. The companies pay well, but it means being locked on a boat for a long time."

"Are you going to join him?" Cheryl felt her insides tighten at the thought of him leaving. And going so far. Sugarcreek wouldn't be the same if he left.

"I have no interest in living where I cannot feel the goot Lord's earth solid beneath my feet." He smiled, but there was a shadow edging it. "The money would be nice. He got a lump sum at the beginning. A bonus, I guess."

"That would be nice." Cheryl could think of a few things she would do with a bonus. Paying off debts would be one of the things.

"He used it to get current on debts. His family has had a hard few years. It will be a blessing to them." Levi filled a cup with coffee and then turned back to Cheryl and the chief. "I need to get going. Thank you for the kaffee."

"Anytime, Levi."

This time his smile reached his eyes, and her heart slowed. She could get used to seeing that special smile on a daily basis. Then he was gone, and she turned back to Chief Twitchell.

"I guess we know where Brandt is going."

He nodded. "And it's time to take him off the suspect list."

"Maybe." It could simply be convenient timing on his part. Maybe accepting the job was a cover to hide where his sudden influx of cash had come from.

"I do have one more piece of information you'll be interested in."

"Yes?"

"The one fingerprint we found from your office came back unmatched. It's almost like the person doesn't exist. In today's world that's hard to believe."

"Why?" Cheryl hadn't been fingerprinted before she came to Sugarcreek.

"So many people get fingerprinted for different licenses and things it's unusual to find prints that we can't trace back to someone somehow. So somehow this mystery person has avoided trouble with the law or never had a reason to be fingerprinted." He shook his head. "That's unlikely."

"I don't know, Chief. There are many people who haven't been."

"Maybe. But it does make me wonder if this person is Amish after all. They'd have a much smaller likelihood of bein' fingerprinted for non-law-related reasons." He put his hat back on. "Well, that's all I have now. Anything to tell me?"

Cheryl shook her head. "Just that I've found Frank Raber's daughter Linda, and she confirms the letters are his handwriting. She was actually pretty shook up by reading them. Sounds like an interesting and sad story. He ended up leaving the Amish community after serving in World War II. Caused a break in his family."

"Let me know if anything else comes up." He gazed at her solemnly. "We are about at the end of this. There aren't many more avenues to investigate."

It was only after he left that Cheryl realized she'd forgotten to mention Rueben's words. She'd tell him next time she saw him, since the chief already believed it must be an Amish person.

CHAPTER TWENTY-SEVEN

Later that afternoon when Naomi stopped by again, Cheryl filled Naomi in on everything the chief had told her—especially about the unmatched fingerprint—and his belief the thief must be someone from the Amish community.

Naomi shook her head. "I don't believe it. Stealing goes completely against the tenants of what we teach."

Cheryl considered that in light of Rueben's comment. "But what if it was someone on rumspringa?"

Naomi worried her lower lip between her teeth. "I still don't believe it."

"Or don't want to." Cheryl sighed. "I can see both sides. It doesn't seem likely that the average Amish person would break into my shop and steal the coins. Yet I can see someone on rumspringa possibly doing it as a part of breaking free." She held up a hand as Naomi began to sputter. "I didn't say it was a good idea. But I could see it happening. The Amish life is very strict. Maybe the person saw it as a lark. A good opportunity to test the strictness."

Naomi shook her head and planted her hands on her hips. "Have you learned so little of our lifestyle? Our faith permeates all we do."

Cheryl hugged her friend and felt the stiffness leech from Naomi's body. "And I love you for it. I'm just saying I have to be careful. Consider all of the options. Even the ones I don't like." Maybe that's what her mom had meant about keeping some white space in her schedule. Not that it wasn't okay to invest in her friends and projects, but to keep an eye on the cost of doing so. If she worked and gave all the time, then she'd be exhausted when it mattered. But if the time energized her, that was important to remember too. Just like she had to remember to keep her mind open to all options when doing an investigation like this one.

As much as it might disturb Naomi, the truth was the evidence pointed to an Amish person being the thief. She didn't like the thought any more than her friend did.

But the truth was she had to find the coins. Whether for Linda or for John-John, she knew the coins belonged with one of them.

"What now?" Naomi's question was one that had cycled through Cheryl's mind since the chief had updated her.

It was one thing to know the thief might be Amish. It was quite another to figure out how to take that knowledge and find the thief.

"I'm not sure. I guess I keep pulling at the strands?"

"And eventually you'll find the right one."

"Eventually. I just wish it was sooner." She sighed. "John-John needs the money now. And even if it ends up not being his, I still want to find it."

"You will."

Cheryl wished she had Naomi's confidence. This one seemed like a puzzle she couldn't quite crack. Yet she had found the identity of the author of the letters. That was something she couldn't forget.

The two worked in companionable silence as Naomi gave Cheryl the jars of jams and jellies, and Cheryl entered them into inventory. Then she handed her friend a check for the jellies and other items that had sold in the last two weeks.

"Looks like the wedding and graduation rush has continued."

Cheryl nodded. "I'm still learning the rhythms of the store." She paused and squeezed Naomi's hand. "Thank you for being such an important piece of this transition. Sugarcreek really feels like home because of the way you've welcomed me."

"You are easy to love, my friend."

Cheryl felt the blessing of those words throughout her soul. "Thank you."

Naomi was packing up her things when the front door opened and Linda Haven walked into the store. She'd changed from this morning. She wore an A-line dress that flared around her knees. This one in a royal purple tone. She seemed a bit freer than she had earlier in the day as she walked toward Cheryl and Naomi.

When she reached the counter, she pulled the baggie from her purse and handed it to Cheryl. "Thank you for the chance to read my father's letters." She smiled wryly as she stepped back. "I didn't expect to be so affected by his words. Even his handwriting."

Cheryl slid them back to her. She'd been thinking about the letters through the day, realizing that they'd already done their job.

They'd given her the clues she'd needed. Now they should remain with the rightful owner. "These are yours. Keep them."

Her eyes misted as she glanced from the letters back to Cheryl. "Are you sure?"

"Positive."

Naomi agreed. "Your father would want you to know his thoughts. Have his writings."

"And there's more." Cheryl smiled at the woman. "I haven't told you the whole story, Linda. We found more than the letters. We found coins too."

Linda's eyebrows shot up. "Coins? What do you mean? Do you have them? Can I see them?"

Cheryl cast a glance at Naomi. "I'm afraid not." She attempted to ignore her Amish friend's compassionate gaze and turned to Linda, accepting her own blame in the loss of them. "I was trying to help my friend Johnson by keeping those coins in my safe, but they were stolen. I wish we knew more about them. I'm not even sure of their value. Personally I think they were worth a lot, since someone worked so hard to steal them." Cheryl went on to tell the woman about her guess that the coins were cash from her father's World War II salary—hidden away and never used.

"I never would have imagined such a thing." Linda sighed. "There was just so much I never knew about my own family."

Cheryl swallowed against the lump in her throat, wishing she had better news to share. "I'm so sorry."

"It's not your fault." Linda retook the letters and clutched them to her heart. "It seems silly, but I knew so little of his time.

The letters are short, but they are his. And this is a true treasure to me—worth more than anything." She glanced around the store and then gestured to the chairs and checkers table. "Do you have a few minutes for me to tell you more of the story?"

The store was surprisingly empty, so Cheryl nodded.

A few minutes later the three women settled at the table. They were different yet tied together by one man's story. Linda in her simple tenderness like her father, Naomi in her Amish roots, and Cheryl in her desire to help others.

Linda's words started slowly. "My mother and father married as he was in medical school. It seems that World War II took a while for him to recover from. His nature was noncombative, but he joined because he felt it was right. Still, he bore the scars of all he had seen, of the men he couldn't help. After they married, medical school was pretty consuming."

She swiped at a tear. "After a few more years, my parents had me and then my sister. Ironically, they had begun to consider adoption, and then we arrived in quick succession. We were close as we grew up, but Anna seemed needier somehow, like she simply couldn't get enough love at home. I never understood why because our parents loved us dearly even if my father sometimes had a hard time expressing it."

"Some of us simply are born with a deeper reservoir that must be filled." Naomi's words were soft but certain.

"That describes Anna perfectly." Linda wiped away another tear. "She needed an abundance of love. As she grew into an adult, she didn't always look for it in the best places. I was away at college and then got married. I always wonder if I shouldn't have stayed home more. Helped her more."

"Surely nobody expected you to do that." Cheryl paused a moment. "God expects us to live our own lives."

"Maybe, but Anna needed more than we could give. Shortly into her sophomore year, she met a man who seemed to promise her the sun, moon, and stars. Instead of believing that wasn't possible or realistic, she absorbed each of his promises and believed them. They eloped when he convinced her our parents' disapproval was ridiculous. By the time we understood what had happened, they had disappeared. He literally moved her across the country away from all she knew and everyone who loved her."

"Oh no." Cheryl could begin to guess where this story was headed.

"It was all we were afraid of. He completely took over her life, and there was nothing we could do. We only got a phone call or hastily scrawled card every year or two. Just enough to let us know she was alive. And to learn I had a new niece or nephew. But she wouldn't come home." She sighed. "She couldn't come home."

Naomi reached across the table and gently held Linda's hand. "I am so very sorry."

"Me too."

Linda gave them a wavering smile. "Thank you. The reality is he held her in a tight grip of control. One she could not escape, especially after the children arrived. I don't know how she stayed, but I understand why she couldn't leave. When their daughter got on Facebook, it gave me a way to connect and try to communicate with Anna. That worked for a year until her husband wised up again. Then he took even that away from us."

She looked at them. "It must be terrible to be so controlled. To lose the freedom to choose who you can befriend, spend time with, and how you will spend money." Linda shrugged. "But there was nothing I could do. They moved again, and I lost track of where she was. Then a year ago I got a call. Their youngest was a freshman in college, and Anna left. She was on the run from her husband. Somehow she'd squirreled away enough money to escape. And that's the last I've heard."

"Is there anything I can do to help you find her?"

"I've had private detectives look for her, but she's disappeared. Thank you though." She glanced down at her hands where she'd clutched them in her lap. Then back up at Cheryl and Naomi. Fire burned in her eyes. "When you find these coins, I want you to donate them to the man fixing the cottages." She sighed, letting the words sink in. "I hope they are valuable. I did some investigating of my own last night of the cottages where the letters were found and the shelter in Millersburg. Your friend is doing a good thing. Anna needed a place like the cottages to escape to when she ran. I was trying to think of how I could help... if I could make a donation of some sort to help them, and now I know how. If the coins are found, I'd like them to go to this cause, even if they're valuable. Especially if they're valuable." She gave them a quivery smile. "I think my father would be honored to know that his hard-earned money was being used to help women like my sister. If the cottages had been finished and if I could have told my sister about them, maybe I wouldn't have to worry about whether she's okay or even still alive. That question and fear haunts me. Literally haunts me each night." Linda gripped Cheryl's hands in hers.

"Promise me that when you find them you will give them to Mr. Williamson."

"I will. Thank you."

"Thank you for the gift of discovering more about my father." With a sad smile, Linda stood and then hugged Naomi and Cheryl before leaving.

Now more than ever she needed to find the coins for the sake of John-John and Linda and the women they both wanted to help.

CHAPTER TWENTY-EIGHT

A sweet sadness filled Cheryl's soul as Linda walked past the Swiss Miss and out of sight.

Naomi turned to Cheryl, and her face was a mix of joy over being able to share Frank's letters with his daughter and sadness over the loss that the woman had faced. No one should have to lose a sister like that.

Naomi sighed. "I do not know about you, but that made me even more determined to solve this mystery. Let us grab a sandwich at Yoder's. We have much to digest."

Cheryl nodded. Her mind also was spinning with the sadness of Anna Raber's story. Tragedy happened to all families, but this was a heartbreaker. "Let me make sure Esther knows we're leaving and she's okay with it."

"She will be." Naomi looked around the store. "It is slow, and she feels bad about being late."

Esther had worked so many extra hours on her own this last week while Cheryl had tried to find the coins and letter writer. Cheryl didn't want to take advantage of her willing heart. "You have raised an amazing young lady, Naomi."

"Thank you." Naomi grinned at her. "I am always glad to hear people love her as much as I do." She grabbed Cheryl's hand. "Now let us get lunch."

Esther slipped out of the back room. "I can handle the store fine, Cheryl."

"As long as you know I appreciate you and the wonderful work you do."

As her cheeks turned red, Esther shooed them toward the door with her apron. "I will see you soon."

The walk to Yoder's was quiet. Cheryl's thoughts filled with all they had learned but remained troubled. While she knew John-John and his ministry would benefit from the coins, she hadn't found them. Knowing it might be an Amish young man seemed like a serious possibility—a small step forward. But the coins themselves were still gone.

No matter how she racked her mind though, she couldn't think quite how to find the next answers. While she knew more people in the Amish community than when she arrived, there were still so many that she didn't know. And if it was a young man, he had most likely helped at the cottages. Then when the coins were discovered, he'd been enticed to take them. Naomi had told her before that many of the Amish youth in the area gave their paychecks to their parents until they moved out of the house. Seeing that large amount of money would be temptation indeed.

Maybe Levi could help her compile a list of which of the men at the work site were participating in rumspringa. It was at least another approach to consider.

Cheryl held the door open for Naomi as they entered Yoder's Corner. Around them the tables were almost full. As she entered, Cheryl recalled her conversation with Rueben Vogel from earlier this morning. It was here the young Amish men had talked about finding treasure. Could they be here now? She quickly scanned the room. There were older ladies eating in pairs and a few families. Mostly there were men having a lunch break from work. Even though it was busy, she didn't see anyone who looked particularly like a troublemaking teenaged Amish boy on rumspringa.

"Welcome to Yoder's." A pretty young server pointed them to the vacant table. "Feel free to take a seat there, and someone will help you shortly."

The table could seat four, and Naomi stared at the empty chairs. "When they are so busy, I hate to take room we do not need."

Cheryl nodded, but as she looked around there was nowhere else to sit. "If we want to eat here, we have to use this table." In a few moments, a waitress set water in front of them. When Cheryl looked up, she startled. It was Leonard Raber's wife.

"Clara? It's nice to see you."

The woman looked frazzled. A few strands of hair had slipped out from beneath her kapp, and her forehead was indented with a map of worry lines. "Leigha will be your server today," she stated simply.

Someone raised his hand from another section of tables. Clara offered an apologetic smile and then hurried that way.

"I don't know that I've ever seen Yoder's with every table full." Cheryl glanced around and grinned. "Maybe some of these hungry folks will shop at the Swiss Miss this afternoon."

Naomi and Cheryl were debating which sandwich and soup combinations to enjoy before they shared one of the large cinnamon rolls when two men headed toward them. Naomi's face lit up as she looked up at her husband. "Seth, how did you know we would be here?"

The man's stern expression softened as he sat next to his wife. "I did not know. I was simply hungry and had no time to travel home for your good cooking."

Levi sat next to Cheryl, and her heart skipped. "Is it all right that we join you?"

"Sure." She tried to keep her smile nonchalant even as his nearness made her sit taller and smile wider. "We were about to order."

When the waitress arrived, they quickly placed their orders. The conversation flowed easily after the young woman left. As Cheryl joined in the laughter, she knew this was what she needed. Where her mother might have urged her to take time for herself over lunch, she needed this time laughing with friends more than she needed a solitary walk. She needed to be around people who cared for others in their community. She needed to be of help.

As they ate Naomi told Seth and Levi about Linda, her joy over reading the letters, and her sad story.

"Makes me glad we can help John-John." Levi took a sip of his coffee. "Makes me want to work harder too."

After their dishes had been cleared but before the cinnamon rolls arrived, Cheryl turned to Levi. "Can you think of any young men helping with the work at the cottages that is in his rumpsringa?"

Levi met her gaze, curiosity filling it. "Why?"

"The chief and I are beginning to think it had to be an Amish person who took the coins." She quickly filled the men in about the fingerprint and what Rueben had overheard. "Also, after Linda's confirmation we also know that the letters are definitely her father's, which reinforces that the money was placed in the walls by an Amish person, probably his mother and stepfather. I'm beginning to believe they died before they could take the coins out and give them to Frank or someone else."

"I wonder how nobody knew about the coins though. It is like they got completely lost to time for a good seventy years."

Levi nodded. "The cottages were almost falling apart before John-John bought them and began the renovations. If the cottages had been simply demolished, we might not have discovered the coins."

That thought filled Cheryl with relief. It was scary to think that so much could have been lost, destroyed. Better for things to be this way... if they recovered the coins.

"As I was thinking about who the boys that Rueben saw could be, I also wondered how they learned about the coins quickly enough to steal them. Then I thought they might be helping with the remodeling. That would certainly explain how they learned about the coins so quickly."

Levi rubbed his hands along his clean-shaven cheeks. "It is true. The coins were stolen almost before people were aware of their existence."

"There is only one problem." Seth blinked slowly. "We know everyone who was helping. I do not like to think it is one of our friends."

"It bothers me too, Husband." Naomi patted his hand. "If it is, they have lost sight of what their faith, our faith, demands."

Cheryl pulled out her wallet to pay her portion of the bill. "Which brings me back to rumspringa. Isn't that the one time that someone who is Amish would consider leaving the confines of their faith? They might be talked into doing things they would never consider at a different time." Cheryl was pretty sure she had that correct, but she wanted to hear it from her friends.

Levi shifted on the bench. "It is true, although none of us likes it. Most people try harmless things like cell phones and a bit of freedom. Others use the time as a license to sin."

Naomi tsked, but Levi reached across the table for her hand. "You know it is true, Maam."

"It does not mean I like it."

"None of us do." Seth's words were firm. "I can think of a couple men at the cottages that fit your description. One is Stephen Raber, although he's only helped a couple times. Another is Brandt Sorenson—although he's not Amish."

"But he's on his way to the Gulf Coast," Levi pointed out.

"Such foolishness. But those are the only two who come to mind. If I think harder, I might come up with one or two more."

Levi looked across the room, obviously deep in thought. Cheryl followed his gaze but then pulled her attention back to the table again when a waitress placed a cinnamon roll between them.

"I think there were just the two around when we discovered and lost the coins," Levi said, picking up his fork. "Many of the young men stayed at home to work on their farms so their fathers and older brothers could help at the cottages."

Cheryl considered the names the two men had thrown out for consideration. Brandt had come upon a large sum of money that paid off his debts and he'd left town, but his new job and signing bonus explained both. If that was the case, that left Stephen Raber—Frank Raber's great-nephew—as the lead suspect. Cheryl scanned the restaurant searching for the boy's mother. Did she know something? Is that why she looked so wary when serving them? Is that why she'd hardly said a word?

A table cleared from the section Clara was serving, and Cheryl narrowed her gaze. Sitting at a far table was Leonard Raber. His scowl was as deeply etched on his face as it had been during her visit to his home. If anything, he looked even less happy than he had then. A hard reality to process, yet it was true. And from the look on his wife's face, he'd managed to make Clara look even more frazzled. With heavy steps he rose from the table and left. Clara glanced up and watched him go, tears rimming her eyes.

A moment later a young man stood and followed Leonard out. The young man, Stephen, was close enough to be with him, but far enough to leave it in question.

Naomi pushed the cinnamon roll toward her husband. "I cannot eat this, not when the thought that you believe one of our own committed this crime and is sitting here."

"Wife, we want the truth."

"Ja. The truth, not goot thoughts." Naomi sighed. "I know we Amish are as sin-filled as anyone, but I don't like being confronted with that reality."

"None of us do." Cheryl turned back to the door in time to watch Stephen Raber slouch toward it. The young man didn't have much more energy now than he did back at his house. She watched as he played with some change, a strange light coming into his eyes as he tossed a coin to his mom before he walked out the door. "Will you excuse me one moment?"

Levi stood so that Cheryl could leave the table. "Do you need help?"

"I'll be fine and back in just a moment, promise." She hurried toward Clara. "Could I see that coin Stephen just tossed you?"

Clara looked at her warily then nodded. "I don't know that it matters. It's just a nickel."

But it wasn't. As Cheryl looked at it, she knew this was much more than a normal nickel. "Can I bring it back to you in a bit?"

Clara shrugged. "Sure. It's just a nickel."

But as Cheryl hurried outside to call Chief Twitchell, she knew it was much more than a nickel.

It was definitive proof of who had stolen the coins.

Chapter Twenty-Nine

As soon as she closed the Swiss Miss, Cheryl headed home. Chief Twitchell had promised he'd meet her there as soon as a string of city meetings ended. By the time Cheryl got home with Beau, she was ready to explode.

She knew she'd identified the thief, but she needed the chief to agree. If he downplayed her determination, she didn't know what she'd do. It all fit. Almost too well.

Beau watched her pace from his perch by the window. The minutes crawled by as she waited for the chief.

A batting at the window pulled her attention to the front yard.

"Beau, what are you doing?"

The cat ignored her, but kept batting at the front window. She couldn't see any birds so was mystified about what held his attention.

"Beau?" She walked to the window and then leaned closer to the panes of glass. On the other side she saw Stephen Raber strolling down the sidewalk. The Amish teen had abandoned his Amish outfit for dark pants, dark shirt, and a dark hat. She might not have thought much of it except he wore a camo backpack hitched over one shoulder and was headed in the direction of the cottages.

"Beau, you are the best." She grabbed her phone and dialed the chief. When he still didn't answer, she tried to leave him a message but groaned when it told her the mailbox was full. Quickly she grabbed a black hoodie and camera before hurrying out of the house. If she was right, this could be exactly what she needed to prove Stephen was the thief.

When she reached the sidewalk in front of her house, Cheryl could barely see Stephen down the street. After a block of walking casually, he had disappeared. "What's he doing? Running a race?"

She picked up her pace and hurried toward the cottages. When she arrived, the cul-de-sac in front of the homes stood empty of vehicles. She didn't know whether to be glad no one was around or worried. The area looked vacant, but she couldn't leave until she knew for sure. She crept to the closest cottage and peeked inside the living room window. Unable to see anything in the growing dusk, she tried the front door. It opened easily, and she stepped inside.

Out of nowhere an arm snaked around her waist and yanked her farther into the home. A shriek exploded from Cheryl's lips. She wriggled and pushed, but the man was too strong. He wore a dark mask and dark clothing. It had to be Stephen.

"I'm the rightful heir so leave the cottages alone." He snugged her closer, his arm tight and unyielding. "I don't want to hurt you, but I will. Back off and leave the cottages and treasure alone."

"Stephen, I know it's you." Her voice wavered, and she tried to swallow against the fear clutching her. "You don't want to hurt me. The treasure isn't yours. I've found Frank's heir."

His grip tightened. "That's impossible."

"No it's not. I found your cousin, Linda Raber. Your cousin wants to donate the coins to this ministry. Just let me go, and we can talk about this."

"You're lying." He yelled, and Cheryl jumped again. "Frank didn't want the cottages, and Linda didn't want them either. My dad did. He worked so hard and lost them. But the coins still belong to us. They gave them up. These cottages were ours. Still would be if someone hadn't interfered."

"How do you know? You couldn't have been very old." Cheryl tried to keep her voice calm.

"I was old enough to see my daed crushed by the loss of this place. All those years ago, and he still uses the tax sale as evidence for why he can't work. It's all vain, he says. So my mom slaves. And he sits around the house because of these stupid cottages. Those coins will show him it's all okay."

Cheryl tried to step away from him, but he didn't loosen his grip. "You can't take what's not yours, Stephen."

"But it is ours." His spittle flew along her cheek. "Daed owned these cottages for years. Before that, my grandparents owned them. These have been in our family since they were built. More years than many people think. Whatever is found here is ours."

"How did you get the coins?"

He smiled and loosened his grip. "It was easy. I just wanted to see if it was true about what the workers had found." His smile slipped. "I didn't mean to take the coins. It was easy to follow you and Levi to the Swiss Miss after you filled your car. There were too many people around to get a good look at the jars when you were here."

"So you followed us?" She knew she should keep him talking. The more Stephen talked, the more he loosened his grip.

"Ja. Then I just had to wait until you left. You didn't latch the back door when you locked it. It was easy to push on it when I noticed the security system hadn't activated. One quick yank and the door opened. After that I went in the store and saw some of the empty jars in the office. I knew the coins had to be there too. Once I saw the safe, it only took a few tries to fiddle with it like on the detective shows. On the third try it clicked open. Once I saw the money, I grabbed the bags and ran."

"Why come back today?"

"There must be more. I want to find it."

Cheryl nodded as another piece of the puzzle clicked into place. "So you came back to the cottages and punched holes looking for more treasure."

"I didn't want anyone else to find it if it was here." His grip tightened once again on her arm, and she wondered how big her bruise would be in the morning. "It belongs to us. I won't let anyone else take it!"

Cheryl bit back a gasp as his fingers squeezed even tighter. She had to find a way out of this mess. Nobody knew where she was or that she'd followed Stephen. She wanted to scream in frustration. If only Chief Twitchell's mailbox hadn't been full. Then someone would have an idea where she was. At this rate, no one would really miss her until she didn't show up at the store on Monday morning.

She didn't have a choice. She had to keep Stephen talking while she figured out how to escape.

"What will you do with the coins? You won't get full value for them if you spend them."

He shook her hard enough that her teeth clicked together. "I know that. I did some searching on the Internet. Each coin could be worth as much as fifteen dollars or more on its own. They're really rare. Put them together, and it could be a small fortune. That's why I will find all the coins that are here. It's my right!"

"So what do you plan to do?"

"I'm taking them to Berlin. I already visited a lady there who knows coins."

Did he mean Suzanne Marshall? Surely not.

"She asked me questions about the coins, and I couldn't answer them. I think she got suspicious about where they came from."

Cheryl's gaze darted around the cottage's front room, but it was empty of everything except a few discarded painting drop cloths. Those would be worthless as a weapon. She had to develop some kind of plan to get away from Stephen, but nothing was coming to her. "So what did you do?"

"Well . . ." His grip had loosened enough that she could slip away. And though he hadn't indicated he had a weapon, she didn't know for sure.

"I decided then that I needed to return the coins since I couldn't get rid of them. Somehow I could do it without getting caught." His voice dropped, and he shuffled even closer. "I was going to bring them back tonight and then leave a tip for the police."

Cheryl looked around the room. The only thing he'd brought with him was the backpack. "You were going to bring them here?"

"Sure. You kept locking the store and arming the security system. There wasn't any way to get in and out without doing it when the store was open. That wouldn't work."

"I guess not." Cheryl tried to get a glimpse of his face by twisting away from him. The mask made it impossible. How could she tell if he was telling the truth without seeing his expression? Was he simply creating a story now that he knew she had identified him as the thief? If so, was he working it out as he talked? Or did he really intend to return the coins? She eyed the backpack again. It didn't look full enough to have the coins, but maybe it had weapons or tools.

"Stop moving. I can't let you go. I need to think."

"So what are you going to do with me?" She twisted her arm sharply, hard this time, and his hold slipped but then tightened again. She had to break free. No one was coming to help her, so she had to do this on her own.

"I will not hurt you." Yet his voice wavered as if he weren't as settled as his words indicated.

This was it.

She couldn't waste any more time. Not while it meant giving him time to decide what to do with her.

Cheryl twisted to the right as hard as she could.

He tightened his grasp, but then she kicked him with all the force she could muster in the kneecap. He howled, but held on, so she lowered her body and dropped. As she did, she slipped out of his grasp. He reached for her, but his fingers curled around her hoodie. She stripped it off and spun toward the front door.

Instead of freedom, she collided into a solid surface. A body. Someone else was there!

Her knees quaked, and her hands shook. Her vision tunneled as she fought to get free of the body. Could it be Leonard Raber? She prayed not as she screamed.

"Cheryl, it's okay." Hands gripped her arms and she tried to shake free, but it was no use. "You're not alone. I'm here to help."

The man's words slowly penetrated, and she stood still. "Chief Twitchell?"

Her racing heart slowed to a gallop.

"What's going on?" The chief looked behind her, a hand on his service revolver.

"Stephen Raber..." She panted as her lungs felt like they couldn't fully expand. "He's in there. And he'll get away. It's him. He's the one who stole the coins. He confessed the whole thing." She explained between gulps of air how Stephen had stolen the coins.

"And it looks like it was my fault it was so easy to get to the coins," she added. Then she told how she'd followed him to the cottages, and he'd grabbed her. "He admitted he did it and claims he was going to return them since he couldn't sell them easily."

"It's okay."

"No it's not. He's going to get away while we're standing here wasting air."

"Relax, Cheryl, we've got him covered." The chief tried to stop her hands which were twisting in front of her.

"But he can't get away. We need the coins!"

He stepped to the side, and she looked out the open door to see another police officer leading Stephen away in handcuffs. She hurried to the doorway and stepped outside. The chief followed her.

As she watched them go, a sinking feeling hit her gut. Had she somehow failed him? Had he been telling the truth? Had he come here to return the coins? She shook her head. It would be up to the courts to figure all that out now.

Cheryl noticed her arms were trembling, and she clutched them to her chest. Then she turned back to the chief. "How did you know to come?"

"I got a call right as I was getting ready to leave to meet you. I'm glad I decided to answer it because it was Clara Raber. She was concerned because she'd found unusual coins in Stephen's pockets when she'd washed his clothes. She was concerned about him." He watched his officer shove Stephen into the back of a cruiser. "She was worried about him and thought he'd headed back to the cottages," he said. "When I got off her call, I saw that I'd missed one from you. I came to your house, and when you weren't there, I followed a hunch that maybe you were headed this way. Something inside just told me you were."

Cheryl felt torn as the cruiser turned around in the cul-de-sac and headed toward town with Stephen in the back. "I hate to see him headed to jail, but I'm so glad we know who took the coins."

"So where are they?"

"I don't know, unless..." Cheryl took a step toward the cottage. "Maybe they're inside."

The chief held up a hand. "Wait here. I don't want there to be any question about evidence being tampered with. Any ideas what I should look for?"

"He had a backpack with him. It didn't look full to me, and he easily carried it." She didn't want to imagine where he could have stashed the coins.

"I'll look around."

Only a few minutes passed before he came back out holding the bag. "I think you'll want to see what's inside."

When she looked inside the backpack, Cheryl stepped back. Inside sat bag after bag of coins. In the same ziplock bags she'd used earlier.

She'd done it! She'd found the missing coins.

CHAPTER THIRTY

A week later Cheryl stood at the front counter of the Swiss Miss while the Vogel brothers engaged in another round of checkers. She heard Ben murmur something, but didn't step closer to hear because the Sugarcreek *Budget* caught her attention. It had a lengthy article detailing all that had happened with the coins.

As she skimmed the article again, she relearned the details of Frank Raber's life and his service in World War II and to the Sugarcreek community before moving to another area as a doctor. Then the article told of how the coins had been discovered and then stolen. After a couple paragraphs, the reporter recounted the story of Frank's daughter and how the coins were being donated to John-John's domestic violence shelter in her honor.

The bell jingled, and Cheryl looked up in time to see John-John walking in. His grin stretched his face, and he walked with the loose stride of one who was relaxed and happy.

He tapped the newspaper. "This story is already doing so much good. You wouldn't believe the calls I'm getting from people who want to support what we're doing at the cottages." His grin stretched even wider. "Cheryl, we'll be able to open even sooner than I thought because of all the donations."

"That's great news!"

"It is indeed." His smile slipped, and he sobered. "I've got to help these women and their families. If I can save even one Anna or my sister, all of this work will be worth it."

The door opened with the accompanying jingle. Cheryl couldn't help thinking the store looked like a major destination with all this traffic before the store was officially open. Her smile faltered when she noticed Suzanne Marshall, the coin collector and appraiser, walking toward her. Cheryl hadn't seen the woman since her pushy efforts to get access to the coins the day the workers discovered the jars. Still she walked toward Cheryl and John-John like they should be thrilled to see her.

"Johnson, I have the best news for you." She spread her arms wide. "I know you didn't ask me to, but I've found a buyer for your coins. This friend loves to collect coins from the first half of the twentieth century but doesn't have much from the World War II era. He's intrigued by the story behind yours."

"That sounds great."

"Now wait a minute, Johnson." Cheryl held up a hand as she studied Suzanne. "How do we know you'll get the best price for the coins?"

"Because I'm excellent at my job." Suzanne stiffened and squared her shoulders toward Cheryl. "I've tried to tell you I could sell the coins from the moment I knew about them."

"Then why didn't you help us when we were asking for information about the coins a week ago?"

Suzanne relaxed. "Is that what you're all concerned about?" She dug around in her bag. "When I was on my way to one of the coin shows, I dropped my phone in a sink and ruined it. The thing is deader than roadkill even though I got it in a bag of rice as soon as I could. I'm back now and want to help." She turned to John-John. "What you're trying to do with the cottages is important. I'd like to help. I'll even waive my commission so all of the proceeds can benefit what you're doing there."

Cheryl swallowed and wondered if once again she'd rushed to a conclusion about someone.

John-John looked at Cheryl, and she shrugged. Then he turned to Suzanne. "Ms. Marshall, how about we head to Yoder's and discuss your recommendations."

The rest of the day passed with the usual work of helping customers, cleaning up behind them, and restocking as needed. Near the end of the day, Fannie and Irving walked into the store. Fannie wore a grin almost as big as the bouquet of fresh flowers in a cut-glass vase that she held. Cheryl watched them walk slowly around the displays, never veering from heading her direction.

"How can I help you today?"

Fannie set the vase on the counter. "You already have. These are a thank-you for the ways you helped me when you came to visit with Naomi."

"Helped you? As I remember it, you helped me."

"No, I was lonely, and your visit and puzzle kept me occupied while I recovered. We're just thrilled with how it turned out, aren't we, Irving?"

Her husband nodded. "I don't know if anything we said helped, but if it did, we're honored."

"It certainly did. I couldn't have tracked down Frank's daughter without your help." They visited a few minutes, and after the couple left, Cheryl locked up the Swiss Miss. As she gathered Beau in his carrier, she thought about all the people who had helped her as she searched for the coins and the author of the letters. Without any of them, she wouldn't have unraveled this mystery.

It was as she gave of herself and her time that she'd learned what she needed to solve this crime. At the same time, she'd discovered the joy of new friends and helping old friends—and that joy was worth more than any earthly treasure, even one hidden away in mason jars.

AUTHOR LETTER

Dear Reader,

I can count on one hand the number of times my grandfather talked about his service in World War II. He didn't talk about it during my growing-up years, and it only came up a few times during the last months of his life. After his death, I became fascinated by World War II. I wished I had asked more questions. I've wondered what it was like for him, and adding the World War II element into *Mason Jar Mayhem* was a wonderful excuse to research a bit more about that time period. In fact, the letters from this book are similar to ones written from Papua New Guinea during that time, where my grandfather also served.

Yet whether or not you had a family member who served in the war, it's always fun to get a glimpse into the past.

Thank you for curling up with *Mason Jar Mayhem*. My coauthor, Cara Putman, and I hope that you will not only be entertained by this story, but that you'll also take a moment to think about the stories that God is weaving all around you every day.

May God's goodness bless you today.

Blessings,
Tricia Goyer

ABOUT THE AUTHORS

Best-selling author Tricia Goyer has published fifty books and more than five hundred articles! She is a two-time Carol Award winner as well as a Christy and ECPA Award nominee. In 2010, she was selected as one of the "Top Twenty Moms to Follow on Twitter" by SheKnows.com. Tricia blogs at ForTheFamily.com, TheBetterMom.com, and NotQuiteAmishLiving.com. She is a mother of six, grandmother of two, and wife to John, and they make their home in Little Rock, Arkansas. To learn more, visit TriciaGoyer.com.

Cara Putman is a homeschooling mom of four who is married to the love of her life. An award-winning author, Cara has published more than twenty books and is an attorney and lecturer at Purdue University. She blogs at TheGroveStory.com, InspiredByLifeAndFiction.com, TheWritersAlleyBlog.com, and CaraPutman.com and serves on the executive board of American Christian Fiction Writers, which is a great resource for anyone who longs to write.

Fun Fact about
the Amish or Sugarcreek, Ohio

Sugarcreek, Ohio, is a small town where everyone knows everyone, but for many years the local population may not have noticed that they had a war hero living among them. Jim Martin from Sugarcreek was only twenty-three years old when he made his first combat jump into enemy fire at the start of D-Day. As he fell through the sky while being fired upon, Jim wondered if that day would be his last. It wasn't.

Jim was part of the 506th Parachute Infantry Regiment, 101st Airborne Division. They were known as the Screaming Eagles, yet after the war Jim returned to the States to lead a quiet life. That is, until he decided to make that jump again.

At ten a.m. Sunday, July 11, 2010, Jim made his final parachute jump. He was eighty-nine years old, and a group of family and friends cheered him on. For this last jump, he stayed close to home in Xenia, Ohio. Also, this time there wasn't a 140-pound pack on his back, and he enjoyed the fall without being shot at.

After the war, Jim worked as a tool-and-die worker, and he was on the Sugarcreek Township Zoning Commission for fifteen years. As within every community, you often don't realize the hero living right next door. Jim from Sugarcreek proves that to be true.

Something Delicious from Our Sugarcreek Friends

Raber's Baked Beans

(Perfect for any cottage raising or community gathering!)

½ pound bacon

2 onions, cut fine

1 large can pork and beans

1 (15-ounce) can kidney
  beans, drained

1 (15-ounce) can lima beans,
  drained

1 cup brown sugar

1 cup ketchup

1 tablespoon mustard

Preheat oven to 350 degrees. Cut up bacon and fry with onions. Mix all ingredients together and bake for one hour. (I add a little Worcestershire sauce.) Makes ten to twelve servings.

Read on for a sneak peek of another exciting book
in the series Sugarcreek Amish Mysteries!

When There's a Will
by Elizabeth Adams

I am sure he will be here soon," Esther Miller said, rising up on
her tiptoes to peer out the front window of the Swiss Miss. "He
is not usually late."

Esther had been standing by that window for the past ten
minutes, peering out, waiting for her brother Levi to arrive in his
buggy. Esther was right; Levi was very faithful with ferrying his
sister to and from her part-time job at the Swiss Miss, the gift shop
Cheryl ran in Sugarcreek, Ohio. She couldn't remember him ever
being late.

"I'm sure he just got confused by the timing," Cheryl said.
Esther usually left by midafternoon, but the past few weeks she'd
been picking up some extra hours since early summer was a very
busy season around the shop. "Why don't I just give you a ride
home?"

Cheryl had already cashed out the register, taken out the trash,
locked up the back door, and was ready to shut off the lights. She
hoped nothing bad had happened to Levi. Esther had already used

the store's phone to call the phone shanty out behind the Miller house, but no one answered.

"I do not want to put you to any trouble," Esther said. She toyed with the string on her apron, which she often did when she was nervous.

"It's no trouble," Cheryl said. "I need to pick up some more of your mother's jam anyway." Naomi Miller had become one of Cheryl's closest friends since she'd moved to Sugarcreek, and she also made the delicious jam that Cheryl stocked in her shop. Besides, Cheryl would worry if she didn't know what had kept Levi. Out on the country roads around town, collisions between fast-moving cars and horse-drawn buggies were not uncommon and often had disastrous consequences. Cheryl wanted to make sure Levi was all right.

Esther nodded. "Thank you, Cheryl. It would be quite a long walk."

"Of course." She gestured for Esther to walk out the front door of the shop, and she shut off the lights and stepped out behind her. The evening was warm, the sky a gauzy light blue, and the soft late-June breeze carried a hint of the sweet scent of summer roses. Evenings like this, Cheryl was pretty sure the little town of Sugarcreek was just about as close to heaven as you could get here on earth.

Cheryl settled in the driver's seat of her little Ford Focus, and a few minutes later she and Esther were passing out of the quaint downtown area of Sugarcreek, filled with shops and restaurants that appealed to Amish and *Englisch* alike, into the glorious open farmland that made this the heart of Ohio Amish country. Cheryl would never grow tired of the sight of cornstalks planted in long, straight rows, and sheaves of wheat rustling in the breeze. High, fluffy clouds scooted across the sky.

She looked over and saw Esther biting her thumbnail. It wasn't as if Levi could text his sister to let her know what was going on. Still, if anything too terrible had happened, surely someone would have found a way to let her know.

Esther let out a breath—a literal sigh of relief—when Cheryl turned into the driveway of the Miller farm and saw that Levi's buggy was parked in its usual spot in front of the barn.

"See, I'm sure he just forgot," Cheryl said, but even as she said it, the words sounded hollow. Esther knew as well as she did that Levi would not forget. He was not the kind of man who took a commitment lightly. They both stepped out of the car and closed the doors, and the sound echoed in the quiet yard. Levi's dog Rover was sniffing around the fence by the entrance to the petting zoo the Millers ran. The barn door was open, and she could hear someone moving around inside, but otherwise the place was still.

"I hope so," Esther said.

Cheryl scanned the fields around the house as they crossed the yard. She didn't see anyone working out that way. They stepped past Naomi's carefully tended pots of zinnias and asters that lined the short walkway that led to the house. The middle porch step creaked as they climbed up. Esther pushed open the door, and Cheryl followed her inside and into the kitchen.

Naomi, her husband, Seth, and Levi were gathered around the rough-hewn wooden table, and they all looked up when they entered the room. Naomi's elder daughter Elizabeth was in the kitchen standing over the stove, stirring what smelled like the most divine soup ever.

"Esther." Levi's face drained of color. "Is it time for you to be done with work already?" He turned his head to look at the clock over the kitchen sink.

"It is past time. Cheryl had to give me a ride home." The hurt in her voice was evident.

"I am sorry. I did not realize." He turned to Cheryl. "Thank you."

Levi seemed confused and genuinely apologetic. Cheryl was glad for Esther, but she got a bad feeling in her stomach. Something was going on. These were some of the hardest-working people she knew. She'd never seen them just sitting around at this time of day.

"Yes, thank you, Cheryl," Naomi said, pushing herself to her feet. "You must forgive us. We did not mean to trouble you. We have had some bad news, and we are still trying to make sense of it. We all must have forgotten what time it was."

"Oh dear. Is everything all right?"

Instead of answering her, Naomi said something to Esther in Pennsylvania Dutch, and Esther's eyes widened.

"*Wirklich?*" Esther then turned to Levi and asked something Cheryl didn't understand. The family spoke among themselves for a few moments. Cheryl felt like an intruder and wondered if she should just come back another time. She was about to excuse herself when Naomi turned to Cheryl again.

"I am sorry, Cheryl," she said. "We are being rude again."

"It's okay. I'll just see myself..."

"I was just about to go outside and get started on my chores," Levi said, pushing himself up. She always forgot how tall he was, and how broad his shoulders were. "Would you come with me?"

Cheryl tried to ignore that thrill that went through her. "Sure." She smiled at him, and he gave the slightest hint of a grin. In his eyes she could see that he was pleased. Cheryl didn't look at Naomi. She knew her friend was worried about what seemed to be a growing attraction between her stepson and her Englisch friend.

"I will explain what is going on," Levi said, and she nodded and followed him out the back door of the house and into the yard. With long strides, he crossed the dirt patch and went around the side of the house toward the barn. Cheryl tried her best to keep up, and Levi, realizing this, slowed his steps. As thrilled as she was with the opportunity to be alone with him, Cheryl knew it was somewhat unusual for an Amish man to go off with an Englisch woman like this, and she realized the circumstances must be difficult indeed.

"My Uncle Silas passed away very early this morning," Levi said. His footsteps crunched in the dirt. "He was my father's oldest brother."

"Oh no." So that explained all the long faces. A death in the family was a perfectly reasonable excuse for losing track of time. She thought she had met Silas at some family events she'd attended with Naomi, though she couldn't be sure. Amish men all had the same wardrobes and wore the same beards, and sometimes it was difficult to keep them all straight.

"Your father must be upset."

"Yes," Levi said. "He will miss his brother."

Cheryl was used to the stoic manner in which her Amish friends often reacted to bad news, so this simple answer didn't surprise her.

They had reached the barn, and as they stepped inside, Levi called out something in Pennsylvania Dutch. A voice Cheryl recognized as belonging to Eli, Levi's nineteen-year-old brother, called back. She turned and saw Eli wave from a milking stool at the far end of the barn. She waved back and then followed Levi the other way, toward the stalls where the family's horses were kept. The air in the barn was cool and dusty and smelled of sweet hay.

"I had been saving up to buy a plot of land from my uncle," Levi said as he grabbed a pitchfork that was resting against the wall.

"Oh." Cheryl looked around at the tall, solid walls of the barn. She trailed her fingers along the soft muzzle of a yearling with a gorgeous reddish-brown coat. He sniffed her hand and then let her pet him. "I didn't realize. Why?"

Levi hoisted the pitchfork and dug the spears into an open bin of hay. Little clouds of dust rose from the hay, and a clean, earthy scent filled the air.

"I plan to have my own farm someday," he said, hefting a load of hay from the bin. "When I get married, I would like to have my own land and my own house." He didn't look at her as he tossed the hay into the first stall. Was he thinking about marriage for any particular reason? Cheryl wondered. Or was this just the kind of thing Amish men did? She noticed that his cheeks had turned a light shade of pink, though she couldn't say whether this was from the exertion or from something else.

"You won't take over this farm?" Cheryl asked. Levi was the oldest of his father's six children, and Cheryl had just assumed he planned to take over the farm someday. She ran her hand down the horse's velvety neck, and then she moved on to the next stall, where her horse, Ranger, was kept. Levi had given her the horse for her birthday, and he was kept here. She ran her fingers along his soft muzzle, and Ranger leaned into her hand.

Levi shook his head and hoisted another batch of hay on to his pitchfork. "In our culture, the farm always passes to the youngest son. So Eli will inherit this farm someday. I will need to buy land of my own." He dropped the hay into the same bin in the first stall. "My uncle Silas had no children, and he was planning to sell me a parcel of his land." The gray horse inside bent his neck and started chomping on the hay.

"So what does that mean, now that he's gone?" Cheryl asked. "Will you still get to buy the land?"

"My father is in charge of making sure my uncle's will is carried out," Levi said.

That made him the executor, Cheryl knew, but she was too thrown off to tell him that.

"Your uncle had a will?"

"Yes. Many Amish people have wills," Levi said. "If they do not, the government can decide how to distribute your things when you die." Another pitch, and hay landed in the next stall.

"I know that," Cheryl said. That was the point of a will, to make it clear how you wanted your assets distributed when you died so you didn't have to rely on the government to do so. "I just didn't realize...I mean..."

"You didn't think the Amish used wills?" Levi said. He straightened up and gave her a wry smile.

In truth, she'd never given any thought to whether Amish people wrote wills. But she did know that they avoided lawsuits, so she had naturally assumed they wouldn't. She was beginning to see that she would need to stop assuming things where Naomi and her family were concerned.

"In any case, my father has seen the will, and he told me today that Uncle Silas left the house and most of the land to his brother Emmon, but he left the parcel of land I had planned to buy to me."

"Levi, that's wonderful," Cheryl said and immediately hated herself for it. "I mean, it's not wonderful that your uncle passed away. What I meant was, it's wonderful that you will get your land and you won't even have to buy it now."

"Yes, it is very kind of him," Levi said. "I was very happy to hear it."

"And your dad knew this whole time? Why didn't he say something to you about the fact that you would inherit the land?"

"Why would he do that?" Levi shrugged. "If I had known I would inherit the land and didn't need to buy it, I would not have been motivated to save my money. It would not have helped things for me to know this."

Cheryl had to admit that might be true in her case, but she couldn't imagine Levi not working hard no matter what.

"Besides, no one knew Uncle Silas would pass away so soon," Levi said. "It was very sudden. A heart attack. He should have had many more years left. I would have bought it from him if he had lived long enough."

Cheryl could see his point. It probably had been for the best that Seth hadn't told Levi about being included in Silas's will.

"In any case, it might not matter because just this afternoon we heard from Jessica Stockton."

Cheryl knew Jessica served as a "Yoder Toter." She had a van and was often hired to drive Amish families around when they needed to go farther than their horses and buggies would allow.

"Why?"

"She said her husband works in the land development department at the county office over in New Philadelphia. He told her that someone came in this afternoon to see about buying the land that had belonged to Silas. He learned that Silas had passed away and thought the land would be available for sale. He did not know the man, but he recognized our name, and Jessica, who has driven our family many times, called here to make sure we knew."

A hundred questions ran through her head: Had word spread about Silas's death so quickly? But even if it had, what would have made him think the land would be available? Wouldn't he assume the land would pass to Silas's heirs?

"I hope he told him it was already spoken for." Cheryl had met Jeff Stockton. He was a straight shooter and wouldn't let this person waste their time sniffing around land that wasn't for sale.

"He did not know, but he did tell him it would be up to the will to say who got the house. But the man told him the land did not belong to Uncle Silas in the first place, so he could not leave it to anyone." Levi pitched more hay into a stall, and Cheryl noticed that his motions were getting stiffer as he talked.

"But that's crazy. Your uncle owned that land, right?"

"We thought so," Levi said. "But now the people at the county records office are saying they cannot find any record that he did."

"What do they mean, they can't find any record? Don't they keep records about this sort of thing?"

"They cannot find it." A load of hay missed the feed bin and fell to the floor.

"What? How is that possible?"

"I do not know." Levi hefted another load of hay and dropped it into Ranger's bin. The physical activity seemed to make him feel better, and he kept moving.

Cheryl puzzled this over. It didn't make any sense. If Silas had owned the land, there should be a record of it with the county. "Is there just no record of Silas owning it, or no record of the land at all?"

"I do not know."

Down at the far end of the barn, they heard the scrape of the milking stool across the floor and the sound of the metal bucket being set down.

"Well, then, where is your uncle's copy of the deed? You should be able to just show it and clear all of this up."

"That is the problem. We do not know where Uncle Silas's copy of the deed is. *Daed* and I went over to his house this evening to find it. That is why I missed picking up Esther," he said. Another forkful of hay came from the bin into the stall. "The deed for the house and the main piece of land is there, but there was nothing for the section of land he left to me."

"Where did he keep his important papers?"

"In his office. We searched everywhere. But we did not find the deed."

Cheryl thought for a moment. "What about mortgage statements? If he'd been paying a mortgage on the land, that would show he owned it, right?"

Levi set the pitchfork down and wiped his sleeve across his face. "Daed says he paid cash. Ten years ago the land wasn't worth nearly what it is today."

Cheryl let her fingers tangle up in Ranger's soft mane.

"So what will you do?" Cheryl asked.

"I do not know," Levi said. "If we do not find that deed, I will lose the land, I suppose."

It couldn't end like that. There had to be a way to fight this.

"You're not going to let that happen, are you?"

"I will try not to." He took in a deep breath and let it out slowly, and then he turned to her. "Actually, we were wondering if you might be able to help."

"Me?" Cheryl wasn't sure what to say. Of course she wanted to help him, but how could she be of any use?

"You know much more about legal matters than we do." His cheeks were still pink, and he picked up the pitchfork again, almost as if he needed something to do with his hands. "We do not understand all of these things. But you…" His voice trailed off. "You are good with this."

Cheryl was touched that he had asked, but she wasn't sure how he thought she might be able to help. She wasn't a lawyer, and she didn't know much about the legalities of buying and selling property. Still, of course she wanted to help however she could. He was probably right that she knew more than her Amish friends did. And she knew how much this land meant to him. She knew what a difference it would make in his future—in the future of his whole family…whoever that might be.

"Of course I'll help." Cheryl didn't know what it would entail, but she did know that she would do whatever it took to help Levi get that land.